SPITE

SPITE

CAT AUSTEN

Cat Austen

ISBN: 979-8-9893873-3-5

Self-published by the author because she's a control freak.

Other works by Cat Austen

Convergence- *August 2022*- a polyamorous, contemporary, romantic suspense.

Aisle 5- *November 2022*- a contemporary, erotic, romantic comedy.

Solace- *Aug 2023*- book one in a mafia why choose trilogy. Dark romcom.

Spite- *November 2023*- book two in the Solace series.

Check out catausten.com, subscribe to newsletter at catausten.com/subscribe, and follow on amazon.com for all new releases.

For the girls who turned their darkness into demons and are working on killing them.

As always, this book is for the stay at home moms. I hope your coffee is exactly how you like it and the Youtube ads during Blippi aren't the stupid five minute ones.

For everyone who read Solace and felt connected to it in some way.

For Ashley and Haley. Thanks for understanding my love language of weird ass TikToks in the middle of the day.

Author's Note

This book contains adult content and is not suitable for minors under the age of 18.

Content includes but is not limited to torture, death, violence, violence with weapons, alcohol use/abuse, marijuana use, discussion of human trafficking, drug distribution. Pregnancy (NOT EMILY), mentions of pregnancy complications (NOT A MAIN CHARACTER).

Dubious consenting exhibitionism and voyeurism, consenting exhibitionism, and voyeurism, use of BDSM bondage, blindfolds during sex, sort of blood play, knife play, wax play, and spanking. Anal activities including rimming, fingering, toys, sex, and prostate milking (can we call it something else? Jfc). Male/male sex, male/ female sex, male/male/female sex.

Devon's bad attitude, Emily being a bitch, the terms "ass blast" and "butt nut," the loss of Milo's virginity, and metaphorical laundry.

This book contains scenes of BDSM that may not adhere to safe practice standards. I encourage you to research safe ways to play if you are inspired. Let's leave the unsafe practices for the fictional characters, babe.

All efforts to keep a detailed content warning list have been made and any missed triggers are solely the author's fault. If content that needs to be listed is found, please contact me at cataustenauthor@gmail.com and don't report to Amazon or your retailer.

The author claims no responsibility for mental health issues or crises that come from reading the material within.

Previously, in Solace (Book 1)

If it has been a while since you've read Solace, here's what you may have forgotten:

Plot: Emily, a suburban kindergarten teacher, catches her mayor husband Gregory cheating with his secretary tied up on the work conference table. He claims Emily wouldn't be into BDSM, so he had to stray. Gregory is a general piece of shit and says he wants to make their marriage work because it would look bad for his career in politics to divorce his high school sweetheart for his secretary. Emily says, "fuck that" and divorces his ass anyway.

Emily feels ostracized by the town, her job, and her family after her divorce. During her post-divorce hair style change she is approached by a woman who gives her a business card with a phone number on it. Desperate to get away she calls the number and gets herself kidnapped. Excuse me, "forcefully hired" by a mafia they call the "family business" and is decidedly Not Only Italian Anymore. It's 2023, baby.

Luckily, her kidnappers- er, new bosses are three hot mafia bosses named Sterling, Milo, and Devon. She struggles to feel safe in their home until they start to respect her and give her responsibility in their business operations. This happens after she kills a dude who tried to kill them.

They find out their leaders, Devon's dad and Milo's uncle (Anthony and Matthew), are getting involved in human trafficking with a mafia from out of town (leaders are Giovanni and Taz).

As a part of a deal with the out-of-town mafia, the guys have to be a part of an MMA fight. Sterling and Milo win but Devon loses. But he was a total asshat about training, so he deserved it tbh.

They plan to confront their leaders about the trafficking, but Emily and Milo are in a car accident and then taken to a basement. They're tortured for information on their mafia operations by Giovanni and Taz. The other mafia believes that Anthony and Matthew are making political connections, and they feel threatened by it. It's a whole Thing.

Sterling and Devon are told that Emily and Milo are dead, and they spiral. But Sterling has a drunken epiphany and sees their Air Tags located in a mechanic shop in town. They sober up and check it out and end up busting the place down and killing everyone to get to Their Babes. Emily and Milo are rescued, and Emily is a bad ass and helps kill Giovanni and Taz.

But not before Giovanni and Taz tell them that Anthony and Matthew are responsible for Milo and Sterling's parents' deaths and paid for Emily and Milo's deaths. It's a sad story, dude.

They finally get to confront Anthony and Matthew and be like "Hello we're not dead, fuckers!" and Devon demands control over the gangs. Surprise! Gregory the Douchebag

Ex-husband is in that meeting as well as other local politicians. Devon announces to the room that Anthony is a terrible person who killed his friends for power. Matthew is like "Omg, you killed my brother?!" and ends up getting shot by Anthony. RIP.

Devon kicks Anthony out and is like "I'm king of this town now. GTFO."

Solace ends with him asking his mom, and other oldies of the family business "Are you with us or against us?"

Romance: Sterling makes videos of him masturbating and role playing for a video service called Personal Cameras, and Emily finds it. Milo catches her just after she touches herself while watching Sterling. It's awkward. Then Milo gets involved and makes a video with Sterling and they go viral.

There's unresolved sexual tension between Sterling and Milo. Sterling is very confused by his feelings for Milo, but Milo is obvs in love with Sterling.

Emily starts to have spicy feelings for her captors and there's a slowish burn until she finally hooks up with Sterling. It's pretty hot.

After they are reunited after being kidnapped and tortured, Sterling and Milo admit their feelings for each other.

Emily has nightmares about being kidnapped and Sterling comforts her with BDSM. He helps her reclaim her body after the torture. Sterling ties her up with ropes and her cries of pleasure call in Milo who thinks something terrible is happening. When he sees what's happening, he says, "String me up, Rope Daddy" to Sterling and he is also tied up.

Sterling puts in the work and gets them both off. It's hot, it's therapeutic.

Emily realizes she might not be so vanilla after all.

Emily

Devon stood breathless and manic eyed as he wiped blood from his lip with the back of his hand. "So... are you with us?"

My heart pounded in my throat as we awaited their answers. The gunshot that killed Matthew still echoed in the room, making my bones feel like sharp-edged ice. The air I gulped down smelled like urine, sweat, and blood and it stuck to the insides of my lungs like sticky marshmallow.

"We're with you, baby," Stephanie said tearfully. Her eyes were fearful and fixed on her son.

"Yeah?" Devon barked at Harold, Victoria, and Brendon. He glared at each of them, looking very much like the mafia boss he was meant to be.

"Of course," Harold replied with a curt nod.

Victoria's chin was trembling, but she nodded, too.

Brendon's eyes were wide and focused on Milo. "Milo,

man, of course I'm wherever you are. Marie would-" he broke off to look at Matthew's body on the ground. "Oh, god." He bent and put his hands on his knees.

Milo's jaw was clenched, and I gripped his hand at his side. He wouldn't look at Brendon, his eyes unfocused and downcast.

"You all say you're with us, but why would we trust you?" Sterling growled. "You three knew our parents. You were there when they died."

"We didn't know," Stephanie urged, her hands out pleadingly in front of her. "Sterling, Milo, we didn't know!"

"Be that as it may, we are going to need time before we can trust you again." Devon cut off his mother's sobs. He looked down his nose at her with stone resoluteness. "I can't trust you and I can't keep you safe from... Dad. You need to hide until we settle this."

She nodded solemnly, looking down at Matthew's body. "Sterling, Milo... your mothers were my closest friends. They both told me as soon as they saw your faces, they wanted out of this business. To protect you, so you never had to-"

"That's enough!" Devon spat, cutting off her reminiscence. "Get out."

Stephanie and Victoria left, but Harold and Brendon held back. Harold looked at the guys with an expression darker and more serious than any I'd seen from the deli owner. "I'm at your disposal," he said.

"Keep them safe," Devon said, meaning Stephanie and Victoria.

"Of course," Harold nodded. "But-"

"Harold, I can't trust you either," Devon said with a sharp exhale.

"I didn't know about Owen and Michael or their wives," he insisted, sounding genuine.

"No, but you were here, at this meeting with local officials. Did you know Anthony and Matthew had been going into business with Giovanni and Taz? That it was going to be human trafficking?" Devon asked, his calm voice delicately laced with venom.

Harold blanched and glanced at Matthew's body. "I didn't know the nature of the business."

"Hm," Devon said with a sniff. "Sounds like blind trust to me. More dangerous than malicious intent."

Harold opened his mouth to argue back but stopped and his jaw clicked shut.

"Leave," Devon demanded.

"I'll leave my line open. You can still contact me," Harold said, looking at each of us.

"No, close it," Milo spoke up next to me. His voice was strained and rasping. "If we find out you had more involvement in any of this, I'll track you down and kill you myself."

Harold nodded again and left, meeting the women in the hallway. I heard their voices as they descended the stairs, planning on how to leave their legitimate businesses while they hid.

"You need to come see Marie," Brendon said to Milo.

"He doesn't need to do *anything*," Sterling snapped, his body still poised for an attack.

Milo put a hand on Sterling's arm to still the beast that was ready to burst from him. "Is something wrong?"

"Not anymore," Brendon said with an exhale.

Milo sniffed and nodded in understanding. "Where is she?"

"At home with Doc," Brendon said with a look like he knew that information would not be well received.

"You said nothing was wrong," Milo accused.

"She- well, she'll definitely want to see you right now." Brendon shifted on his feet and looked at the door.

"Fine. Sterling, go with Milo and Brendon. Emily, stay with me," Devon said and wiped his bleeding lip on the sleeve of his white shirt with a wince.

Milo gave my hand another squeeze before leaving with Brendon. Sterling stooped to kiss my sweaty forehead before following them out. Devon and I stood in silence as we heard their boots thump down the stairs. He was the first to move. His movements were jerky and fast. He cupped my face in his hands and his sharp inhale trembled and caught in his throat. Tears gathered at the bottom of his eyes. His terrified gaze was on me, but his mind was elsewhere as he swallowed his choked breath. "Fuck," he said with a shaking exhale. I gripped his hand on my face with my hand that wasn't in a sling and felt the swelling and wetness of blood on split knuckles. He closed his eyes and took a long, steadying breath before opening again. The tears were gone, the desperately fearful expression erased, and the cool demeanor of a mafia boss remained. While I felt good being trusted with a glimpse of his true emotions, I didn't know what to do with it. I didn't know how I could help him. He stepped back from me, and the scent of blood and urine in the room replaced his cologne and sweat.

"In that cabinet are cleaning supplies. We need to..." he

said, his voice even and calm, as he gestured to Matthew's body.

"We have to... his body?" I didn't even know where to start.

Devon's lip twitched at one side in the only smile he could muster right now. "What do you think we do with bodies?"

"Um, feed them to fish. Or maybe pigs," I said, thinking back to the only clichéd information I knew.

Devon smiled for real this time. "We just make a call, actually. We have a funeral home we're connected to. Sonny's family has worked with ours since before our fathers were in power."

"Sonny?" I asked as we gathered rubber gloves and bleach from the closet.

"He's an asset to us. He does a beautiful service for people within our family and he cremates the bodies we need disposed of," Devon explained.

"Handy," I mumbled as I put the glove on my good hand.

I wiped down the table and chairs with the bleach to remove fingerprints and any blood splatters. I did my best to not look at Matthew's body on the ground for the thirty minutes it took for two men to arrive to remove the bloodied body. A third man came in, wearing a crisp suit and gelled hair. I assumed him to be Sonny. He spoke quietly with Devon, getting Matthew's name and confirming details that seemed to have been made in advanced. The man seemed shocked to hear it was Matthew Holden he was taking, but Devon entertained no other friendly conversation. As soon as Matthew was gone and it was just me and Devon again, we looked at the large pool of blood on the floor.

I gagged. Devon echoed me compulsively. "Don't you start," he grumbled at me as we both wiped our watering eyes.

I gagged again. "Sorry, that was the last one," I said through chattering teeth. He gave me the middle finger as he tried to stifle his gag against the back of his hand.

Once our stomachs settled, Devon and I got to work, clearing up the blood from the floor. We were silent as we worked, only murmuring to each other when we needed the other to hand us something. I remained quiet out of respect for the man whose blood we were cleaning and for the man in front of me, getting bleach on the knees of his expensive pants. Devon seemed to be planning and plotting in his head like the leader he was trained to be. Trained by a man who had betrayed his own so deeply.

"Hey, um, Mr. Bilal?" a voice came from the door and we whipped around to see the young gangster that had guarded the entrance earlier.

"Tommy, what are you still doing here?" Devon asked, his posture relaxing when he realized who it was.

Tommy gulped as he saw the last remnants of the blood on the floor. He couldn't have been over twenty-one. "Um, I was wondering if you wanted me to go and stand guard at your house. I've been security there a few times, so I know how it's done."

Devon hung his head. "Did my father call the gangs out?"

"Yes, sir," Tommy said with a nervous nod.

Anthony wasn't stepping down without a fight. We had expected it to happen, but it didn't change the shock and betrayal of it. He was going to use his control of the gangs to cripple Devon's power.

"Then why are you still here?" Devon asked him and sat back on his knees.

Tommy looked at Devon with his chin held high. "I heard what you all said in there. I know what Anthony did to your families. I can't work for him like that anymore."

"You're going to get yourself into trouble going against the Prospect Kings' orders," Devon said.

"Prospect Kings?" I asked.

"One of our gangs," Devon replied. "One that doesn't tolerate insubordination."

Tommy shook his head. "They won't notice me missing."

"They will," Devon said. "And I'll end up cleaning *your* blood off the floor."

"Anthony needs to be stopped. I heard you say he was involved in human trafficking. We have enough trouble on these streets. We don't need that bullshit."

Devon nodded and sighed, thinking. "Can you drive by the house and just let me know how it looks? Monitor it but don't interfere with anything you see. I don't want you getting hurt."

"On it," Tommy said before leaving.

Devon looked at me for a moment, letting me see a glimpse of his exhaustion.

"Tommy looked to me for an order earlier. When all the politicians were scrambling to leave," I said quietly.

"He respects you," Devon said and got back to scrubbing.

"I don't know why. I haven't done anything to earn it," I said, joining him.

"Not that they know of yet. But you definitely had a hand in taking down Giovanni and Taz," Devon reasoned. "He trusts you because we do. Because I, as their leader, had you next to me."

"And why do you trust me?" I asked, not looking at him.

Devon was silent for a minute. I was just thinking maybe he didn't trust me after all when he spoke. "You could have run many times. You could have called for help. You could have taken a car and left the house. You could have freed Marcus instead of killing him. You could have bitten off Sterling and Milo's dicks."

I snorted a laugh as we stood up from the now clean floor.

"And you're here elbows deep in blood, laughing at a joke, because I asked you to help me," Devon concluded.

"I think that just makes me... sociopathic, not necessarily trustworthy," I mumbled.

"Well, that makes two of us. Or, really, *four* of us," Devon said as we carried the mop bucket of bloody bleach water down to the bathroom.

"You are what you eat," I said lightly.

He chuckled. "Then I must be a laxative brownie."

I stumbled on the stairs. He shot me a sly look over his shoulder.

"How-?"

"I know how to use the cameras in the house, too," he said as he dumped the bucket of water into the utility sink.

"But..."

"But it's not your blood in this bucket," Devon said and turned to look me in the eye. "Emily, I get it. We had you caged like an animal in our house. You could have stabbed us with a kitchen knife. But all you did was make us sick.

Just... don't tell Milo or Sterling it was you. Or Harold, for that matter."

"Why?" I asked. Meaning why can't I tell them and why am I still alive and *why* is he so nonchalant about it?

"Milo and Sterling were on rounds with Harold that night and... well, they had to pull over," Devon said, and I could hear the amusement in his voice.

I bit my lip. "Our secret?"

"Our secret." He confirmed. I wanted to ask why he didn't seem to care, but I didn't want to change his mind by accident.

We slipped out the back door of the deli and headed towards his SUV. I hopped in the passenger seat and he removed his bloodied white shirt before getting in. Leaving him in a crisp white undershirt. Our coats were still heaped in the back seat and I vaguely noticed neither of us reached for one to keep warm- we were barely feeling our bodies amongst the emotional turmoil of the day.

Devon rested his head back on the seat of the car for a moment before turning on the engine. He opened his phone and pulled up the app for the security cameras. He handed me his phone. "Check each room to make sure it's empty."

I did as I was told and saw nobody in the house and nothing looked amiss. "All good."

"None of the sensors went off. But just to be on the safe side, keep an eye on the doors," Devon instructed me.

I switched between the doors and the larger windows as he drove. There were so many questions and concerns speeding through my mind, but none seemed like the right thing to say or ask. He had just stood up to his father and sent his mother away. A man he had trusted his whole life was just killed in front of him. And everyone expected him to lead us into a new war against his father.

2

Milo

Brendon refused to speak more about Marie until we got to their house. The fucker acted like he had some sort of secret. If nobody told me what was going on as soon as I saw my sister, I was going to freak the fuck out. All he had said was she wasn't injured, and she was with Doc.

While he had insisted she was safe, I didn't believe him entirely. For years I'd been the only one to keep her safe and just because Brendon was around now, didn't mean I'd stopped. Being a big brother never stopped. Especially in the world we lived in. I'd monitored the cameras outside her house, and she hadn't left since she'd heard I was killed in the accident. I had assumed it to be grief that kept her home. That feeling of responsibility for her sadness weighed me down like an anchor. Only Doc, Brendon, Stephanie, and Victoria had gone in or out of the house since the night of the accident. I saw Harold dropping off food from the deli, but Matthew had never visited his grieving niece. I had assumed it to be an aspect of his own grief and guilt over his responsibility in my alleged death. His reactions when he saw me alive and well seemed genuine. But... he was Anthony's confidant and fellow leader. It was possible his cruelty and deceit had matched Anthony's.

Past tense.

Because Matthew was dead. Dead at the hands of his closest friend. His fellow leader. The man that had also killed his brother and his friend.

I would not cry in this car. I shifted in the passenger seat of Brendon's car and felt Sterling's eyes on me. At least he was here with me. Sterling knew me as well as I knew myself, so he surely knew how I was feeling. At that thought, Sterling reached over the seat and squeezed my shoulder. I tilted my head so the side of my face rested on his tattooed hand. He squeezed again and returned to his seat. As simple as the contact was, it steadied my heart enough to not blubber in front of my brother-in-law.

The twenty-minute ride to the suburbs was excruciating. I had left my tablet in Devon's car and driving through Cleveland provided insufficient cell service to run the security camera app on my phone. My fingers on my unbroken arm tapped an anxious rhythm on my knee. Sterling used to say it looked like I was typing on an imaginary keyboard over my legs. I wasn't. I just needed something to do with my hands before I went fucking stir crazy with the lack of a task.

When we pulled up to Marie and Brendon's cookie cutter suburban home, I was out of the car before Brendon had fully parked. Sterling was hot on my heels behind me, likely knowing how out of my mind I was. Brendon swore as the car rocked when we jumped out. But he was not far behind us.

I knew running in there was going to shock her. She thought I was dead. As I came to this realization, I was nearing the front door and Doc came out. He looked at me like I was a kid running with scissors, or glitter, or whatever the fuck parents hated that kids ran with. "Milo, wait!" he hissed and held up his hand.

I skidded to a stop, and Sterling almost mowed me over. Newton's first law riding on eighty pounds of cheeseburger and muscle. I bit my tongue at the impact of his chest to my back. "Why?" I asked Doc.

"If you go speeding in there right now, you'll give your sister a heart attack," he scolded me in the way only Doc could.

I huffed.

"He's got a point," Sterling admitted.

Sure, Doc was right, but I was never one to accept an error report. "I need to see her."

"I didn't tell him." Came Brendon's voice from behind us. Doc nodded.

"Tell me what?" I growled, wanting to scream it.

"Oh, your sister is safe, Milo," Doc assured me.

I saw red. Why did they feel the need to keep telling me this?

"Here," Sterling said with a warning hand on my chest. I was practically vibrating with rage and anxiety. "Why don't I go in with Brendon and Doc and tell her Milo is alive, and then you can come in? No heart attacks and you still get to see your sister."

All I could do was nod my agreement. The three men entered the house, leaving me cold on the stoop without a coat. Brendon could have at least tossed me his fucking car keys so I could wait in the heat. Fucker.

Now alone, my mind had nothing to do but run through scenarios where Anthony harmed Marie to get to me. While simultaneously reliving the sight of Matthew's body jerking as a bullet struck him directly in the heart. I closed my eyes and ran through each scenario I could control. I had learned long ago I required control in my life and the unknown and uncontrollable gave me anxiety. The only way to snap out of it was to troubleshoot it. Lean into the perseveration. Prescribe the compulsion. A data server giving me problems? I had to check it seventy-five times. And by the time I got to check twenty or twenty-five, the compulsion was gone, and I could stop on my own. Thinking about Anthony hurting Marie? Plan her security. I had cameras outside her home, but I could do inside. There were bodyguards at the salon she worked at. I could have them here. She could go into hiding with Brendon, away from Stephanie and the others.

I was calculating the cost of more cameras when the door opened. "Okay, your turn," Sterling said brightly.

Jumping up, I asked him, "Is she okay?"

"Yeah, pissed as all hell. We only told her about you and Emily, not Matthew. She thinks we played a joke on her. Your funeral was supposed to be next Saturday," Sterling said as he led me up the stairs.

"Sonny's going to be pissed," I said as he led me to Marie's bedroom. "I had plans for an expensive service."

Sterling held me back from running in at a

sprint, and we entered at a walking pace. Marie gasped when she saw me. She was pale and her face looked thinner than when I'd last seen her. Oddly, she was in pajamas and sitting in her bed in the middle of the afternoon. I went directly into her outstretched arms as her tears came in gasping sobs.

"You tricked me! You made me think you were dead!" she sobbed into my shoulder.

I murmured back, "I'm sorry, I'm sorry. I'm so sorry, but I'm here now." My voice cracked.

Behind me, I heard Brendon try to get Sterling to leave with him to give us privacy. Sterling refused. He didn't ask Doc.

I pulled back and looked at her. "What's wrong? Why are you still in bed?"

"I was grieving for my dead brother!" she scolded me and smacked my arm in the cast. "And... I'm pregnant."

"Pregnant doesn't mean you have to stay in bed," I said without thinking.

"Milo, social skills," Sterling coughed behind me.

Oh. Oh!

"You're having a baby?" I asked, my voice full of amazement.

She nodded tearfully up at me. I hugged her against me and let out an excited laugh. "Congratulations!"

"Thank you," she sniffled and grinned.

"When am I getting a niece?" I asked her. Picturing myself holding my sister's little baby gave me feelings of joy and pride.

"Mid July. And it could be a nephew," she said.

"Brendon doesn't have enough testosterone to produce male sperm," I said dismissively.

"Hey!" Brendon scolded from behind us.

"I don't think that's how it works," Marie giggled.

"Why are you in bed?" I asked, looking down at her pajama clad body. I noticed they were weird collared and button-down pajamas like Emily had. Was that a requirement to live in the suburbs? Was there a welcome wagon carrying mayonnaise casserole recipes and collared pajamas that came around? Disgusting.

Marie looked at Doc, who was waiting patiently and quietly in the corner.

"She had a small bleed. Nothing serious and nothing to worry about," Doc said in that doctory way that made even the worst news sound benign.

"Um, it definitely is something to worry about!" I snapped and stood up. I didn't want to jostle her too much and cause another bleed.

"Milo, stop," Marie sounded annoyed. "It's not abnormal. I was just so upset after you had fake died that I irritated my placenta."

"Okay," I said, sounding anything other than mollified. "Is your placenta... um, soothed?" I asked, thinking of the news I had to give her about Matthew and our parents.

"She's alright. I'm here to monitor," Doc said quietly.

"What happened? Sterling said you and Emily were both fine, and Giovanni and Taz were dead," Marie said warily.

The joy I felt at her news gave way to fear and grief. I looked down at our hands. "Well, I'll start at the beginning," I said with a sigh. "After you were born-"

"Milo, please, current events," Marie said with a look like she couldn't believe I was talking about her birth.

"After you were born, our parents decided they didn't want to be in the business anymore. They wanted our family safe and whole," I said slowly.

"Well, fuck all that did," Marie muttered amongst fresh tears.

"They were almost out, but Anthony thought they couldn't be free with the knowledge of the business they had," I said and stopped when she gasped.

"Anthony killed our parents?!" she shrieked.

I nodded.

"Does Matthew know?" she asked urgently.

"When Matthew found out, he attacked Anthony. And Anthony... shot him," I said in a low, quiet voice. I tried to emulate Doc's soothing voice.

"What?! Doc, go to him! I'm fine!" Marie insisted and shooing Doc.

"I didn't get a call," Doc said, hearing this information for the first time with Marie. He looked at the three of us that were there. We all bowed our heads. Doc cursed under his breath.

"He's dead?!" Marie sobbed.

I nodded. The memory of holding his hand as the light faded from his eyes replayed in my head. Marie leaned into me, breaking me out of the memory. I held her tightly with my good arm as she cried.

"Did Matthew know about our parents?" Marie asked thickly through her tears.

"I don't know. He seemed upset when we confronted Anthony," Sterling said. "But I don't know how much he knew or didn't know."

"He had his suspicions," Doc supplied. "We all did."

"Why did you never say anything to us?" Marie asked Doc.

"I've worked for this business since I was finishing med school. I had loans and a fiancée, and I had hoped to make some quick money so I could buy us a house. There were a few jobs I did successfully. Then, when I tried to retire from being the mafia's physician, they threatened my new wife and our unborn child. Your leaders have never been against corruption and blackmail. I knew this extended inwards to their own members when, not long after I attended the births of four heirs to the family business, some new parents left. While I was neither witness nor confidant for the crimes, I knew Anthony and Matthew just as well as the deceased," Doc explained.

We all read between the lines of Doc's story. If I had ever doubted my involvement in this business, it felt more re-solved in my need for revenge on behalf of my parents. "Doc, if you ever want to leave, you are not bound by us," I said, thinking of Doc's wife and their daughter. I'd met both of them before, and they didn't seem like they were upset with Doc's job with us. But Doc wasn't going to be forced to work with us anymore.

"Seriously," Sterling agreed. "You don't have to work with us."

"Thank you, boys, but I've made peace with my job. I won't abandon you," Doc said, and patted Sterling's shoulder.

"You need to hide, though," I said and looked at Marie. "Both of you."

Marie looked at Brendon helplessly.

"I know you don't want to be a big part of the family

business, but Anthony might use you to get to Milo," Sterling reasoned.

She nodded and sat back against her pillows with a sigh.

I was desperate for her to agree to go into hiding with Brendon, but also desperate for her to stay somewhere I could protect her. Losing control over her safety made my stomach churn, though I knew she'd be safer far away from here.

"Okay," Marie whispered.

"We'll figure something out," Brendon said. He was a lawyer for our family and his own, so he couldn't simply disappear- they'd have to get creative.

"And you?" I asked Doc.

He shook his head. "No, I'll send my wife and daughter out, but I'm staying. I wasn't at today's meeting, so I can go to him and agree to allegiance on his side. I can help you with information when and if he calls me."

"Doc-" Marie started in protest.

"No, I've held onto secrets and guilt long enough. It's time for me to make it right," he interrupted sternly.

I didn't want another good person to get hurt at the expense of our family business, but he had made his decision. Doc on our side could be the biggest asset we have if he was willing to be in the crossfire.

3

Emily

Devon pulled his SUV up next to a rusted black pickup truck outside our house. He rolled down his window as the driver of the truck did the same. It was Tommy.

"Nobody in or out," Tommy said confidently.

We had known this already by looking at the cameras, but it was nice to have someone on our side.

"Thank you, Tommy," Devon said. "I'll call you directly if we need any more help."

Tommy lit up with pride and nodded before driving off.

It was odd, pulling into the driveway without two gangsters guarding the gates. Devon had to type in a code to open the gate, something I hadn't realized needed to be done since the gate was always open for us. Devon parked the SUV, and we gathered all the stuff from the backseat. The bundle of coats in my arm smelled like the guys and it comforted me as we walked into the empty, quiet house.

There was something eerie walking into a quiet house after a traumatic day. Even though we'd been quiet cleaning and driving, it felt wrong for it to be so calm. Dropping the coats and our shoes off in the hall, we went straight to the kitchen. Devon opened a bottle of bourbon and poured two glasses. He handed me one before downing his and refilling it. I held my breath and drank mine down. Bourbon was not my choice in drink, but I wanted a bit of alcohol to blur the edges of my fear and anxiety. My arm was aching, too, as my ibuprofen wore off. I could use some numbing.

Sterling and Milo came in soon after, looking weary. Devon and I stood up straight from leaning on the island when they came in. My heart jumped in my chest when I saw them, realizing we were all together again and safe after the meeting. I hugged them both but lingered on Milo. He breathed in my hair like he was steadying himself. I was doing the same, my nose buried in his chest. I had thought it was him who had been shot. He had shouted just after the gunshot and thought I was about to lose him. Gripping him tighter, I let some of my fears relax.

"How is Marie?" Devon asked as he poured two more bourbons for the guys.

"Pregnant, and going into hiding," Milo replied.

"She's pregnant?" I asked and pulled away to look up at him. "That's wonderful!"

"Uncle Milo," Devon said with a fond smile.

I had forgotten that even though Marie didn't want much to do with the mafia business, she had grown up with Sterling and Devon, too. Not just Milo. She was also their sister.

"Please, you're all uncles to that baby," I laughed.

"Then I'm happier she's hiding," Devon said and slid the two fresh drinks across the island.

We gathered around the island and sipped our drinks. The pain in my arm faded to a dull ache.

"They're all in hiding and the gangs have been called out by Anthony," Devon said.

Sterling and Milo both stiffened. "All of them?"

"Did you not notice the gate?" Devon snapped.

"But *all* of them?" Milo asked, sounding defeated.

"Yeah, as far as I know," Devon replied.

"So, we attempted to take over the business, and we failed other than getting our family in danger," Milo summarized in a flat voice.

"Well, Tommy was there, and he agrees with us. Maybe the gangs would agree with us if they knew what was going on," I suggested.

"We can set up a meeting. Make them see how being on our side would benefit them," Devon agreed.

"Unless they kill us instead," Sterling murmured.

"We have to try," I said.

"Do we though? Do we have to do anything?" Sterling asked. "Do we even have to stay here?"

"We have to get revenge for our parents and Matthew," Milo snapped and slammed his glass on the counter.

Devon shifted. "Revenge isn't going to change anything," he said. "They're not coming back. And revenge will only result in more deaths."

"Are you seriously still trying to protect your father?!" Milo snarled. I'd never seen him this angry before. That was saying something because Milo was nearly always angry.

"I'm not protecting him. I'm protecting *you!*" Devon shouted.

"Oh? Then what did you say to him after he shot Matthew? Before you *let him go?*" Milo barked.

Devon's eyes flashed like his control had snapped like a rubber band. "I told him that if his goal was to break my brothers to keep me in power, then he failed. If he had hoped to ruin you two to go back to a single leader, then he failed. Because I would spend my last breath, my last drop of blood, to make sure we stayed together and led together."

I gasped at his words and looked at Sterling and Milo. They were both frozen in shock, having not expected Devon to defend them. Sterling moved only to hang his head and breathe deeply.

Milo swallowed. "Thank you," he said hoarsely.

Devon waved it off, but the tension left his shoulders as he sighed. "I am truly sorry about Matthew," he said after a moment.

"Doc told us Matthew may have known about some or both of our parents' deaths," Milo grumbled.

"Maybe, but he was still the man that raised you and Marie," I interjected.

Milo practically crumpled as my words hit home. Sterling caught him as his grief over his uncle, the disaster that was the family business, his closest family outside of this room having to go into hiding, and his three near-death experiences overwhelmed him at once. It was like a dam broke and his tentative hold had cracked. Sterling held him tight, and I rushed to hold him as well.

I looked back at Devon and he appeared lost. His expression

was unsure, like he didn't know if he deserved to be a part of Milo's grief. Like he felt responsible for it. I was about to tell him to come over when he jerked out of a thought and mumbled, "I'll go contact the gang leaders for a meeting." He left the kitchen for the office before I could tell him to stop.

Milo calmed down under our touch and when his breathing evened out against Sterling's neck, we pulled back. His face above his beard was splotchy, but his eyes were dry. Sterling fixed his crooked glasses and clapped a hand on his shoulder. "Let's go get a shower, clean the day off of us."

Sterling led us to his bathroom and started the water. When it was on, he turned back to us. "Well, get naked. Or do I have to strip you?"

"I would like to be stripped," I said brightly. "Please."

Sterling laughed, and even Milo smiled.

"Alright, well, you asked for it," Sterling warned before he roughly stripped me, but was gentle with my broken arm. I giggled the whole time.

"I can't get my cast wet," Milo mumbled. "I'll wash up later."

"Nah, I'll help you. The shower is big enough you both can be out of the spray," Sterling said as he undressed himself.

He helped Milo undress. A bit more awkward than with me, but effective. We stepped into the shower, inhaling the steam and scent of Sterling's soap. Here, with them, I finally relaxed. It was just us in this bathroom. We were safe with each other and there were no hard expectations. There were no stakes to consider. No threats. No anger. No violence.

Sterling washed and I watched raptly. When we first stepped into the shower, it had been a congenial, friendly endeavor. But now, the air of the shower was thick with lust.

I watched Sterling tip his head back with his eyes closed, his tattooed throat exposed. I watched his throat bob as he swallowed. Soapy bubbles slid down his body, curving around muscles and tangling in the hair of his legs before washing down the drain. I looked up to see Milo watching also, his cock already standing tall. We made eye contact, and I bit my lip. He smirked and reached his hand down to his erection.

Sterling finished up and looked at Milo and his eyes widened as he saw what Milo was doing. "Here, let me," Sterling said as he lathered up his hands. He ran his soapy hands over Milo's body with calm reverence, giving special attention to the places Milo liked most. Milo leaned back against the glass window, his eyes hooded and on Sterling. I slid around the shower spray to touch Milo. The need to feel and taste his smooth skin was overwhelming. I licked up his neck, tasting salty sweat and soap, and ran my hand over his lathered chest. He groaned as I sucked at his pulse point on his neck and his eyes fell shut. Sterling and I ended up on our knees in front of Milo after Sterling carefully rinsed him off with the handheld showerhead.

We sucked and stroked, our tongues warring for drops of pre-come. Milo was trembling and breathlessly moaning soon after we started. "Fuck, stop," Milo said. We backed off immediately. "I want to come in Emily's pussy."

"Not a chance," Sterling chuckled darkly.

"Why?" Milo almost whined as Sterling gripped the base of his cock. Hard.

"Because you should not lose your virginity on a day like today," Sterling said calmly.

"I think we're past losing my virginity, Sterling. You've

literally tied me up and made me come with fucking BDSM, and I've had both of you suck my dick at the same time. Let me fuck-" a shout of pleasure when I deep throated him while Sterling massaged his balls cut his angry rant off.

I giggled around his cock and then gagged when the vibrations of my voice made him thrust deeper. I sucked him hard and long, and Sterling bit his thigh while massaging his balls.

"Let me see you come down her pretty throat. Come on, that's my good boy," Sterling praised in a deep, growling voice. "Make her wish it was her pussy you were filling. Fuck yes, come on."

Milo came with a shout and a snarl as he grabbed my hair tight in his good hand. His grip made my eyes water as I swallowed him down. When his cock stopped pulsing in my mouth, I came off of him with a sucking pop.

Sterling washed Milo's over sensitive cock again, making him hiss through his teeth. Then they converged on me, washing me and touching me. They overwhelmed my senses until I wasn't sure who was washing and who was touching me. There were hands and lips, tongues and teeth, soap and water everywhere. Sterling pressed me against the glass once I was rinsed and mumbled something to Milo. Milo mumbled back, but I was too focused on their touch to hear their words. After a second, Sterling easily lifted me into the air. I squeaked in shock as my wet skin slid against the window, reaching an area that had not been warmed first by Milo's body. I was in the air, held up by Sterling's arms, with my thighs over his shoulders. This was not something to be nonchalant about- I was not a small woman. But he lifted me like I weighed nothing. Licking a flat, wet line over my pussy, he moaned deep in his throat. I looked out at the foggy mirror and saw our reflection. Sterling was devouring me and moaning while Milo kneeled below me, sucking Sterling's cock with vigor. It was probably the most erotic thing I'd ever seen.

"Oh my god, don't drop me," I breathed between moans. "I'd kill Milo."

"No, you'd only snap my spine and paralyze me," Milo said, his voice rasping but matter of fact. I couldn't even be insulted because he was entirely correct.

"Social skills, Milo," Sterling scolded and his piercing gray-blue eyes fixed on me. "You're not going anywhere." He winked, and I settled back against the glass, watching Sterling's eyes roll back as Milo sucked him and then watching our steamy reflection in the mirror. He swirled his tongue and jolts of pleasure coursed through me, making me whimper and shiver.

It wasn't long before I was gripping Sterling's hair with my unbound hand and rolling my hips. His grip shifted from my waist to where my hips met my thighs, his thumbs securely trapped in the fold there and holding me still against the glass.

"You're fucking drooling and dripping on my head," Milo chuckled hoarsely below me.

Sterling gave an apologetic slurp against my pussy and the sensation ricocheted me into my orgasm. I bit my lip as I screamed and tried not to thrash. He sucked hard on my clit and it almost hurt but sent me spiraling. My body felt like pins and needles of pleasure shot through my arms and legs originating at my clit. Sterling's arms trembled as he held me and I thought it was because I was becoming too heavy. But his eyes rolled back and then shut tight before he moaned long and low against me as he came. I heard Milo sputtering and coughing and laughing below me.

"Dude," Milo laughed through a cough as Sterling set me down gently next to him. "You gotta give me a warning next time."

"My dick was in your mouth, I think that's warning enough," Sterling panted as a few more streams of come trickled out.

"No, it's not," Milo and I both said. Sterling was gifted in the ejaculation department. He always came more than anyone I'd ever seen.

"Whatever, you liked it," Sterling said, rinsing off.

"Choking to death? Yeah, it was a blast," Milo said sarcastically.

"Like a firehose," I said, and both guys laughed.

We finished up in the shower and separated to our rooms to get dressed. I was in my room, just finishing drying my hair when my phone chimed. The only people with my new phone number were in this house. I heard a loud laugh down the hall and it sounded like Sterling. Eagerly, I picked up my phone.

Apparently I was part of the house group chat now. Smiling, I opened the text. It was a picture from Devon. It was clearly a picture from when we were in the shower. Milo's back was pressed against the glass of the window, making his butt cheeks flatten. The light and angle prevented me and Sterling from being visible on our knees. I giggled, looking at the picture.

Sterling replied in the chat, "Our first group chat and it's Milo's booty cheeks!"

I replied with two peach emoji.

4

Milo

It was three in the morning, and I was still awake. Sighing, I looked over at Emily and Sterling. Emily was asleep on her side, her peaceful face tilted up toward me. Her red hair was pushed back from when she tried to stay awake with me and let me talk about computers until she finally fell asleep. She had murmured "Talk to me about anything that will calm your body for sleep," and tried so hard to keep her eyes open while I droned on about how IP sub-netting works. She did pretty well, even asked what a few jargon terms meant, but ultimately fell asleep.

Sterling was flat on his back, snoring like a lawn mower, sprawled out and taking up most of the bed. He had handed me a weed gummy and told me to get too high to stay awake. He had promptly taken two, ate Emily out again, and then fell fast asleep. Maybe there was merit to his methods. I picked up the gummy and chewed it. Ugh, it had a horrible fruity and skunky flavor. I put on my glasses and got up to go get a drink.

Down in the kitchen, I got a glass of water and stood against the counter drinking.

"Emily, is that you?" Devon's voice called out from the office.

Startled, I replied, "No."

"Oh, Milo, come here," he called back.

Looking down at my body, I realized I was just in a pair of boxer briefs. Not really caring about my state of undress, I padded to the office.

"What's up?" I asked, my voice thick with exhaustion.

"I'm working on tracking down some of our gangs. My dad's in the wind so I haven't found him. But I'm looking at some of the security feeds you have for some of our gangs," Devon said and sat back in the creaking leather desk chair. He rubbed his hands over his face and scrubbed over his stubble.

"What did you find?" I asked and leaned against the desk. Long ago, I had hacked into the existing security camera feeds of the hideouts and strongholds of our gangs. Or I had discreet cameras hung outside the locations that didn't have their own. One or two of them had outright asked me to help them with security setups, so I had easy access to those.

"The Prospect Kings and East Side Warriors moved for Anthony quickly. One went to his house and packed up his shit, and the other went somewhere else. I haven't seen them show up on any of our cameras. They seemed to have gotten calls right about the time the meeting ended, so I'm assuming it was him," Devon explained. He did a double take at me, leaning next to him. "Do you have to be so naked next to me?"

"You called me in here, not the other way around," I argued blandly.

"Emily and Sterling didn't put you to sleep?" He smirked with a tinge of bitterness.

"No," I replied simply, not trying to rub it in that he wasn't included. I suspected he had feelings for Emily, and I'd never been on this side of the situation before. "Did they empty his safe?"

"No, they seemed to not even know about it," Devon said, returning his attention to the computer.

"We could get in there," I suggested and crossed my unbroken arm over my chest and cast.

Devon made a face like he was considering it. "It's something to think about."

"It could cripple his financials," I assessed.

"Are we safe here, Milo?" Devon asked suddenly.

"Is that why you're not sleeping?" I asked, looking him over. He was in a pair of gray sweatpants and a black zip up hoodie, his hair mussed and his stubble thick. It had been a long time since I'd seen him this casual.

"Part of it," Devon yawned.

"Our security system is the best we can get without guards. And we have weapons in every room," I explained. "We'll see any attack coming."

Devon exhaled tensely.

"What?" I asked him, warily.

"Milo, I'm sorry," he said and looked up at me.

"For what, exactly?" I asked.

"For what my dad has done. I had no part in it, but... he's

my dad and I... feel responsible," Devon said, his voice rasping with thinly controlled emotion.

"I don't blame you," I said, even though my chest tightened. It didn't make logical sense to connect blame for my parents' and Matthew's death to Devon but yet those words burned on my tongue.

His golden-brown eyes were on me intently as he studied me.

"Matthew was a good-"

"Don't," I snapped, ashamed of the desperate hoarseness in my voice.

He looked away and nodded. He understood that while I didn't blame him, I still associated his family with my losses. Not only my parents and uncle, but my intended right to rule the family business at his side.

"How is Sterling doing?" Devon asked after a moment.

"He'll be fine. He doesn't remember his parents. It's only ever been just him. He didn't have a baby sister crying for her mom or an uncle who talked about how much more than parents we'd lost," I said, ignoring the crack in my voice.

"Do you mean leadership?" Devon asked.

I nodded. "Matthew was always talking about it."

"I'm sorry about that, too," Devon whispered. "My father was always adamant ... well, you know."

I nodded again. The strongest leaders were from the strongest surviving bloodlines. I knew the belief well.

We were silent again, and Devon returned to the computer. I watched him for a few moments before something occurred to me. "Was that Gregory Ambrose, as in Emily's ex, at the meeting?"

Devon scoffed. "Yeah, she said everyone in that room was local politicians. I guess Giovanni and Taz were right."

"They were absolute jackasses, but they weren't lying ones," I mumbled.

"My dad had us bring in Emily as a political tool. A connection for insider information. And maybe even as a bargaining chip. And while that didn't work out, he still had mayors and commissioners and trustees in that room. He put out the hit on her because he had all he needed, and she was useless to him. By then, she knew too much," Devon explained angrily.

"Do you think they're all going to stick with him after that meeting?" I asked him.

Devon shrugged. "I think it scared them at the moment. But they'll all go home, have a drink, fuck their wives, and then realize they love the danger and the adrenaline and be back for more."

I snorted in derision. "You're probably right. I can start identifying them from the footage and then monitor them. Maybe they'll lead us back to Anthony."

"Start with Gregory," Devon said.

"Why?" I asked.

"He's the weakest link. He just saw his missing ex-wife in the arms of the mafia he was getting into business with. He's going to panic and get sloppy," Devon reasoned.

"Don't downplay her. She wasn't in our arms, she was standing next to us," I lectured him. Emily wasn't an accessory. She was one of us.

"I had to hold her up after she saw Gregory there," Devon argued.

I felt momentarily bad for not being there for her when she needed me, but I had been occupied at that moment. Oddly, I felt grateful Devon could be a support for her. I sighed and ran my hand through my hair.

Devon's eyes looked me over. "So, why are you awake?"

"Couldn't sleep," I grunted.

"Obviously. Are Emily and Sterling asleep?" he asked.

"Yeah, they're out," I said, thinking back to our activities in the shower.

Devon chuckled.

"What?" I asked him.

"You got this look on your face like they had every reason to be sound asleep," Devon explained.

"Oh, they do," I said with a laugh of my own.

"And you're not a part of it?" Devon asked, looking me over again.

"I am," I defended.

"You still a virgin?" Devon asked with a sly grin.

The heat of a blush crept up my neck and down over my chest, confirming Devon's question.

"Well, get on that. Literally. We could die tomorrow," Devon laughed.

"They won't let me," I grumbled, that weed edible making my lips looser. "You'll probably fuck her before I do."

Devon's face shuttered instantly. "I don't think so."

I shrugged, and a chuckle slipped. "Whatever you say. You could absolutely jump in and she'd love it."

"I'm not into group shit," Devon said, but wouldn't make eye contact.

"It's hotter than you'd think," I said, and yawned.

"That's because you are attracted to the other guy involved," Devon defended.

"You're not attracted to me or Sterling?" I asked him, shocked and a little offended.

Devon peered at me suspiciously. "Milo, are you high?"

"Yeah, but do you think me and Sterling are ugly?" I said before I could stop myself.

"Objectively, you both are... attractive," Devon said hesitantly.

"Are you not attracted to Emily, then?" I asked, feeling like there was no way he couldn't be.

"Of course I'm fucking attracted to Emily," he snapped at me.

"Then what are you-" I began, but he stood up abruptly.

He got in my face. His expression warned of a brewing storm. I wondered for a moment if he was about to kiss me. Wait... *what?*

"The way I fuck is not conducive to two more dicks in the room," he said low and growling in my face. His breath smelled like whiskey and like he'd eaten a peanut butter sandwich. God, that sounded good right now.

"I'm not sure what you mean," I said, my voice breathless.

Devon shook his head. "You're too high to have this conversation."

"Why does it matter?"

"You're hard," he said and looked down.

I looked down, too. And there I was, high as a kite, with my boner pressing into the leg of my lifelong friend. I laughed, and it sounded more like a giggle. Devon stepped back with a chuckle of his own.

"Thanks, this conversation has exhausted me enough to go to bed," Devon said and shut down the computer.

"Happy to help," I said. "But when you dream of being in bed with Emily, make sure you picture me and Sterling there, too."

"Good night, Milo," Devon drawled as he left the office.

Still uncomfortably hard and high, I went back to Sterling's room on a mission. He and Emily were exactly as I'd left them. I stripped off my boxer briefs and climbed clumsily between them. I rubbed the head of my dick over Emily's cheek and then Sterling's lips, leaving a shiny line of pre-come on them. Sterling's brows twitched, but neither one woke up. Grinning, I decided to leave a little gift instead of waking them up to suck me off. I stroked my cock hard and fast. Just as I was about to come all over their faces, I tipped my head back.

I heard a sleepy male grunt and a quiet feminine giggle. My head dropped back to look at their faces to see them hooded eyed and smiling at me.

"No, go back to sleep," I groaned. "I was going to paint your faces."

"Do it," Sterling murmured. "Paint us. You fucking slut."

"I'm the slut? You're the one asking for it," I breathed.

Sterling smirked before reaching up and spanking my ass hard. I jerked toward them with a moan in reaction, and Emily giggled again.

"Whore," Emily whispered.

"Our whore," Sterling grumbled deep in his chest as he massaged my balls. Emily stroked up my thigh, her nails lightly raking over my skin.

Their gentle touches brought me right back to my climax. "Fuck," I moaned.

"What a dirty boy. Wanted to mark us while we slept. Wanted to jerk his massive cock on our faces. Wanted to show us how mad he is that he hasn't fucked Emily yet," Sterling growled out.

"God, I want to fuck you," I groaned as my legs shook.

"Show me how much, all over my face," Emily moaned.

At the sound of her quiet and sleepy moan, I let go. I came in hot streams over their faces with a shout. Sterling used his shirt to wipe them both up.

"Milo, go to bed," Sterling chuckled.

I could only grunt in agreement before I collapsed between them.

5

Milo

The bed was empty and cold when I woke up. I felt simultaneously sad I was alone and happy they'd let me sleep in. Getting up, I slipped on the pair of mostly clean jeans and sweater I'd abandoned at the foot of Sterling's bed yesterday. I stopped in my room to grab a laptop and went to meet the others. Descending the stairs, I could smell toast and coffee. I heard Emily's voice and the guys' voices reply as if she'd been asking questions.

"Bananas?" Emily asked them as I entered the kitchen.

"No, I'm allergic," Devon replied.

Emily was leaning against the kitchen island, pen and pad of paper in hand. I kissed her on the cheek before going to the coffeepot.

"Did you know that people with banana allergies are often also allergic to latex?" I said as I poured my coffee.

"Alright, I'll scratch latex bodysuit for Devon off

the list," Emily said dismally and pretended to scribble on her notepad.

"Where's my kiss?" Sterling demanded.

I grinned and turned back to oblige him. What I had intended to be a brief peck on his cheek like the one I'd given Emily was hijacked by Sterling and turned into a lip biting, sucking kiss. When I extracted myself, Sterling's pupils were blown wide with lust and my heart jumped in my chest at the sight. Not even in my wildest dreams did I think I would ever get to experience Sterling in this way. I went back to fixing my cup of coffee like I wasn't hard in my jeans and red up to my ears. Emily was smiling widely as I passed her again, and Devon was watching me from over his mug.

I suddenly remembered last night when I was high and got turned on by Devon. Well shit. That's embarrassing. I made my coffee and sat at the island between Devon and Sterling. Devon was still staring at me. "Oh, did you want one, too?"

Emily whimpered. Devon shot her a warning glance before responding, "No."

"Are you sure?" I pried with a smirk. Devon was too easy to get all pissy.

Sterling adjusted his pants next to me.

"I'm sure," Devon said, a blush high on his cheeks. *Too easy.*

"Maybe another time then," I said and sipped my coffee.

"Um." Emily started and cleared her throat. "Apples?"

"Sure," Devon said at the same time Sterling said, "In a pie."

Emily wrote something on the paper.

"Are you making a grocery list?" I asked.

"Yes. Is there anything you want from the store?" Emily asked me.

"Coffee, whiskey, and... maybe some good steaks. We haven't had them in a while," I said as Sterling slid the plate of toast over to me.

Emily wrote on the pad of paper.

I unlocked my laptop and chewed my toast as Emily listed basic food items and meal ideas. Not caring much about what else they bought at the store, I only replied to direct questions. As a morning routine, I browsed the news, browsed Reddit, checked on a few forums I interacted with, looked over some server logs, and checked my emails.

"Milo, listen up," I heard Devon's voice come into focus with the use of my name.

I blinked and looked up. Sterling ran a soft hand down my back, and Devon was looking at me for confirmation of my attention. Emily had an eyebrow quirked at me. She had put her list down in front of her. I had been hyper focused on my tasks that I hadn't heard the end of the shopping conversation. Devon and Sterling knew to use my name or a light physical touch to pull me out of a tunnel of concentration.

"Listening," I said, my voice grumbling from being unused for a time.

"Okay," Devon began. "We've had time to sleep, and time to think about the events of yesterday. We need to make plans for going forward."

"Do you want me to get the big notepad and markers?" Emily asked, pointing towards the office.

"No." Devon smiled at her. "I think we'll be fine without."

"Okay, because I kind of feel like we all have different goals here. So, it's going to be hard to plan for anything," Emily reasoned.

Devon sighed. "Well, what do you want, Emily? What is your goal?"

"I think we need to find out why Anthony and Matthew were meeting with politicians and local officials. If you've been operating the family business under their noses this whole time, then why were they just now getting involved?" Emily asked.

"I don't know that yesterday was the first meeting," Devon said, adding to everyone's suspicions.

"Gregory was there, and he has never met with them before," Emily argued.

"You didn't know he was fucking his secretary. Why would you know about his meeting schedule?" Devon said coldly.

Hurt flashed across Emily's face.

"I never thought I'd say this, but Devon, social skills," I muttered.

Sterling snorted next to me and proudly smacked my thigh. I was successful in erasing that hurt look from Emily's face, at least. A soft smile played on her lips.

"I'm sorry, Emily, but it's the truth. He could have been working with Anthony and Matthew for a time before you came to us," Devon said, only slightly softer this time.

Emily nodded. "I was probably going to be collateral for Gregory's compliance before they realized they didn't need me."

"Now, you're one of us instead," Sterling said and smirked lasciviously at her.

"Anyway," Devon said. "Milo, what's your goal?"

"I want revenge for my parents and uncle. For Sterling's parents. For trying to have me and Emily killed. I want him to pay," I replied darkly. As I spoke all of Anthony's sins out loud, a feeling of putrefaction and rage simmered in my stomach. I regretted the toast I'd eaten.

Devon nodded solemnly because he knew my answer already.

"Sterling?" Emily asked.

"I only want us all together and safe. I want to get the fuck out of here," Sterling said and rubbed his hand over the back of his neck. "There's nothing for us here. We don't have control over any gangs or businesses anymore. We're free of this shit."

"Devon?"

"I want to rebuild. I want a chance to build a life for us here," Devon said.

Some of the anger from my stomach reared up to my chest. "You just want your turn to rule the world. Well, look at where that got us. Maybe it's time someone else ruled."

"I've been training for this my whole life! Of course, I'll be in control!" Devon shouted back at me.

"In control of what?" I snapped, my teeth tight and lips curled.

"Alright, let's settle down," Emily soothed.

"We can barely trust our family as it is," Sterling said. "So, I don't see why we'd stick around to have power struggles over nothing."

"Do you mean Stephanie and Marie?" Emily asked, confused.

"Not Marie. We can trust Marie and Brendon," I said. If there was anything I was sure of, it was Marie's loyalty.

"I don't know about that," Devon said.

"What?!" I shouted. "Of course, we can trust my sister and her husband!"

My heart hammered in my chest with indignant anger. How dare he suggest we can't trust my *sister* to be on our side?

"Brendon's family ties to the Irish businesses and families in the area are important in considering his loyalties. Where do they stand? And Marie would go wherever he went," Devon said, a bite of anger still in his slow and calm voice. He sounded just like Anthony. My stomach boiled.

"Marie would never take the side of someone who wanted me dead and killed our uncle," I snapped. The thought of Marie betraying us was so ridiculous I could have laughed if Devon wasn't serious.

"Let's get back to the plan," Emily said, trying to redirect us. Her voice was soft and soothing, like she was directing children to join story time on the carpet.

"I think we need to hold off until you hear from the gangs and try to get a meeting," Sterling said pensively.

"Are you saying we should base our decisions on if we can get gang support?" Devon asked.

"I do. I think we should see if we even have business to run, you know?" Sterling said with a shrug.

"If they want to work with us, we stay and continue the fight against my dad. And if they are against us, then we can leave," Devon elaborated.

"And we turn in Anthony before we leave?" Emily asked with a wince. "So he can't control the business anymore?"

We were silent as we considered.

"Our concern is selling out Anthony will get our own

names and the names of the rest of our family associated with the crimes," Devon said carefully.

"Devon is trying to protect his daddy," I spat.

"I am not!" Devon shouted next to me. "I'm keeping *our* names protected!"

"And you're underestimating my ability to get us new identities and a plane ticket out of here in less than twenty minutes," I shot back. We'd been over this, and Devon still ignored my skills and instead protected his dad. It made me sick to know I shared a house and a life with this man who so readily discounted his chosen family.

Devon gave a groan of frustration. "I don't want to flee. Our lives are here."

Emily was watching Devon narrowly, like she was figuring him out. "I think you're worried if we leave Cleveland, you wouldn't have the power over our group that you have here, and the lack of control scares you."

Devon glared at her. "No."

She smirked. "I think I'm right."

She was. I knew it. Everyone knew it.

"The gangs and suppliers are going to need to be paid the same, if not more, than what they were getting before. Or more than what Anthony is offering them to keep them on his side," Sterling said.

"I have the spreadsheets of what we were giving each of our gangs before the split," I mumbled as I pulled them up on my laptop.

Emily asked about who does our bookkeeping- something either Devon or Sterling could answer, so I focused on the screen of my laptop. Logging into a few websites in separate tabs, I switched to the tab with my bank account. With a sickening lurch in my stomach, I saw the total of my accounts at zero dollars. Panicked, I opened the recent transactions and saw a line where my accounts were drained of every penny yesterday afternoon to cash at the bank.

"Oh no," I said hoarsely as I switched to Devon's account. Sterling and Devon leaned over to see what I was looking at, and Emily came around the counter.

"Milo, I've told you not to hack into my bank account. That's private information," Devon muttered as I scrolled on his account page. I ignored him. As if *any* information was private when I was involved.

"Nothing. There's nothing there," I grunted.

"What the fuck?!" Devon said and stood up from his stool.

"Check mine," Sterling said urgently.

I opened the first of Sterling's accounts and saw his money was missing from that one, too. "This is your first one," I explained. "The one you got paid into by Anthony."

"Check my other one," Sterling said in a rush. I opened the tab that had his Personal Camera's deposits. It was untouched and had a remaining balance. He let out a relieved sigh.

"How'd he get your money?" Emily asked.

"Technically they were joint accounts. It's easier to pay us without direct deposit slips and tax form bullshit," I explained. "He transferred us money every month as payment between connected accounts, so his name was on our shit."

"Can you take it back?" Emily pressed. "If the accounts are connected you should be able to."

I was already opening Anthony and Matthew's

main accounts. "Nope, he emptied them both to cash. Must have pissed the bank off doing that, too."

"Fucking hell!" Devon shouted and Sterling hit the granite countertop.

"Wait, if you're not getting paid by Anthony anymore and he stole your money, how are you going to pay bills?" Emily asked and looked down at the grocery list.

"I guess we'll have to make some more videos," Sterling said and nudged me.

"I'll get the chocolate strawberries and Viagara," Devon said sarcastically as he poured another cup of coffee.

"We only have utilities and property taxes," I explained to her. "This house is technically Sterling's."

"You own this house?" Emily asked, looking shocked.

"Yeah, why?" Sterling asked.

"It's not decorated like you own it," Emily said and looked around. "This is a nineties era Tuscan winery kitchen."

Sterling shrugged. "This was my parents' house. It's decorated how they liked it."

"Except for the cells in the basement," I clarified. "They didn't have on-site torture chambers in the nineties."

"An upgrade, I'm sure," Emily mumbled.

"So, how are we going to make the most money with these videos?" Sterling said and rubbed his hands together.

"Do we need another guest star?" I asked, looking at both Emily and Devon.

Emily looked at Devon as if she hadn't even remotely considered she could be on the channel and was assuming I meant only him. Devon was leaning against the counter next to the coffeepot and his eyes shot up towards me. "No."

"I think we can make it a series," Sterling said thoughtfully. "What if we do a mixture of scripted stuff and natural stuff?"

"Wait, what if you pretend to break the fourth wall?" Emily asked excitedly.

"What do you mean?" Sterling asked.

"I mean, what if you have a video where you two are discussing the popularity of your first video as if you're not filming and it's found footage you're posting? And it's you two saying how much you enjoyed doing the first video and then saying you should go further to test it out. It can be like a hidden story line. The scripted stuff can vary and then the fake found footage," Emily said quickly.

"You seem to have had a fully formed idea just occur to you in completion," Devon said with sarcastic awe. "It's almost as if this was a fantasy of yours."

Emily blushed and rolled her eyes. "I may have fantasized about it."

"Isn't it like... the definition of queer baiting?" Sterling asked hesitantly.

"No, because we'd actually be doing the gay stuff. We wouldn't be faking it to get views and then not following through with it," I grumbled.

Devon shifted uncomfortably. Internally, I laughed at him. Sure, it was probably kind of weird to see your two longest friends become romantically involved. But his discomfort was a pleasant bonus. I knew Devon wasn't homophobic, so I wasn't offended that he was uncomfortable.

Emily flipped her notepad to the page after the grocery list. "Okay, let's plan out a video schedule. You should film one and have it posted today, so we have more money for the gangs and any bribes we will need right off the bat."

"First video should be another scripted one," Devon muttered, like this was the actual last conversation he wanted to be having. "Then it should end with Sterling thinking he's hitting stop on the recording and then video two can be the fake found footage where you admit you like seeing each other's junk."

Emily giggled. "And Sterling can be like 'Oh, all I can think about is if I can fit your monster cock in my mouth' and Milo can tell him to try."

Sterling's eyebrows shot up. "Emily!" He stretched out her name. "That's dirty!"

She blushed even deeper, and I grinned.

"We didn't get anything figured out," Emily said. "See? This is why we need the big paper and markers."

Devon rolled his eyes and snapped at her, "If we want to buy out the gangs, we need money. And in order to get money we need to exploit those two. No board needed. Now, I'm going to contact more gang leaders to set up a meeting." He left with his coffee and an irritated expression.

We spent the next thirty minutes planning out scripts for today's videos. One where Sterling is my personal trainer, and we jerk off in the sauna. Then one where we break the fourth wall and then touch each other. Despite Emily's idea for the script, we decided on keeping it to only hands on each other. Then the next video could be blow jobs to create a slower burn and stretch out the videos with anticipation. Besides, we hadn't gone further than that in real life, let alone on camera. I wasn't about to have our real first time having penetrative sex be on camera for views. The thought of getting there with Sterling sent a jolt of excitement through my spine, and I was ready to film.

6

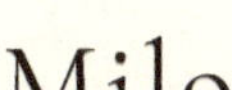

Milo

After breakfast, Sterling and I went to the gym to get some shots of us working out for marketing and for the story we're creating. I've shown him the data from his videos that says most people fast forward until they see naked skin and don't listen to the story. But Sterling's vision was the story lines brought people in to watch his porn. Not his pierced dick or tattoos. His delusion was... adorable.

Sterling had us getting closer and closer during our work out videos. Carefully positioned in the camera shot and posed in a way that highlighted important features to create tension and a sexually charged atmosphere. I didn't realize how much work went into his videos. Sometimes he would send me a text with some editing suggestions, but other than that, it was a few clicks on my end in Adobe. I was impressed with him. My arm in a cast didn't deter him one bit.

"Okay, now let's get a shot in the shower. I want it to be

you looking out the corner of your eye at me by the sink and swallowing like you're turned on and nervous. Try to blush or something," Sterling directed, purely businesslike.

I didn't think I could blush on demand, but I'd do the rest. Carefully avoiding getting my cast wet, I washed my body. While we had been mostly filming, I had worked out enough to break out in a sweat. Though that could have been because I was near Sterling the entire time. He got the shot he wanted on my second take and went to strip out of his clothes. He directed me to film him in the shower and we'd pick the best shot later.

Heading to the sauna, I was already hard. I'd been teased by the sight of Sterling, sweaty and then naked for too long to not be able to touch him. Sterling handed me a bottle of water as he set up the phone tripod. "Drink the whole thing," he instructed as he changed the angle of the phone. "You have to come twice."

I finished my water and handed him his. "Well, actually, I don't think it's based on our hydration if we can come more than once."

He shrugged. "Can't hurt."

We were silent while he checked the frame again. "You know," he said as he came out of the sauna. "The first time I got turned on by you was in this sauna."

"Really?" I asked, a bit more excited than I'd intended.

He smirked at me. "Yeah, we were training for the fight, and we gave each other massages."

I moaned, remembering. "Fuck, I loved that. The only reason I won that fight was because I was obsessed with having your hands on me while we trained."

Sterling looked shocked. "Really?"

"Yeah," I grinned. "We should start this video with a massage for old time's sake."

Sterling agreed, and we waited for the ten second countdown on his phone. Sterling entered the shot first and sat on the bench, his white towel tied around his waist. I entered just after him and sat on the bench opposite him, but still in view. We chatted for a moment before I pretended the shoulder of my unbroken arm was stiff.

"Oh, I can massage that for you. Help you relax," Sterling said, his tone a mixture of helpful professionalism and restrained lust.

"Yeah, um, sure," I said, feigning shyness, and rotated on the bench.

I was facing the camera with Sterling behind me as he put some oil on his hands. The smell of the oil took over the eucalyptus scent of the sauna with an almost spicy, woodsy scent. I inhaled deeply as Sterling massaged my shoulders. He was intentionally gentle on my injured arm, not wanting to hurt me. The moan I let slip was genuine. I hadn't realized I was carrying so much tension in my shoulders.

"Normally, after a big workout and I need to relax, I come in here and... well, work some other muscles," Sterling said huskily after a few moments.

"What do you mean?" I asked, playing dumb.

"You know, I jerk off," Sterling said with a chuckle.

"Oh. Well, don't stop on my account. I can close my eyes," I said with a chuckle of my own. It was a call back to the day Sterling first asked me to be a guest star on his channel. He had said he'd close his eyes while I masturbated next to him. I fought a grin at the memory.

"In that case, I'm already hard. Don't mind if I do," he said and plopped back down on his bench, untying his towel.

My eyes went straight to his cock, erect and his piercing, shining in the ring light attached to his phone tripod. My gulp was also a genuine reaction to the flood of saliva in my mouth upon seeing Sterling's cock. I closed my eyes, as promised, as he used some of the massage oil on his cock. The slow slide of his skin made me intimately aware of my erection. I adjusted my towel and kept my eyes closed.

Sterling's voice was deep and growly when he spoke. "You can do it, too. I swear it's a game changer for post work out relaxation."

I gave a hesitant glance over at him and saw he was watching me as he stroked himself. Untying my towel and grabbing some oil, I allowed myself to finally touch my cock. It was throbbing with the need for release after all this teasing. I had no doubt I'd be able to come twice. With a long exhale, I leaned against the wall on the bench, facing Sterling. I stroked myself at a slow pace and kept my eyes closed until I heard Sterling's soft moan. My eyes opened to meet his instantly as he panted. We stared at each other with hooded eyes and open mouths and heaving chests. I wasn't touching him, but I loved this.

He scooted on the bench so he could reach down to his balls easier, and his knees knocked against mine. I couldn't help the curl at the corner of my mouth as I pressed my leg against his intentionally. He gave me a small wink in return as his fist moved with a tighter grip.

The only sounds in the sauna were our heavy breathing, the sound of slick skin on skin, and occasional moans and sighs. Sterling had his lip trapped between his teeth as he groaned. His abs were jumping and twisting as he neared his orgasm.

It had only been a few minutes in here and he was already about to come. I was close, too, but I wanted to enjoy this. This was the best I'd felt in days, and I didn't want it to be over already. "Wait," I whispered hoarsely. "Slow down."

"What?" Sterling looked startled. I thought it was an authentic response since we'd not scripted this part.

"I said slow down. Make it last. It should feel like it drains your muscles, right?" I asked, my voice cracking as I fought a moan.

"Right. Like this?" Sterling asked as his fist slowed.

"Yeah, like that. That's good," I replied and moaned. "Fuck. Match my pace. Hell yeah, that's hot."

"You're telling me to relax but look at your shoulders," Sterling huffed. "Relax your shoulders. Your whole body. If you're all tensed up it almost hurts when you come. If you're relaxed, it feels like an orgasm throughout your whole body."

Both of us intentionally relaxed our shoulders against the bamboo of the sauna. Our sweaty legs rubbed against each other, and I felt when Sterling trembled. I licked my lips, knowing he was about to come. Feeling the crescendo of a building orgasm to match his, I wanted to wait until he came. I wanted to come with him.

Sterling gave three sharp breaths before he arched against the bamboo and his fist took on a slower but tighter pace on his cock. Come poured from him in thick streams and I watched it land on his abs and roll back down his body. The long, hoarse groan that came from him as his eyes screwed shut was what sent me over the edge. I came with a shout which ended with a moan. I felt come slide down my abs as well, mirroring Sterling. Focusing my eyes on him, I watched as he licked his lips and a last surge of come came from him with a grunt.

We sat, catching our breath for a few moments, before I put my towel back on and pretended to be modest and respectful. He cleared his throat as he put his towel back around his waist after wiping some of his come off his chest. Most of his come had slid down and puddled on the towel he was sitting on, so he was now sitting on it.

"Thanks for the training today. I'll see you for our session on Thursday?" I asked, standing.

"Yeah. See you later, man," Sterling said in a deep, casual tone.

He got up from the bench as if he was pressing stop, jostled the phone, and sat back down. I went back into the sauna and asked, "How do you think it looked?"

"I think it was good," he said with a nod as he wiped up more of his come. "We were in the shot the whole time. I don't think we left the screen at all. We both came, so I think it'll work out fine."

"Well, let me know if you need to film it again," I said and sat back down in my vacated spot.

"You're down to film again?" he asked excitedly.

"Yeah, I really like doing this. The two times we've made videos I've come the hardest in a long time. I think I enjoy being watched," I said casually.

"By me or by subscribers?" he asked, his steel-blue eyes intent on me.

"Maybe both," I said after a shy look.

"Hm," Sterling said with a dark smirk. "I think I like being watched by you, too."

I gulped and said in a fake nervous voice. "Imagine how many views we'd get if we kissed or something."

Sterling grinned now and shot across the small sauna to sit next to me on the bench. We had angled the benches before filming today so the camera would still get a good view of both of us when we were together on one side. "We should try to see if we can even stand to kiss each other before we try to kiss on camera," he said, his voice gravelly.

I leaned forward and caught his lips with mine. Despite having just come, I felt my cock twitch beneath the towel when our lips touched. We kept it light for a second, like we were evaluating our feelings, before his lips opened to suck mine between them. I gripped his hair tight at the nape of his neck and groaned into the kiss. Sterling trailed fingertips down my back and made me shiver and gasp into his mouth. He pulled back from the kiss as his fingers touched the top of my towel. "What if we touched in our next video?"

I nodded and bit my lip. "I think we should practice now, though. I've never done it before."

"Me neither," Sterling breathed as he slowly untied my towel. His breath ghosted over my face in hot gusts. I untied his towel at the same time and tipped my forehead against his.

I was hard again, which was not shocking, considering I had Sterling touching and kissing me. I could probably get hard, come, and get hard again all night with Sterling. He was also hard and gasped when my fingers hesitantly touched his cock. When his hand wrapped around mine, I moaned and shivered. We both stared at each other with shock as we held each other's cocks. It wasn't all fake. I was endlessly in disbelief that Sterling, my oldest and closest friend, loved me how I loved him. My cock was still so sensitive that the bite of painful oversensitivity had me breathing like a bull. He poured oil over his hand on me and my hand on him and we started hesitantly stroking each other. I hissed out a breath through my teeth, trying not to shake too much.

Sterling tensed up next to me and kissed me hard. His strokes on me were fast and shaking, and his frantic pace and heavy breathing had me closer than I thought I could get this quickly for a second climax. We both danced at that edge of orgasm for what felt like hours. It was likely only a minute or two, but that edge was sharp and biting the second time around. Thankful for the oil, or we'd be fucking chafed, I reveled in the feel of his hand on me. I tried to relax into the orgasm, but that feral animal in my chest had me growling and thrusting.

Under my hand, Sterling was no better off. Or worse off, depending on the angle. His eyes were unfocused, and he was hunched over like he was fighting the urge to push me off him. Like my hand on him was almost too much to handle. And to think he was worried about *me* not being able to come a second time. Oddly enough, seeing his pain was what sent me over that jagged precipice. I'd Google that later. But my second orgasm ripped through me in an almost painful, tearing, scratching wave. My teeth ground shut as I breathed and growled through it.

His hand stuttered as he tried to coax me through it and my hand on him had completely stopped stroking. When I realized my inaction, I started stroking him hard again, with a twist at the top. He took his hand off me and I shivered. But he didn't put his hand down. He brought it to his lips. He looked at me as he panted and licked my come off the back of his hand. Sweat was dripping down the side of his face as he licked and moaned like it was the best thing he'd ever tasted. He held his hand out to my mouth with a quirk of his eyebrow. I licked his hand tentatively, tasting myself on him. He smirked at me before he gripped the edge of the bench on both sides of his body and curled over further, his stomach and chest rippling with convulsions. He gave a sharp cry of pleasure as he came. Spurt after spurt shot from him and he tried to turn his head away but, to my delight, come dripped from his cheek. It honestly impressed me he could still come so much the second time. Maybe there was something to hydration after all.

When his orgasm let go of him, he slumped back against the wall. He wiped his eyes, and I realized they were watering.

"Wait, why are you crying?" I asked, horrified I could have hurt him.

"I'm not *crying*," he insisted as he wiped the come from his cheek.

"You're literally crying," I said.

"I don't know. I think my eyes are watering because I came so hard two times in like thirty minutes," he said and chuckled breathlessly.

"Oh, in that case, I don't feel bad," I said.

"For what?" he asked me, his eyes meeting mine.

"For this," I said as I shoved my come covered hand in his mouth. I gripped his chin with my thumb and had all four fingers in his mouth. I felt his mouth fill with saliva and then he gagged at the pressure on his tongue. He was glaring at me and trying to push me off. "No, suck my fingers clean. You made a mess."

He rolled his eyes and obliged me. He glared the whole time, but I heard him gulp and felt his mouth constrict as he sucked. Once I was satisfied, I pulled my hand from his swollen lips.

"Well, what did you think?" I asked him, still breathless and shaky.

"That was..." Sterling stopped to swipe a thumb over his lips, gathering the last of his come I'd smeared there. "Super fucking hot." He shoved his thumb between my lips, and I smiled around him and sucked.

"Next video we touch each other?" I asked him once his thumb was clean. I leaned back against the warm wall of the sauna again.

He was slouched next to me, still trembling and breathless. He smiled at me; one I'd never seen in his videos. It was just for me. My heart jumped in my chest despite still beating at a faster pace than usual. This man was going to give me a heart attack before I could go out, guns blazing, like in the mafia movies.

"Absolutely," he said after a moment. His voice was quiet and low, and he leaned over to kiss me. His lips were soft and slightly sticky against mine and his tongue was a teasing swipe against my own. He pulled back with a sighing groan and grinned at me.

Getting up, he went to the phone and laughed. "Oh shit! It recorded that whole time!"

"Post it," I said with a chuckle. "It was hot."

Sterling stopped the recording, and I heard the chime. "Nice job," he said.

"It's tough being the breadwinner of the family," I said with a long-suffering sigh.

He snorted. "Speaking of bread. I'm fucking starving."

"When are you not starving?" I asked, as we headed to the bathroom to clean up.

"When I'm fucking or eating," Sterling said as if it were obvious. "Duh."

7

Emily

I was in the kitchen, picking the wilted leaves out of a salad that had technically passed its "Fresh By" date two days ago, when my phone rang. Startled, it took me a minute to realize it was my phone. It was a FaceTime call from Devon. I clicked to answer it.

His face came into view, slightly out of frame and bathed in fluorescent lighting. "Hey," he said, his voice sounding slightly irritated. "I stopped at the store with your list. You said flour. What kind? There's about twenty here."

Several questions occurred simultaneously, and only one came out of my mouth. "How do you look so good under grocery store lighting?"

His eyes landed on the phone screen, and a smirk graced his lips. "Because I'm good enough to eat, baby," he whispered, dipping his head closer to his phone and then nodding politely to someone as they passed.

I snorted. "Show me the shelf."

He switched the phone to the back camera and stepped away from the shelf to get it all in view. I had intended on going to the store on my own or placing an online order, but making Devon do it was thrilling in its own way. "The all purpose flour is fine... the one on that top shelf. No, over. One more... yeah, that one. And then get that one labeled 'pasta,' I want to try it. Oh, get some good cheese, too."

"I'm in *this* aisle right now," he grumbled as he switched the phone back to the front camera. His handsome face came back into view.

"I thought you were meeting with Doc?" I asked him as I continued making lunch.

"Yeah, I was. He says hello and says you can probably get a real cast soon. He gave me the supplies for it in case he's with my dad," Devon said, his eyes looking at the shelves he passed.

He had his shoulders hunched like he was leaning on the cart and the phone was in the child seat. My belly felt warm with affection. Devon took my grocery list and did the shopping for me. Devon. Leader of the mafia. Well, *sort of* leader of the mafia.

I directed him for a few minutes to different brands of food and household items while I arranged some crackers and cheese on a plate.

"Fine, I'll get a jarred sauce," he sighed.

I giggled and opened my mouth to make the same joke I've made before.

"Don't say it," he said in a rush, and looked around. "I

know we're not the *you know what*, but we can still enjoy homemade marinara."

"Homemade sauce is a labor of love. You kidnapped me, so you get jarred sauce," I said.

"I'm hanging up. Bye," Devon snapped as he ended the call.

I put the plate of crackers and cheese and a bowl of salad on the island. Sterling and Milo were still filming. It had been a while, so I figured they'd want to eat when they were done. A solid three minutes passed before Devon was calling again. I smiled and answered. His face was centered on the camera now.

"Hello," I said, as if he hadn't just hung up on me and was calling me back for more help. I propped the phone against the empty fruit bowl on the counter.

"You wrote tampons. Which flavor?" he said with a smirk.

I told him my preferred brand. Last month, my first menstruation with the guys, I had used pads supplied by Doc. And he had those big hospital grade ones. No thanks.

First Devon was getting groceries, and now he was picking up tampons for me. I felt like if I mentioned this change, he'd get all grumpy again and we'd end up with no food in the house and the wrong type of tampons. I decided not to rock the boat and thanked him instead.

"So are the guys still filming?" he asked as he put stuff on the belt to check out.

"Yeah, I haven't heard from them. But lunch is ready for you guys," I said and leaned back against the island, watching him on my phone.

"Thank you, Emily," he said, and then greeted the cashier.

"When was the last time you were at a grocery store?" I asked as the *beep beep beep* racked up a total.

Devon smirked. "You know the one down the street from us? On the corner? We do a lot of business with them."

I understood his meaning and laughed. "Why not shop there, then?" Stepping out of the camera's frame for a moment, I poured four glasses of water.

Devon looked around and then said quietly, "I wanted to go somewhere where my dad would never have reason to show up or know I'd been there."

I heard footsteps coming down the hallway upstairs. "Oh, the guys are done," I said, but didn't hang up.

Devon was paying the cashier and leaving the store when Sterling and Milo entered the kitchen. I was setting glasses of water on the island when I was promptly scooped up by Sterling. I squeaked and looked up to lock eyes with Devon in the phone camera. He looked confused about what was happening.

Our questions were answered when my back met the island countertop. I opened my mouth to protest and tell them Devon was on FaceTime, but Milo's mouth covered mine and Sterling tugged down my leggings and panties.

"We thought it wasn't fair you didn't get to have fun with us," Sterling said, his breath ghosting over my bare pussy.

I wanted to tell them about Devon, really; I did. But when Sterling's tongue met my skin, it was game over. I kind of forgot about Devon on the phone. Sterling's tongue lapped at me, and he slid a finger inside. I moaned against Milo's mouth as he pulled down my loose top to get to my breasts.

The surrounding air smelled like the soap from the gym

shower. Water from Milo's hair dripped onto my face. I gasped into Milo's mouth as Sterling tapped at my g-spot.

"That's a good girl. Come for me," Sterling said before sucking at my clit. "You made us lunch and we'll make you come."

My right knee knocked into the salad bowl, but Milo caught it before it fell to the ground. Sterling put a hand over my pelvis so I couldn't thrash about as his other hand tapped a vicious rhythm on my g-spot that had me seeing stars and screaming. I loved the feeling of both of them worshipping my body so much I didn't allow myself to come yet. I wanted to feel them on my skin longer.

Trembling and moaning, my body felt like it was going to explode. I felt hot all over despite the cool temperature of the room and the cold granite below me. Sterling alternated between sucking on my clit and licking me from my opening to my clit as his fingers pumped inside me. Milo pinched my nipples as his tongue ravished my mouth. This felt like a claiming, not just pleasure. It was not just letting me have some fun after their videos. This was intentional.

They had planned this. They walked down here discussing this. The realization that they talked about sex with me to-gether sent me over the edge. I felt my muscles clamp down on Sterling's fingers and Milo gave a sharp pinch and tug on my nipples. A scream flew from my throat, and I gripped Sterling's wet hair tightly with my unbroken hand.

As I came down from my climax, panting and shaking. Milo was grinning at me. "She should get two. We got two."

"Agreed. Milo, you come down here and taste her," Sterling directed as I unlatched my trembling fingers from his hair.

I was barely gasping in air to tell them about Devon on the phone- I'd remembered- when Sterling barked out a surprised laugh. "Milo, we've had an audience!"

Too embarrassed to look at the phone, I turned my head. Milo laughed as he came around to take Sterling's place. "Devon, tell us who makes her scream louder," he taunted, as he leaned over to lick up my arousal. With a quick movement, he had me flipped over on my stomach with my ass in the air.

Sterling was grinning down at me like he was going to devour me. Again. He smoothed back my hair before he gripped the base at my scalp in a tight, almost painful hold. I hissed and pushed into the hold. When Milo's tongue teased at my pussy, I cried out, my voice echoing against the counter. Both Milo and Sterling chuckled darkly, and I heard a sharp exhale from the phone. Turning my head, I saw Devon in his car, still watching. Watching me.

Part of me felt humiliated Devon was seeing this, but... he could have hung up. Instead, he was watching as his closest friends went down on me just inches away from the lunch I'd prepared. Milo gave a strong suck on my clit and my back arched, pushing my ass further into Milo's face. My eyes fluttered closed, and Sterling turned my face back to him. When I opened my eyes again, he was watching me with a smile still on his face. But that smile was more amused than hungry. "You like being watched?" he whispered in my ear. His hot breath tickling my ear and neck, he continued. "Do you like knowing tonight Devon's going to touch himself, thinking about your body?"

I didn't answer him, not wanting him to know my feelings.

I closed my eyes again and gave myself over to the pleasure of Milo's tongue and fingers.

A sharp tug of my hair had me gasping and looking up at Sterling. "Answer me. Do you like knowing Devon's sitting in his car, fighting the urge to come in his pants?"

I swallowed before nodding.

Sterling pulled away with a smirk. "That's my girl. Give him a show."

Milo moved faster and faster in and out of me and sucked harder and harder on my clit. I bit my lip to keep in my scream, but my second release felt like an explosion of light inside my body. It felt like it went on for ages as I shook and screamed, but it was surely only a few seconds. When I opened my eyes again, I was flat on my stomach on the counter. Hands were roving over my sensitive skin, making aftershocks of pleasure shoot through me. Sterling licked the sweat from my neck, and I giggled drowsily.

"He's almost home," Sterling whispered.

My stomach and heart clenched with anxiety and humiliation. I sat up as quickly as I could and fixed my shirt. Looking around, I spotted my leggings on the floor close to my phone. Quickly, I picked them up and shoved into the leg holes. Not looking at Devon's face on the phone, I hung up.

Sterling chuckled. "Damn, Emily."

I took a moment to fix my clothes and then reached under the sink for some antibacterial wipes. I tossed the canister to Sterling, and he caught it easily. The few seconds of silence as I gathered myself were enough to conquer my humiliation and... shame at what had happened. If Devon didn't like what he saw, he could have hung up. He must have been enjoying the show. I stood up taller and moved out of the way for Milo to wash his hands in the sink.

Sterling finished wiping down the counter and washed his hands. We chatted about the video they'd filmed and their plans for the next one before Devon came in carrying an armful of grocery bags. "Well? Am I doing this alone?" he snapped at us.

Sterling rolled his eyes. "Alright *Mom*, I'll get it." He waved a dismissive hand at me and Milo, so we stayed seated.

I helped unpack the groceries from the bags with Milo and between the four of us; we got done quickly. As I was putting the last box of crackers into the pantry, I felt someone behind me. The door slammed shut, closing us in darkness. Hands spun me roughly and they slammed my back against the shelf of the pantry. I gasped as glass containers rattled above me. My heart choked me with fear. Had someone got into the house? We had the door hanging open while we unloaded groceries. Were we under attack? I didn't hear the guys fighting outside the pantry.

A large hand wrapped around my throat and squeezed, tilting my face up. Hot, panting breath fanned over my face. It sounded like they were breathing through their teeth with barely restrained ferocity. I tried to gasp in a breath, but I couldn't. I scrambled to grab onto the man in front of me to push him off me. To fight. My fingers gripped and slipped on his silk shirt.

Devon.

"You do not want to tease me, Emily," he ground out through his teeth.

Knowing it was him didn't relax me. It made lust and

arousal mix with my fear. I still pushed at his hard chest, not particularly wanting to be choked out. He loosened his grip only slightly. Just enough for me to suck in a thin breath.

"Dev-" was all I could whisper before he cut me off.

"You don't know what you'd be getting yourself into," he growled in a breathy whisper, his nose at my neck. He inhaled long and slow, like he was smelling me.

"What if-" I took in a strained breath. "-I want to find out." New wetness threatened to soak my leggings. I hadn't found my panties when I got dressed.

"Fucking hell, Emily. I am not gentle. I am not nice. You're not ready for my needs," he said, his voice low and gravelly.

Something about the way he said it, and the painful press of his belt buckle against my hip, had me believing him. "Okay," I said, my voice thick with his hand around my neck.

He stepped back and was out of the pantry in a second. The light from the kitchen made me blink. When my eyes adjusted, I saw Sterling and Milo sitting and eating their lunch, leaning to stare at me in the pantry with eager faces. I shook my head to tell them nothing happened and caught my breath. Disappointment and frustration taking the lead.

Later that evening, I was with Sterling watching a movie in the den. Milo had gone up to bed an hour before, looking exhausted. Sterling had fallen asleep about ten minutes into the movie, but his presence and arm around me was comforting and warm. I was drowsy, but still awake when Devon came in and gestured for me to follow him. Slipping out from under Sterling's arm, I followed him to the kitchen. He was wearing gray sweatpants and a zipped up black hoodie. I'd never seen him like this, and I stared, taking it all in.

He pushed up his sleeves as he sat at the island. There were medical supplies on the granite, and I relaxed when I saw it there. "I'm going to put your cast on. The lighting in here is best," he said, looking over his supplies.

"Okay," I said and sat in front of him. "Do you know how?"

"Yes. Doc was my mentor for a few years. I followed him around to some of his calls," he replied and unlatched my sling while gently cradling my elbow. "Your bullet wound is closed enough I can put this on now. It'll be itchy with the healing scabs, but I want you to be able to use this arm later."

"Thank you," I said quietly and watched as he picked up what looked like a long sock from the countertop.

A look of gentle concentration took over his features as he carefully slid the white sock over my arm. He cut holes for my fingers and thumb and trimmed off the end. He was silent as he worked, and I took the time to watch him. His eyelashes were dark and long, framing his amber eyes. His hands were smooth and strong. The cuticles around his thumbs looked like he bit them, a habit I'd never seen with him. I wondered if it was recent stress that led him to the habit, or if he did well to hide it.

The slight movements of my arm made it throb, and I fought back tears as Devon steadied my elbow in his hand. I sniffed, and he looked up, his eyebrows high, a slight wrinkle on his forehead. "I'm sorry, baby. Once we get it wrapped, you can take a break and get some medicine," he soothed quietly.

I nodded and let him work on wrapping my arm in padding. Breathing slowly and steadily, I tried to focus on anything other than the pain. I could see down his hoodie from his collarbone to his navel at this angle. His skin was smooth and free of blemishes. Despite the pain in my arm, my mouth watered with the desire to taste his skin. One bare foot was on the bottom rung of the bar stool I was sitting on, and I looked at his strong thigh next to mine. The gray sweatpants clung to his thighs and looked like they were made to show off his cock. Realizing I was staring at his dick outline, I blinked and looked away.

"Doc also sent me with some other medication for you," he mumbled. He nodded with his chin, and I followed the gesture to see a pack of a few months' supply of birth control pills.

I blushed. "Did you ask for it, or did he assume?"

Devon smirked as he cut the end of the padding. "He asked me if it was necessary."

"I had meant to ask him before he left back when he was taking care of me and Milo," I said, leaning into the awkwardness.

Devon nodded and swallowed. "Alright, the padding is on. We're halfway there. Want to stop for medicine?"

"Yes, please," I replied, thankful for the awkwardness because it had distracted me from the pain.

He opened an unmarked orange prescription bottle and handed it to me before getting a glass of water. I swallowed the pill quickly, trusting he was giving me painkiller and not poison.

"You'll have to have this cast on for probably four weeks since you've been in the sling for a little while," he explained as he put away the supplies he was finished with. He had a large black toolbox filled with medical supplies on the counter and he dug through it for a moment. "Do you want plain white, pink, or black? I got you pink since you're... you know, a girl."

"Black, please. It will match more of my clothes," I said. "But thank you for considering my vagina in choosing cast colors."

He shot me a look and gathered what he needed from the toolbox. "Brat," he muttered.

I smiled. It was always fun to annoy Devon.

He settled back onto his seat and started wrapping my arm in the black plaster material. A dull ache reverberated through the bones in my arm as he wrapped it, and I eagerly anticipated the painkillers kicking in.

"Why haven't you slept with Milo yet?" he asked as he carefully wrapped my arm with black plaster.

"We didn't want his first time to be while he's in the throes of grief," I said, not expecting that question.

"We?"

"Me and Sterling," I replied.

"Not Milo?" he pressed.

I sighed. "I also don't want us to have broken arms. Please don't act like me and Sterling are being exclusionary about it."

"I was only suggesting that maybe he doesn't want to wait anymore," Devon defended.

"I know he doesn't," I said. "But I don't want it to be anything other than perfect."

"You think highly of your... skills," he said, and I knew he was teasing.

"I know what I have," I said with faux confidence.

He chuckled as he finished wrapping my arm. "I guess if your motives are truly to make it special, then I approve."

"Oh, good. I'll make sure I run everything through you first," I said sarcastically. "Sterling likes to tie me up, is it okay if we-"

Devon grabbed my face, my jaw in the space between his thumb and index finger and squeezed. His eyes flashed with a feral lust and anger. My lips puckered before opening against my will. "What did I say about teasing me?" he growled. "You need to stop."

I gave a slight nod, and he pulled away.

"I'm finished. You should go to bed," he said without looking at me. He put his supplies back into the toolbox, facing away from me.

"G-good night," I stammered before leaving to go up to my room.

That night I dreamed I was tied up in the pantry with bandages instead of rope. It was dark, with only flashes of light as the door opened and closed. I couldn't tell whose hands were on me, but I trusted them. I knew it was one of my men. I knew they wouldn't hurt me.

8

Emily

The morning Devon lined me and Milo up to remove our casts was a stressful one. We'd been working on tracking down gang members for a month and finally had a meeting set up with a few of the leaders and their seconds.

"I can't have us walking into the meeting looking like we can't handle ourselves," Devon had grumbled over breakfast. This had pissed off Milo, resulting in Milo trying to put Devon into a chokehold with his cast and Sterling having to intervene.

Directly after breakfast, Devon had us sit outside so he could saw off the plaster casts. I was sitting on the cold front steps in my bra next to a shirtless Milo. We didn't want to ruin our clothes with the plaster sawdust, so we sat shivering together in the icy air of late February. Devon, with an expression like a disappointed father taking his teenager's door off the hinges, sawed through Milo's cast first with a small cast saw. When it was finally off, Milo groaned with relief. Devon stepped back and looked him over.

"Oh, good. I didn't cut you," Devon said with a relieved sigh. I wasn't sure if he was kidding or not.

"Wait, that was your first cast removal?!" Milo shouted and clutched his arm.

"I've done one before, but Doc was there for it," Devon said with a shrug and turned to me.

I gulped and held out my arm. I was desperate for it to come off. It smelled bad and itched unbelievably. If he cut me, it would heal. Closing my eyes, I waited until cold air hit my skin. When it did, I could have cried with relief.

My cast was off, and I flexed my arm carefully under the guidance of Devon. He declared me and Milo healed, and I went immediately to shower. I couldn't wait to wash my hair and body without help or struggle. While it had been nice to have one of the guys wash my hair for me, it wasn't the same. And shaving my legs left-handed had gone poorly, so I was excited for a Full Diva Shower.

After an ibuprofen for some residual soreness, I felt euphoric. I could use my right arm again! Milo and I had made the mistake of high fiving with our newly healed arms, but both of us almost keeled over with the pain. We decided to never speak of it again.

Early that afternoon we met in the office to discuss strategy for the meeting again. We had done almost nothing other than discuss what we had hoped to gain from the meeting for weeks. Devon stood in front of us at his desk while we sat in the stiff-backed chairs. He crossed his arms over his chest, his button-down shirt rolled up to his elbows, showing off his tan, corded forearms.

"Alright, we're going in strong but friendly. That means we greet them formally and respectfully. We ask about their members, wish their families well, and then we tell them what my dad had been up to with Giovanni and Taz. By bringing their families into their minds and then telling them my dad threatened their safety, we may gain more of their alliance. Then, we tell them who took out Giovanni and Taz and see if it gains more of their trust," Devon recited our well-rehearsed plan.

"We can offer each of them ten percent more money per delivery and service rendered than they were getting before plus five thousand cash for each leader," Milo said reading from his tablet. "If they give us push back, we can go to seven thousand cash, but we'll be eating ramen for the foreseeable future."

"Until you two finally fuck on camera, that is," Devon reminded.

Sterling and Milo both rolled their eyes and shifted in their seats. Their videos had gone almost viral. Fan edits were all over Twitter, Instagram, and TikTok. Devon and I had done nothing but make fun of them about it. Their fake storyline (though, really, not fake at all) of two best friends experimenting and falling in love with each other had been a massive success. Their scripted videos outside of that fourth wall breaking storyline had done fantastic as well. They were raking in more money for each video than the combined salaries of a kindergarten teacher and town mayor. While Devon and I poked fun, we were both grateful for their work.

"They'll work with us for sure," I said confidently. We were appealing to their families and the safety of their city. I couldn't see a scenario where these people didn't side with us.

"I hope you're right," Devon said, staring at me.

Our meeting was being held in a building that had been abandoned for months. Milo had put in security cameras and Tommy had set up a table and chairs and some battery powered lighting. I offered to bake cookies, but the guys stared at me in horrified disbelief before Tommy, of all people, gently reminded me this was a gang meeting, not a PTA meeting. Instead, I was put in charge of packing up bottles of liquor.

We arrived at the meeting place forty-five minutes before the meeting was set to begin. The guys looked over the place, and I poured them and myself drinks. Tommy didn't come to the meeting, as his alliance with us was dangerous until his gang leader came to our side. Milo kept the security feeds open on his laptop and we remained in nervous silence. Devon had made sure I was armed like the guys were, and I felt more comfortable with the weapons this time.

I felt bone chillingly nervous this meeting would go poorly, and we'd be in danger. But I felt less connected to the outcome. Over the past month, Sterling had whispered to me and Milo every night in bed about his daydreams about a house on the beach, a cabin in the woods, a mountainside hideaway, anywhere with us. I had to admit living in a secluded space, just me and my men and nature, was appealing.

"Car pulling up." Milo broke the tense silence.

I moved to sit down at the table, and Sterling pulled me back up by my upper arm. "Stand. I need you to be able to run. Only sit once everyone else is sitting. I'll stay up with you," he muttered to me. Devon turned to nod at us, drink in hand.

Milo was the only one that remained sitting since he was working on the laptop. He moved his chair back from the long table, so he only had to jump up if he needed to. He adopted a seemingly relaxed position with his legs spread and boots planted on the dirty cement. I did my best not to focus on the fit of his jeans.

An older man came into the room, his hand on his hip holster. His eyes were furtively glancing around the building, and he peered into the room before stepping in. His hair was fully gray, and he had a fair complexion. "I'm the first here?" he asked, his voice sharp and deep.

"Yes, Cormac. Welcome," Devon said. His voice was friendly, but businesslike.

"That's Brendon's dad," Sterling whispered to me.

We all exchanged pleasantries until two men in their forties entered the room like Cormac did, hand on holster and glaring around the corner. They both had dark skin and close-cropped hair. Sterling informed me they were leaders of the gang Tommy was in. Pleasantries and introductions were made, and a light conversation ensued.

More and more gang leaders filtered into the room. Devon poured them drinks and asked about their families and members by name. Everyone glanced at me with confused interest but didn't ask questions. It felt odd, knowing some leaders in this room had once been rivals until Anthony and Matthew and my men had recruited them to work for the family business. Sterling, Devon, and even Milo were talking to the men and women in the room like they were equals and friends. They spoke about family members, gang members, and restaurants and businesses in their districts. Everyone was smiling and talking loudly by the time Devon motioned for everyone to sit down. Sterling, Milo, and Devon had been holding out on their charm. I felt slightly jilted that these gang members got charming, smiling men and I had gotten angry and rude ones when we met.

Everyone sat down, and Sterling tapped my elbow, telling me to sit with him. I sat between Sterling and Milo while Devon stood at the head of the table. The chatter died down, and they passed a few bottles of liquor around for refills.

"Good evening, everyone. I know this was an unconventional setting and method of having this meeting. And I know you're all wondering what's going on within our family business. To explain, I will start at the very beginning, over three decades ago. Thirty-three years ago, Owen and Kristen Hawthorne welcomed Sterling into the world. Their view on their involvement in the family business changed, and they wanted out. They spoke of resigning their position. Three months later, I was born, and then three months later Michael and Meredith Holden had Milo. Owen and Kristen sold off some of their holdings in the business and purchased a house outside the city. Soon after, they were killed. We were led to believe it resulted from gang retaliation. Then, when Michael and Meredith had their second child, a little girl, they looked at her and knew they could never leave their two children parentless. They were giving their holdings away to get out of the business when they, too, were killed. Michael's brother, Matthew, came into power beside my father. A rival family business had been around when the deaths happened, were implicated in the crimes, and then left town," Devon began the story and stopped for a sip of his drink. He had the attention of everyone in the room. He spoke confidently and calmly. A natural public speaker if I'd ever seen one.

"Do you mean, oh, what was his name... Giovanni?" Cormac asked, snapping his fingers as he tried to remember. Cormac and a few other people were old enough to have been around thirty years ago. They looked like they were recalling the situation, like they hadn't thought of it in years.

"Yes, Giovanni and Taz." Devon nodded.

"There was a war, if I'm not mistaken," Cormac continued.

"You're right," Sterling added. "We won, and Giovanni and Taz moved their operations to Akron."

"It wasn't until they returned late last year that we learned the truth about our deceased leaders and parents. Anthony sent Milo and Sterling to meet Giovanni and Taz, taunting them when they thought they were meeting with Anthony and Matthew to make a business deal," Devon explained.

A few men *tsked* in irritation at the trick. Devon nodded. "It was a move we weren't aware of, and we were pawns in it."

"You guys fought for him at his club. I saw it," said one leader.

"They forced it upon us. Neither of us wanted the fight or the deal once we found out the nature of the business. Anthony and Matthew were working on making a deal to share in human trafficking with Giovanni and Taz," Devon said and paused.

The men and women shouted their disapproval. Not directed at Devon, knowing there was a reason he was telling them, but sharing their distaste.

"Man, there's enough of that around here," a man spat dismissively. "We already fight that shit every day. We don't need more."

"We have missing children every day in my district," another man shouted.

Devon held up his hand with a solemn expression. "Please, I know you're upset. But Giovanni and Taz are gone. Before their deaths, they were the ones to inform us about Anthony and Matthew's involvement in the deaths of our leaders and parents."

"Matthew killed his brother?" Cormac shouted in shock.

"We believe Matthew suspected his brother's death and may have had an involvement in the deaths of Owen and Kristen. We will probably never know because Anthony killed Matthew," Devon said and paused again.

The bottles of liquor went around again as the gang leaders reacted in anger and shock at the news.

"We put a stop to Giovanni and Taz's business in trafficking when they tried to kill Milo and Emily at the direction of Anthony," Devon said and gestured to me and Milo.

"Emily?" one woman asked.

"They kidnapped me to be used a political pawn," I said. My voice was clear and confident. "My ex-husband is a local mayor. Anthony and Matthew were working with local politicians at the time of Matthew's death. We are unaware currently the nature of their business."

"Kidnapped?" the woman, who spoke before, asked and looked at Devon.

"I choose to stay now," I explained. Sterling put a hand on

my thigh under the table. Milo smirked down at me, and I smiled back at him.

"Oh!" the woman said, her eyebrows high. "You go, girl."

A few chuckles and quiet wolf whistles sounded around the room.

"This is the woman who helped kill Giovanni and Taz and survived torture at their hands. Do not underestimate her," Devon said with a slight warning to his tone. He quirked an eyebrow at me.

My heart swelled as Devon answered a few questions about Giovanni and Taz's death and businesses in the area. He had spoken so highly of me to these people. Nobody had ever done that for me before. With Gregory I was his "beautiful wife", but he never vaguely threatened a room full of hardened gangsters to not underestimate me. Sterling's hand squeezed my thigh, and he slid me my untouched drink. I drank it down in two gulps. The whiskey stung my throat and made my eyes water, but I welcomed the settling warmth in my stomach.

"As you can imagine, when Anthony was confronted with Milo and Emily being alive and with the news we were aware of his part in the murders, he reacted poorly. He killed Matthew when Matthew expressed anger towards him. I demanded he give over power of the business to us, and he refused. We know he has contacted you about continuing business and we urge you to remain with us instead," Devon said and made eye contact with everyone in the room.

A few people shifted in their seats. Others remained stoic.

"We can offer you ten percent more for each delivery and service than you were making before the split," Milo spoke up. "In addition, there would be a five-thousand-dollar bonus for each of you in this room."

Cormac was the only one who felt comfortable speaking up. "Milo, you know I love your sister like my own daughter, but I gotta tell you Anthony has more financial stake in my businesses than some of my own family members. He's been slowly buying out my older guys as they retire."

"Brendon and Marie are not safe as long as Anthony is around," Milo bit out.

Cormac looked torn. "If I side with you, me and my family lose everything. Gentlemen, and lady, this isn't personal, this is business."

"Anthony killed Marie's parents and her uncle. He tried to have me, her brother, killed. And you're choosing to protect him?" Milo shouted.

I put a hand on his shoulder to calm him. His muscles were tense under my fingers, and I leaned into him.

"Listen, I'm sorry about your parents and all, but Anthony upped our cut by thirty percent," one man said. "I've got families who are counting on that money."

Devon nodded solemnly. "I understand."

"You said the trafficking was done, this is personal stuff now," a woman said slowly, like she wasn't trying to start a fight.

"We don't know he's given up on the trafficking. He's been working with politicians. He may make connections that won't throw him in prison," Sterling said.

"It doesn't make sense," said the leader of Tommy's gang.

"He had us take Emily to hold over Gregory Ambrose, a

mayor. We believe he has something held over all the other politicians as well," Sterling explained.

"Regardless, without proof, there's nothing we can do about it," Tommy's leader said. "I don't want any more trouble in my streets, but I can't destroy my operations or get my people involved in a war because of a family disagreement."

"Then I need a vow," Devon said sharply, demanding attention. He hardened his face into the steely expression I'd seen before. With fury coming off him in waves like hot asphalt. "I need a vow you will not hurt my remaining family." He gestured to the three of us sitting at the table.

Nobody spoke. Nobody could make that vow or even make eye contact with us. A chill ran through me, cutting through the warmth of the liquor.

Slowly, the men and women got up and filtered from the room. Devon pressed his palms to the table and hung his head between his shoulders. When the last man left, he slapped a hand on Devon's shoulder and squeezed before wordlessly leaving.

We were silent until Milo said, "Everyone pulled out of the lot." I watched the headlights of the last car leave the parking lot on his laptop screen.

Devon let out a scream of anger, startling me. He flipped the table, making all the liquor and clear plastic cups go flying. Milo caught his laptop just in time. "FUCK!" Devon bellowed and turned away from us, his hands in his hair.

I stood up. "Devon," I whispered hoarsely.

"They couldn't even promise not to kill you!" Devon shouted, turning back to us. Desperation and fear covered his features. I had seen him like this only once before, just after the meeting when everyone had left, and Matthew lay dead at our feet. My heart clenched, feeling terribly sad for his pain. Devon picked up a bottle of liquor that hadn't broken and took a drink from the bottle. I approached him, wanting to hold him. He was facing away from me and didn't see me come up. He finished the nearly empty bottle and threw it into the concrete. I shrieked in shock as glass shattered around me. He spun around to see me there and reached out like he was going to throttle me or grab me. But he stopped himself and turned away again.

He needed to know we were safe and here with him. I reached out to him.

"Emily," Sterling warned behind me. Maybe Sterling and Milo hadn't seen Devon like this before. Maybe he had only shown me a glimpse that day and it was the first time he'd shown anyone.

"No, it's Devon. He needs us," I whispered, and my hand touched Devon's back. He was sweating through his silk shirt, his body feeling like a heated stone under my fingertips.

Devon spun around again and grabbed me around my middle. He buried his nose in my neck and held me so tight it felt like my ribs could crack. He took in a shaking breath against my skin, and I curled my arms around his neck, raking my fingers through his hair. I soothed him with whispers and assurances we were here and safe. He didn't fail us. Because I knew that was what he was thinking and feeling. His desperate last plea for them to promise not to hurt his remaining family was his last-ditch effort to protect us. And I loved him for it.

When he calmed enough to set me down, I realized Milo

and Sterling also had their hands on Devon. Their devotion to each other was stronger than ever, and I felt incredibly lucky to be a part of it.

"You know, I never realized how close in age you all were until your speech," I said, to break the tension.

Devon briefly smirked down at me despite his still strained breathing.

"Devon's birthday is next week," Sterling informed me.

"Why did nobody tell me?!" I asked them with a gasp.

"Are you going to throw me a birthday party?" Devon asked sarcastically. "Who are you going to invite?"

"Maybe I would want to get you a present and bake you a cake," I insisted and smoothed down the front of his shirt. "Maybe we could go out for your birthday."

"Out?" he asked, watching my hands on his shirt.

"Yeah, like out to eat or dancing or something. See a movie or go bowling," I suggested.

"Devon doesn't bowl," Sterling and Milo said simultaneously.

Devon grinned at me.

"There's a story there and I know it," I said and poked Devon in the chest.

"I'll tell it to you over a drink," Sterling said and slung his arm over my shoulders. "Let's go somewhere and get drunk. Let off some steam."

"Can we go dancing?" I asked as we gathered the stuff we'd come in with, leaving the broken liquor bottles and cups. "I don't mean to be tone deaf for the evening, but me and Milo got our casts off. We just did something big and scary, and it's Devon's birthday."

"It's not my birthday yet," Devon said as we walked towards the door.

We started an off-key chorus of "Happy Birthday" as we got in Devon's SUV. He smiled and shook his head as we finished the song at different times. Sterling finished with a metal scream and Milo attempted an opera style note and I did my best Britney Spears impression. I had beaten them to the car, so I waited at the passenger side door. These men had yet to catch on that I would get the front seat every time.

"Never sing to me again," Devon demanded without heat as we got in the car.

"Do you know of any clubs we can go to?" I asked the guys.

"No, we're too old for clubs," Milo said.

"Oh," I said. I really needed to get this anxious energy out of my system. Maybe it was the whiskey and the stress, but I needed to move my body. I turned on the radio and Devon smacked my hand away from the controls. I returned the smack to the back of his hand and fiddled with the dial, searching for a good radio station.

"The only club I know about is a sex club," Sterling said.

I craned around in the seat to look at him. He shook his head. "I didn't partake. I met with a guy there to make a deal. I learned some cool stuff, though."

"There's a club near one of our businesses," Devon sighed his long-suffering parental sigh as he drove.

"Yay!" I said and wiggled with excitement. I settled back into my seat, not caring about the gang leaders at the meeting. We could leave everything tomorrow. I could still have my men and a new life. These men who treated me with respect and like an equal. Like a force to be reckoned with, and not just the mayor's wife. I felt powerful and sexier than I had ever felt in my life.

Sure, I wanted to know what Gregory had been doing with Anthony. But in the end, it didn't matter. I didn't want him anymore. I wanted nothing of that life anymore. Everyone from that life, including the woman I was, was dead to me.

9

Emily

We pulled up to the club, used valet parking, and paid the cover fee. The bouncer at the door arched an eyebrow at us as we approached but said nothing as we gave him our IDs. Milo had mine in his pocket. Something I was grateful for as I hadn't needed an ID or wallet for months.

"It's fake... Savannah," Milo whispered in my ear as we walked in.

I laughed out loud. "How did you know the name I had on a fake ID in college?"

He grinned secretively.

The floor of the club opened with bars wrapping around a pit of dancing people and flashing lights. At the front of the club, I took in the surroundings. A song I didn't recognize was playing, and I felt weirdly overdressed. I was wearing a pair of skintight medium wash jeans, black heels, and a black blouse. The last time I was in a club, peplum tops and sock buns were in style, giving more of a business casual look than the crop tops and miniskirts on the surrounding girls.

The excited, empowered feeling drained out of me like someone had pulled the plug. Milo was right. We're too old for this.

"I'm going to get us drinks," Sterling shouted to our group and walked towards the nearest bar. Girls' heads turned to watch him as he passed, but he didn't look at any of them. They giggled behind their hands and pointed as he moved through the crowd.

Okay, well, maybe *I* was too old to be here.

Milo grabbed my hand and was pointing to the ceiling. I looked up and blinked as lights flashed over my eyes. There, nestled amongst the lights, was a big contraption of plastic and computer wires. I felt Milo's breath on my ear as he spoke, but I couldn't hear him. He was most likely telling me the brand and the model number of gear the club used to get internet service. I could not care less, but that was Milo's favorite hobby wherever we went. Then he would say something ridiculous like, "I hope they downloaded the security patch last week, or they're bound to get hacked." It was cute. I smiled up at him and gripped his hand tightly in mine.

Devon was looking at me with a crease between his brows. "What's wrong?" he asked me. I was mostly reading his lips; the music was so loud.

I gave a little shrug. "Just feeling old."

Anger flashed in his eyes, and he leaned down to shout loud enough in my ear that I could hear every word. "You are the most powerful woman in this room. In this city. And you're worried about your age?"

I looked up at him from beneath my lashes as Sterling approached us. He handed me something pink and fruity looking and the guys some shots. I cocked a questioning eyebrow at him, and he smiled. "I asked the little girl next to me what she wanted to drink, and she told the bartender. I don't know what she said, but I figured you'd like it."

"Wait, you made a girl think you were buying her a drink and took it for me?" I asked with a laugh.

He shrugged and grinned at me. "Maybe."

"Babe, that's so sweet!" I crooned sarcastically. "Let's drink these and then go dance," I shouted to them.

"We don't dance," Sterling said with a wrinkled nose.

"But you will for me!" I said confidently and drained the sugary drink. A shudder ran through me as I handed the glass to a random man as he passed.

I was still holding Milo's hand, so I dragged him down the few stairs to the dance floor. There was resistance in his arm as he hesitantly followed me into the mass of people. I looked back once to see Sterling attached to his other hand and Devon taking the rear as we wove through the crowd to a less crowded area. Once we had found a space I felt worked best for our group, I stopped walking and turned into Milo's body. I let go of his hand and put my arms around his neck. His hands moved to my waist, and I stepped closer. Swaying to the beat of the music, I let my hips rock against his. I felt someone step up behind me and I expected it to be Sterling. The hands that stroked up my arms and caused goosebumps to erupt from my skin despite the heat of the building were tan and clear of tattoos. Devon had rolled his sleeves back up, showcasing those amazing forearms again, and I fought the alcohol fueled urge to bite them. I licked my lips and Milo smirked down at me. Sterling's face appeared behind Milo, and he said something in Milo's ear. Milo's smirk turned into a full laugh and his head tipped back onto Sterling's shoulder.

We danced like that until the song changed and I spun around in their arms to face Devon. I looked up at him while I swayed, pressed between them. His eyes were serious despite the atmosphere and seemed almost sad. I moved my hand to hold the side of his face and stroked his cheekbone with my thumb. Milo kissed down the side of my neck and his hands slid up under my shirt. He sucked and bit my sweaty neck and my eyes fluttered closed despite my efforts to decipher Devon. When I opened my eyes, Devon was smirking down at me.

The song changed, and Milo spun me around again to face him. I laughed as I nestled against the bulge in his pants, rocking to the music. I trailed my fingers up his chest, feeling his muscles and the heat of his skin through his button-down shirt. There was movement behind me, and Sterling pressed hard against my back. I smiled, feeling as safe as I'd ever felt. Their hands were everywhere on me, and I closed my eyes, enjoying the feel of a buzz and these men.

Sandwiched between them, I didn't think about my age again. I didn't think about a single person other than us. I didn't need to. Nobody else mattered. All that mattered was their hands on my sweaty skin, the bass line of the song playing, and the promise of later tonight. I slid my hands up and around Sterling's neck behind me. His sweat slick skin was radiating heat, and I tugged the hair at the base of his hairline.

I closed my eyes and enjoyed the feel of the music beating through my blood and bones like I was an instrument.

This was the release I was looking for. It's different from exercise or sex. I couldn't remember the last time I allowed my body to *move* in a way that felt intuitive and cathartic. And while we were technically only swaying and grinding to the music, it felt good. Strobe lights flashed against my closed eyelids, and I smiled while Sterling and Milo peppered my skin with kisses and little nips with their teeth.

A tug on my arm jerked me from my trance, and I opened my eyes to see Sterling and Devon talking. Or, rather, trying to read each other's lips. Devon gestured for us to follow, and we chained our hands together to get off the dance floor. Was something wrong? Was Anthony here?

I gave Devon a worried, scared look when he looked back to check we were all following, and he smiled and shook his head. My anxiety relaxed marginally. He led us up a flight of stairs and passed a security guard, who nodded to us. A sign labeled this area as VIP. I'd never been in a VIP section before. My anxiety turned to excitement.

Upstairs was completely deserted. A railing overlooked the club and there was a private bar. This bar had no staff tonight, though. Small tables and booths encircled a much smaller and cleaner looking dance floor. It was dimly lit and strobe lights from the club below streamed into the space.

"I bought out the VIP section since we aren't paying any gangs," Devon said with a smirk that poorly belied his disappointment in the meeting. It was still loud, but he could shout to be heard. He gestured to fresh drinks for us on the table. We each took our drinks, and I moved to the dance floor. I danced and drank, looking down over the crowds of club goers. My drink was still a fruity liquor but was a vodka cranberry this time. I sucked it down. It was hot in this club.

When a song changed to one I recognized, I spun to tell the guys, and saw them sitting and watching me. They were lined up in a rounded plush booth, relaxed, and drinking from their glasses of whiskey. All three of them staring with lazy, hooded eyes.

A second of embarrassment that I was drunkenly swaying and shaking my ass to an *audience* passed through me. Directly after it was that feeling of empowerment I thought I'd lost earlier. The alcohol, their lustful stares, the tension reduction from the meeting and planning for the past few weeks, and the music fueled my confidence. I had never felt so desirable as I did at that moment. Three powerful and sexy men were watching me dance. *Me.*

Standing where I was, with them sitting where they were, I felt like I was dancing on a stage. Who dances on a stage? Strippers. It surely was hot in this club. I walked toward them, licking the last drops of my drink from my lips. Setting the empty glass down and taking a step back, I looked at each of them like I could devour them in a minute.

I undid the first few buttons on my blouse and looked up at them under my lashes. My black lace bra peeked out. Sterling sat forward in his seat, watching me intently. Milo adjusted his cock in his pants. Devon watched me and sipped his drink. He tipped his head to the side and narrowed his eyes in challenge when we made eye contact. Like he was daring me to continue. Daring me to strip bare right here in this club. Their approval and Devon's challenge spurred me on and I slowly, while swaying my hips to the music, undid the rest of my shirt.

My jeans were next. I unzipped and unbuttoned the fly and slid them down my legs. I'd worn a matching panty and bra set, anticipating a fun night after getting my cast off. Now, I was in a black lace thong and bra, and I kept my feet in my black heeled shoes. I was smoothly shaven now that I could do it on my own, so I felt sexy and confident. Swaying to the beat, I turned my back on them to make sure nobody down in the club could look up and see me. Belatedly, I realized people might see us up here. Wasn't the biggest part of being in VIP being *seen* in VIP? I didn't hear him approach, but Sterling roughly pulled me back to the table that stood in front of the booth.

I gasped as he bent me over the table and reclaimed his seat. I made eye contact with Devon as Sterling roughly pushed aside the string of my panties and his tongue met my pussy. Closing my eyes on a moan, my body relaxed. He kicked my feet apart more and pressed me so hard into the table I was sure I'd have bruises on my hip bones. Milo gripped the back of my head and turned my face to him. He kissed me in long sips that had my lips tingling. Wetness came easily to my core, and I moaned into Milo's mouth. This was too good.

I snaked a hand down to open Milo's fly. He pulled away from my lips to help pull his cock out and I remembered Devon there, too. I looked up at him to see him still in his seat next to Milo, watching and drinking. His eyes were hooded and full of a threateningly dark desire. Was this the teasing he had talked about? Oh, well.

Sterling's mouth left my pussy, and I felt him stand up.

Devon reached forward and took something from Sterling with a nod. He sat back in his seat, lounging with his legs spread and a joint between his lips. He kept his hooded eyes on me as he lit it with a black lighter. His corded forearms taunted me yet again. I swallowed hard as we maintained our eye contact, and Sterling returned to his job of eating my pussy. My eyes rolled back and interrupted our staring contest.

Milo kneeled in the booth and roughly turned my head so I could suck his monster cock into my mouth. I could see the intrigued look on Devon's face when he saw what his lifelong friend was packing. When I bobbed my head and then took Milo all the way down, I saw Devon's eyebrow quirk like he was impressed before he drained the last of his whiskey.

The smoke of the joint, more sickly sweet than skunky, swirled around us as Devon exhaled. He had exhaled almost directly into the gap between Milo's pelvis and my face. I couldn't help but breathe it in. I didn't care. I didn't exactly have a job that did random drug screens anymore. Milo stroked back my hair as he thrust into my mouth with un-forgiving force. He hit the back of my throat, my teeth, my tongue- but didn't care. I gagged and my eyes streamed, but still he fucked my mouth.

Someone thumbed away the tears that streaked down the left side of my face, and I opened my eyes to see Devon with his hand outstretched. He wasn't looking at Milo or Sterling. Devon was only looking at me with those eyes that threat-ened danger and pleasure at the same time. He sat back and licked the tears from his thumb before taking another hit off the joint.

My legs shook, and Sterling gripped my ass in both of his hands as he licked and swirled his tongue in me. I felt the tingles of an orgasm begin at my fingers and my toes, making my limbs shiver with anticipation. I wanted Milo to come with me, so I reached out and pulled him closer by the backs of his thighs. His hand slapped down on the table next to me as I almost made him fall off the booth in my eagerness to swallow him whole. My gag reflex became nonexistent when I came, so I shoved him down my throat until my nose met his pelvis. He was directly above me, so I heard him let out a growling scream as he came down my throat just as my orgasm took over completely. He was so far down my throat I didn't need to swallow. I couldn't breathe, his cock obstructed the gasps my body desperately wanted to take. I felt him pulsing against my tongue and his body shook as I tapped the back of his thighs to signal I needed air.

Just as black dots swam before my eyes, Devon reached over and pushed Milo's stomach, so he backed away. The joint between his lips. He looked irritated that Milo almost suffocated me. Milo collapsed back against the booth and my orgasm ended with me back at the precipice of another. But as Sterling sensed my orgasm ending, he pulled me up from the table. Not missing a beat, he shoved the table over with ease. It tumbled until it was upside down and it shattered our empty glasses on the dance floor. I only glanced at it in shock before I was shoved to my knees in front of Sterling. He was sitting back in the booth, legs spread, and pulling his cock out of his dark jeans.

Eagerly, I kneeled between his knees and took him into my mouth. If the table had still been there, I'd have been under it. I knew my makeup was entirely ruined, but I didn't care as I looked up at him. He smiled as he lounged back in the seat, gathering my hair up in one hand.

"I'm going to be quick," he said, but I mostly read his lips. He was grinning self depreciatingly and gave a small shake of his head.

I smiled around his cock, and he tipped his head back against the top of the booth. His neck and tattoos peeking out over his shirt were the sexiest things I'd ever seen. His chest rose and fell like he was panting. I couldn't help it; I snuck my hand back down to my pussy and rubbed over my sensitive clit. Jolts of oversensitivity like electric shocks coursed through me, and I moved to dip two fingers into my pussy. I moaned around Sterling's cock.

Spreading my knees so I could reach better, I slammed my g-spot until I made myself scream. This time when my eyes watered, it was from pleasure and not from choking. But I kept myself on the very edge of my orgasm until I saw Sterling look back down at me and tap my jaw in warning. I was thankful Milo and I had conditioned him to give us a warning. Coughing up come hours later was not a fun activity.

As soon as I felt the first spray of come, I tried to push him further down my throat like I'd done with Milo. But it was too much, and I had to pull off him as I gasped and screamed. I came around my own fingers, dripping onto the floor, while Sterling covered my face and neck. We both came for what felt like forever.

I opened my eyes to see Sterling and Milo kissing slowly. A new plume of smoke curled around me, and I turned around to look at Devon. Would he want me to touch him, too? I crawled towards him with my bottom lip between my teeth. He was still watching me, sprawled out in the booth. He smirked as he saw me inch closer to him. I gently ran my nails up his thigh towards his fly and looked up at him. I knew I looked ruined, but he saw how the mess was made.

He was hard in his pants, I felt him under my fingertips. I undid his belt and unzipped his fly. Feeling eyes on me from Sterling and Milo, I continued. He was wearing gray boxer briefs, and I could see a wet spot where his pre-come had soaked the fabric. I stooped, intending to lick over it, but he caught me by my jaw. Lifting my chin up towards him, he held so tightly I was sure to bruise. A flash of desperation and anger crossed his face, and I felt confused. His jaw muscles feathered as he glared down at me, the joint bouncing on his lips. He squeezed my cheeks until my mouth opened and pulled the joint from his lips. My hands still rested on his thighs, waiting for his consent.

His nose brushed mine, and I thought for sure he was about to kiss me. My breath caught in my chest with the anticipation. Instead, he said, "Tongue out."

I obliged, not understanding what he was doing. He pulled back slightly and spat directly onto my tongue. Flinchingly, I tried to pull out of his grip, but he clenched my face. I pushed his thighs, trying to get away from him, but he didn't budge. Instead, he brought the joint up to my mouth and put out the burning cherry on my spit-soaked tongue.

It didn't hurt, but I felt the heat all the same. After putting out the joint, he let me go roughly and stood up. Humiliation and shame filled me as I crumpled on the ground. I spit the ashes out and gagged. Milo's gentle hands helped me sit up in the booth and Sterling gathered my clothes.

Devon had left.

While dressing me, Milo's jaw was clenched, and his eyes were glaring behind his glasses. Sterling was stoic but kept gently touching my hair and face. I was almost more embarrassed they had witnessed my rejection than I was over Devon pushing me away. Once I was dressed, I slapped away their hands.

"I'm going to the bathroom," I said and raced down the stairs to the club.

I knew I looked thoroughly ravished and ruined, but I needed to get to the bathroom. Pushing through people towards where I had earlier seen a restroom, I moved quickly enough they didn't see my face. There was a line for the bathroom, but I pushed past all the women waiting. A few girls shouted, but most didn't care or notice.

Once I was in a stall, I was sick. I wasn't sure what made me sicker, a belly full of liquor and come, or the sting of humiliation. Likely both. I heaved until there was nothing left. I tidied myself up in the sink of the crowded bathroom, completely ignoring the surrounding women. A few offered to help, and I politely refused, so they didn't call the police or something.

I expected at least one guy to be out in the hallway waiting for me, but there was nobody. I went back to the VIP area and the security guard turned me away. He held up a hand and shook his head.

"I was just up there!" I shouted over the music.

He shook his head.

I patted down my pockets and found I had my phone in my back pocket. It was a miracle it was still there, honestly.

"We're out by the valet," Milo had texted.

"Are you okay?" Sterling said five minutes later.

"If you're not out in five minutes, I'm coming in," Sterling had said... twelve minutes ago.

They must have gone to a different bathroom.

"I'm headed outside," I texted and typed out "Sorry," but erased it. I wasn't sorry for having to use the bathroom and I wasn't sorry for being difficult to find.

I pushed through the crowds of people again towards the door. Once I got outside, the cold air soothed my overheated skin. I breathed in big gulps of the crisp air and looked for the guys. I didn't see them anywhere. Irritated and still drunk, I started walking. I didn't know where I was going, but I knew I wanted away from that club. The music was loud, it smelled terrible, and the rejection from Devon was still hot in my veins.

"Hey!" a male voice shouted.

I turned, expecting it to be one of my guys, but it was someone unfamiliar.

10

Emily

"Can I borrow your phone?" the guy said.

"Um, sure," I said, deciding to help someone in need. It was well after one in the morning. If someone was asking for help, then they probably really needed it. I approached him and handed him my phone.

He took it and I watched as he sent a quick text for someone to pick him up. "You okay?" he asked me, looking me over as he handed back my phone.

"Yeah," I said and looked around me, hoping to catch sight of Devon's car or one of the guys.

"You alone?" he asked.

I shrugged, not wanting to admit it.

"Wait, do I know you?" he asked and looked me over again.

"No," I said and tried to take my phone back.

He held firm. "Wait," he said and then barked out a laugh.

"I have seen you before. You were getting the shit beat out of you with Giovanni and Taz."

My chest squeezed with panic. "I don't know what you're talking about," I said as simply as I could.

"No, it was definitely you. You killed my bosses and now I don't have a job," he retorted.

"I don't know who those people are. You have the wrong person," I said and backed away.

He smirked, and my blood ran cold. "It was you, and now you're all alone."

I turned and ran down the street. It got darker and darker without streetlights or open businesses the further I went. The man's footsteps thundered behind me. What were the odds I ran into someone from Giovanni and Taz's gangs? I cursed my luck twice over as I stumbled on my heels. A hand grabbed me by my hair, and I was painfully yanked backwards. I cried out in pain as I struggled to stay on my feet.

"Come here, you stupid bitch!" he shouted and shoved me against the brick wall of a building. My head painfully bounced off the brick and I screamed in terror. I hoped someone, anyone, heard my scream. He clamped his hand over my mouth. I kicked and hit him as much as I could, but he leaned forward so he pressed his entire body against mine. It was difficult to move now, and my hands scraped against the rough brick.

"You lost me my fucking job!" he growled in my face. He reached a hand down towards his pants and I couldn't tell if he was reaching for a weapon or his dick. Either way, I didn't feel like finding out. I bit down on the hand covering my mouth and tasted blood. He howled in pain and was suddenly away from my body. I thought he'd stepped back, but a second later, he was flat on his back and Milo was on top of him. Milo landed punch after punch to his face, and I stood, shaking and spitting out his blood. I gagged at the taste and the fear.

"Emily!" Sterling's voice sounded as he approached at a sprint from the direction of the club. He looked at me up and down and saw no physical wounds. He gave the guy on the ground a solid kick to the ribs and helped Milo up off the unconscious and bleeding man.

"Does he have a weapon?" I asked, my voice hoarse from screaming and gagging.

Sterling squatted down to look him over. Milo shook out his fists like they hurt as he moved towards me. His eyes were wide behind his glasses, and I could barely see his fearful expression in the street's darkness.

"Are you okay?" he asked and held me by my shoulders.

"I'm fine," I said, my voice cracking.

"No weapons," Sterling said. "But here's your phone."

"Then he was about to assault me," I said angrily and pocketed my phone. "He was reaching towards his pants, and I couldn't tell if he was going for a weapon or his dick."

Sterling spat on the man. "Fucker."

"He used to work for Giovanni and Taz. He recognized me," I said as rage filled me. He was going to assault me. If Milo hadn't come out of nowhere, I could have been raped.

Sterling stared at the man for a moment as he considered the next move. I heard tires of a car squealing around the corner. I looked up, expecting it to be the cops or the person this piece of trash had texted to pick him up, but it was

Devon's SUV. He squealed to a stop next to us and got out of the car. Devon rushed over to us and looked at me, and then at the guy on the ground.

"What happened?" Devon asked.

I filled him in as my fear relaxed and my adrenaline filtered out of my blood. I felt exhausted and I leaned against the brick for support.

The guys all exchanged serious, dark glances before turning to me.

"It's your call, Emily," Sterling said. His voice was deep and intense.

I looked down at the man on the ground. He twitched as consciousness crept back in. Disgust and rage ran both hot and icy in my veins, feeling like needles. This man thought he had power over my body, and he was going to abuse that power. But now I had it over him.

"Kill him. But he might have information about the guys Giovanni and Taz had, and where they ended up. Maybe something about the politicians. We need to move, though, because he used my phone to text for a ride before he recognized me," I said coldly. The tone of my voice shocked me. It was hoarse still, but confident and threatening.

Milo *tsked* and grabbed my phone from my pocket, unlocking it and typing away. "I need you to know my security systems only work as long as you don't give people the keys to the castle."

Sterling rolled the guy over while Devon got zip ties out of his trunk. Once the guy was zip tied, he woke up again. Sterling punched him and he returned to unconsciousness.

Sterling and Devon heaved the man into the trunk, and I got into the passenger seat.

The ride home was tense and quiet, and Milo typed away on his tablet. "Good news is no security cameras in the area saw us."

"How do you know?" I asked and looked back at him in the back seat.

He looked up at me with an irritated expression. "I know."

"Yeah, but how?" I pressed.

Devon and Sterling were both fighting grins. Devon was biting his lower lip and focusing on the road intently.

Milo sighed. "It's my job to know."

"I thought it was your job to suck off Sterling on camera?" I teased.

Sterling snorted a laugh.

"I'm in charge of digital security. I have access to every security camera in our city," Milo said. He sounded defensive of his technological prowess.

I opened my mouth to retort, but the guy in the trunk shuffled around and started kicking at the trunk door. Sterling rolled his eyes and took his gun from where we stored our weapons under my seat. He held it to the guy's head without saying a word.

We were pulling into the garage a minute later. Sterling and Devon accompanied our guest to the basement where the metal rooms were. I changed my clothes and shoes while Milo iced his knuckles. We met Sterling and Devon in the basement, where they were watching the man cry and blink through blood.

Devon was standing arms crossed, next to the table of

weapons, and Sterling was prowling around the man dangling from the ceiling. I recalled the vision of Marcus, the man I'd killed last year, strung up the same way. It was also how Milo and I had been hanging at the hands of Giovanni and Taz. The memory of killing Marcus didn't make me sick anymore. It felt like the turning point in my life and the relationship with the guys. In a horrifically deformed way, it felt like a first date. That butterfly feeling that felt like a new beginning. The start of a new story.

Sterling's body and face changed when he was like this. I watched with a dampening core as he prowled around the dangling man. His shoulders were high, and his jaw clenched tight. He wore only an undershirt and his jeans now; a few splatters of blood dotted the front of him. His expression was beastly. He was no longer the Sterling I knew.

Milo came in behind me, holding two folding chairs and his tablet. He opened the chairs and gestured for me to sit. I obeyed and he sat next to me. He unlocked his tablet and read from the screen.

"Timothy Wheeling," Milo said. "AKA Hot Wheels to his friends. Car jacker originally from Akron. Worked for Mack's side of the illicit business controlled by Giovanni and Taz. Let me guess, now that they're dead, you are no longer relevant?"

Timothy grunted and nodded.

"That's a sad story," Devon said with zero empathy. "But it doesn't give you the right to assault a woman."

Timothy looked up and blinked away some of his blood. He glared at me. I smiled in return.

Devon saw the exchange and tossed Sterling what looked

like a metal meat tenderizer. Like from a kitchen. "And not just any woman. Our woman."

That feeling of power and a dangerous thirst for blood had me standing from my chair. I felt the eyes of every man in the room as I approached the table of tools. I looked them over and wiggled my fingers in the air like I was perusing a pastry case and choosing the perfect one. "Hmm," I hummed as I picked up a pair of brass knuckles. Though they weren't brass, they looked like they were made of stainless steel. I slid my fingers through the holes and admired how it looked on my hand, like I was trying on diamonds.

"Beautiful," Devon murmured. I avoided looking at him because I was still upset with him.

I turned to Timothy and approached him. He watched me warily.

"You tried to hurt me," I stated.

He glared and spat at me. Bloody spit landed on my shirt, and I slowly looked from the wet spot on my black shirt to his face. He smirked in triumph. I raised my fist and let it come cracking down on his ribs. He grunted and swung in the chains.

I should have felt horrible. I should have felt disgusted with myself.

But... I didn't.

I smiled and hit him again, enjoying watching the bruises form before my eyes. It was like watching kindergarteners paint with watercolors. They would over saturate their brushes with the watery paint and the color would bloom outwards on the paper. Timothy's skin bloomed after each punch to his body with the metal in my fist. It was lovely.

My men let me paint by number until I tired myself out and my arm ached. I gingerly took off the metal knuckles and placed them carefully on the weapons tray. When I looked up, Devon had a crease between his brows, but he said nothing. Sterling was crouched behind Timothy and looked like a tattooed gargoyle. He was watching me with barely restrained lust.

Milo was sitting forward in the chair, his tablet sitting forgotten next to him. He was in the shadows of the spotlight that shone on Timothy, so I couldn't see his face.

"Milo, can you take me to bed? I'm sleepy," I said to him, my voice sounding eerily innocent. He jumped up from the chair and escorted me out of the basement. Halfway up the stairs, he slammed me against the wall, his mouth crashing into mine.

"Fuck, that was hot," he said as he pulled away.

I smiled. It had been... fun. I recognized that was an inside thought and kept it to myself.

"Let's get a shower and go to bed," I said. "I'm exhausted and my arm hurts."

"Yeah, beating a man half to death will do that," Milo agreed as we continued upstairs.

"Here, come shower and sleep in my room," Milo said as we approached my room.

"I've never been in your room," I said. He had always put his laundry in the hall when I was doing their chores. It had been a while, so I figured the guys started doing their own laundry. Nobody had complained, though.

"I don't let anyone in my room," Milo said slowly.

"Not even Sterling?" I asked.

Milo gave a snort. "He occasionally gets in."

I giggled as he opened his door. Inside was both shocking and exactly what I'd expected at the same time. The wall that was taken up by a long dresser and a TV in my room was occupied by a long black desk with a computer and three monitors. Two more TVs hung above the monitors showing the house's security cameras, and both ends of the desk were cluttered with laptops, tablets, phones, and bundles of wires. Manuals and books were stacked on a tall bookshelf along with spare keyboards, network gear, and other technology items whose names I didn't know. The long windows of his room were blocked off with the same blackout curtains as Sterling had, and a clothing rack and a small set of drawers stood in front. He had a walk-in closet the same as me, judging by the doors in the same spaces as my room, but his clothes were out in his room.

"Why not use your closet?" was all I could think of asking.

"It's the server room," he said simply and went to the closet door. He opened it and the dark room was lit with only green and blue flashing LED lights. "This is how the business operates."

"I guess you don't use the cloud," I said, taking it all in.

"Emily, there is no cloud. It's just someone else's computer," he said and rolled his eyes. "But I back up all our data here and to one trusted 'cloud' source. It's overseas where there are considerably fewer laws governing technology."

"Oh," was all I could think to say as I turned away from the server room. His bed was messy and slept in. There was a mug on almost every flat surface in the room, and I smiled.

Despite all the mugs, his room still smelled like his clean soap. I never wanted to leave.

Milo stripped and put his dirty clothes in an overflowing hamper near his door. Maybe they weren't doing their laundry after all. I followed suit and found him in the bathroom, starting the shower. His bathroom was identical to mine and Sterling's, though his windows faced the front of the house.

My head throbbed with a hangover, but the water felt fantastic. I knew the guys had been barely buzzed, but I'd been drink for drink with them all night.

"Headache?" Milo asked as we toweled off.

"Pounding," I pouted.

"I'll get us some water and ibuprofen. Hopefully, we can fall asleep before Sterling finds us and keeps us awake with his snoring," Milo said as he stepped into a pair of loose boxers.

He handed me a pair of boxers and a t-shirt before leaving. When he came back, I was finger combing my hair and sitting on his bed after running to my room to brush my teeth. "Sorry I didn't make the bed," he said with a small blush.

"No, it's perfect. It smells like you," I said and sniffed a pillow.

He chuckled awkwardly, like he didn't realize that was a good thing. "If you say so."

"Have you ever had a woman in your bed?" I asked him after I swallowed the pills and chugged my water.

"Nope. Well, Marie and I used to cuddle and sleep as children. But no, no other woman," Milo said and stepped into the bathroom. I heard him brush his teeth.

He climbed into the bed next to me and we lay facing

each other. Our wet hair made patches on his pillowcases. He watched me carefully before speaking. "Are you alright?"

"Yeah, I'm great," I said. "I mean, all things considering. How are you doing?"

He sighed and rolled onto his back. "I'm... alright."

I traced the veins on his biceps with the tip of my finger. "Do you want to talk about Matthew?"

"Not really. Sure, I miss him and I'm sad he's gone. But... from the time we were kids, he always told us our life was dangerous, and it would likely kill us before we had the chance to get old. Me and Marie knew we'd lose him eventually. So, it's not shocking he was killed. What's shocking is that it was Anthony that did it. And then realizing everything my parents and Matthew had died for was for nothing. I'm not safely out of the mafia like my parents wanted. And I'm not the leader like my uncle wanted. I have nothing these people gave their lives to provide for me. To top it off, I don't even have a way to get revenge. Anthony is in hiding and the skills I worked my whole life for can't find him."

"We'll find him," I whispered. "You will grow old. And honestly, if we don't find him, we can leave. You know how Sterling feels. We can go live in the woods with him. Make him chop wood shirtless all day. You and I can become porch raisins and watch Sterling do manual labor."

Milo chuckled and turned his head toward me. "Is Devon allowed in our log cabin in the woods?"

I gritted my teeth. "He can live in a shed on his own."

"It's probably for the best. He's insufferable now, I can't imagine how he'd be without his empire to run."

We laughed softly before Milo kissed me.

"Goodnight, Emily," Milo said and turned off the light.

"Goodnight, Milo," I replied in the darkness. "Sorry I didn't pop your cherry tonight."

"It's alright. I'm expecting flowers and dinner first," he said. "I'm not some cheap whore."

I giggled again as my body relaxed for sleep.

11

Milo

I woke up with Emily in my arms and to the feeling of Sterling climbing into bed behind me. He was freshly showered, and his skin was warm and damp as he settled down behind me. I turned my head and cracked an eye open.

"Timothy said they've all scattered. Most went back to Akron, but a few hot shots thought they could run the game after their bosses were gone. He wasn't invited to join any of the new gangs," Sterling whispered as he pulled the blanket over him.

I *hmm*'ed in sleepy response as Sterling curved his body around mine, which was curved around Emily. It's not that I didn't care about what Timothy told them, but I didn't care right now, sandwiched between two people who wanted to be around me. Two people who liked me and made me feel amazing. Tomorrow I'd think about other people.

Sterling finally settled down and stopped moving, spooning

against my back. His arm was around my middle and his hand rested on Emily's soft belly. He sighed contentedly against the back of my neck, and I stroked his arm lightly. Bumps rose on his skin, and he shivered. I smiled and fell back asleep.

After breakfast the next morning, Emily said she wanted to "work on computers" with me. As much as I loathed teaching people about computers and acting like they'd ever be at a level comparable to mine, I wanted to spend time with her. In my room with coffee in hand, I turned on my computers.

"Is there something specific you wanted to see?" I asked her as I pulled over my old desk chair I kept in the server room. It was rare for anyone to be in my room, so I hadn't needed a second seat before.

"I wanted to see if I could find anything leading to where Gregory is. I mean, I know he's probably at our- *his*- house, but... I don't know. It freaked me out seeing him at that meeting," Emily said and sat in the seat.

"Devon and I agreed he might be our weakest link to finding Anthony," I said.

"Oh?" Emily looked surprised. "Because I know him?"

"Sort of. We figured it freaked him out to see you there, and he was going to get sloppy," I said and turned on my monitors. The whirring of my computer waking up was a comfort to me. I took a sip of my coffee as my computer started up.

Emily watched curiously as I typed in my password. I had intentionally used an operating system that looked complicated to the average user. That, in and of itself, deterred most "normies". My password could be "password" and most people wouldn't be able to find where to type. And my keyboard had no printed letters on it. It was just a bunch of blank, black squares and rectangles.

"Did you want to see the security camera I placed outside the house?" I asked her.

"My house?" Emily asked, her eyebrows raised in shock.

"*This* is your house," I said and gestured around us. "But yeah, Gregory's house."

"Sure, that's a good start," Emily said and rolled her chair closer to me.

Shaking off the discomfort at not starting my morning with my usual routine, I pulled up the security footage of Gregory's house. It was a cookie cutter colonial style home with flower boxes in each window. I had this camera installed to monitor Gregory not long after we'd... acquired Emily, but I'd never looked at it much more than checking the alerts of people coming and going. Seeing the home she'd shared with him and had hoped to raise his babies in had stung, even back then. But before, I had mistaken my jealousy for disdain for their lifestyle. There was nothing wrong with the suburban life they had been leading. In fact, now that I knew it was what my parents had wanted before they were killed, it made it seem like a goal of sorts.

We watched the security alerts of people coming and going for a few minutes. It was mostly Gregory, coming in and out at normal working times. A few times a week, the secretary went in at night and left in the morning. I glanced at Emily to see her stoically watching. It didn't seem to bother her, but I could have been wrong.

"Before everything happened, and I left, we had been talking about getting a new mattress. We had like... body shaped sunken holes in the mattress," she said and stopped to laugh. "We were waiting for Black Friday sales after Thanksgiving. Did he buy a new one or is his new girlfriend sleeping in my imprint?"

I snorted. "Well, I watched all the comings and goings until about a week ago already and there's been no delivery. I think she's sleeping in your hole."

Emily giggled. "Do you know how much sweat and skin a mattress absorbs? I bet she smells like me when she wakes up."

"I would say that's gross, but you smell nice," I said with a shrug as I opened the last security alert.

"Thanks, Milo," she said and rubbed my shoulder.

"This is the last time he left the house," I said and checked the date. It was yesterday morning.

"He looks terrible," Emily said and peered at the screen.

"How so?" I asked. He looked normal to me.

"His hair isn't done," she said. "He's very particular about his hair. And his shirt isn't ironed. He has always put a lot of effort into his appearance. He felt a leader must always look strong and put together."

"He's not wrong. I mean, look at Devon," I said as the video ended with him getting into his car and driving away.

Emily giggled.

"The Starbucks closest to his house has a security camera by their back door and over their counter. He gets a coffee every morning," I said and logged into the store's system.

"Wow, you are a stalker," she said and sat back in her chair.

"Mhm. So, it takes about six minutes for him to get there every morning, give or take a minute. He chats up the blonde barista whenever she's working. But she's twenty years old and a college student. She flirts back because he tips well on Fridays."

"It's scary that you know this," she said and stared at me.

"It's my job," I said quickly.

"It's your job to know about the blonde barista?" Emily quizzed me.

I sighed. "No. When I first started watching his coffee run, I thought she was his secretary, and she had gotten a new job after all the drama. But she's not. He just likes blondes."

Emily touched her dyed red hair, self-consciously. It was naturally a soft brown color that made her big blue eyes stand out like sapphires.

"Submissive blondes," she muttered and spun in slow circles with her chair.

I couldn't comfort her on this and not sound insincere, so I pulled up his phone records and the security footage of his office. "He gets to work about four minutes to eight every morning. He always greets security."

"Charles."

"Now, who is the stalker?" I teased.

She spun back to look at me with a grin. "He's a very nice man. His wife is a nurse, and their daughter played the part of Baby Jesus in the manger two Christmases ago at their church. She pooped so loud it got picked up by the microphone and her little baby farts echoed through the speakers. They had to stop to change her before they could continue the production."

"What an enchanted world you lived in," I said dryly, and turned back to the computer.

She smiled again and leaned back in her seat.

"Anyway, Gregory hired more security. It's Charles on the first floor and then another guy on his floor by the elevator," I continued.

"He must be nervous," she said, no concern for Gregory in her voice.

"Yeah, and he's keeping a gun in his desk," I added.

Emily shuddered. "I never want to see Gregory holding a gun. I once asked him to help me hot glue something for my class and he couldn't even aim that."

I smirked, feeling superior to Gregory for a moment. We'd been trained with guns as soon as we could hold them up. "So, besides his security and gun, here are his phone records."

Emily sat up and squinted at the document on my computer. "That number comes up a lot."

"That's Clara. The secretary," I replied. "He calls and texts her the most. Every Sunday he talks to your parents, though."

Emily rolled her eyes.

"And his internet history shows him Googling his name a lot. And yours," I said.

"Is he looking for me?" she asked.

"He was. And now it seems like he's trying to find us through you," I said.

Emily let out a long breath. I opened up a tab and logged into the bank page.

"How do you get into the bank system that easily?" she asked, awe in her voice.

I chuckled. "I would say I hacked in, but that's false. I watched one teller type in her password. So, I remote into their system- okay, that's a bit of hacking- but I just log in with her info. I was able to take the easier route in."

Emily shook her head with a small smile on her lips. "It's still very impressive."

"I know," I said and turned back to the screen.

There were lines after lines of normal bank activity. Emily scooted closer to read the small text. Starbucks, a local Italian restaurant, phone bill, and utilities. Then, peppered within normalcy, are transfers to another account.

"I don't know that account," Emily said and pointed to the line on my screen.

I looked it up within the bank's system since it was created at the same branch location. "Clara Palmer."

"Ew, he's paying her?" Emily practically shrieked.

"Wait, he's depositing cash. Large amounts of it," I said as I continued to scroll. "Does he take cash donations to his campaign?"

"That's illegal. Well, that amount is illegal, for sure," Emily said, her brows furrowed.

"It's probably Anthony then," I said. "He knows how not to have money traced."

"Well, Gregory doesn't," she said and gestured to the screen. "He's sending it to his secretary."

I snorted. "Yeah, and look, she's cashing it out immediately."

"Do they think they're laundering it?" Emily asked me through a laugh.

"Probably. I guess it's good most people don't know how to do it," I said and turned in my chair until our knees knocked.

"How would he even explain that amount of cash flow? Everyone in town knows his job," Emily said.

She had a point. "Want to fuck it all up?" I asked her with a mischievous smirk.

She looked like she was considering it. An impish sparkle shone from her eyes as she looked at me. "How?"

"Flag his transactions as suspicious. Gets people asking questions and making assumptions," I said, my hand on the mouse, ready to make it happen.

"Do it," she said eagerly.

I highlighted the cash deposits and the transfers to Clara's account and marked them as suspicious activity to be reviewed by the bank team. Anybody would assume he was taking illegal cash donations, not receiving money from the mafia.

"So, this is what you do all day?" Emily asked me.

"Yeah," I said, giving her the easiest fraction of the truth.

"You cyber stalk people."

"I monitor people who need to be checked in on. I manage the house's finances. I keep our names out of police reports, official documents, and the news," I corrected. "And I maintain the hardware and manage the software used in the business, as well as our network and cyber security."

"That's a lot," she said.

"It is a lot, especially when pretty girls give strangers their phones," I said pointedly.

"Oh, sorry," she said and looked down.

"It's okay, you already have a new number and SIM card." I waved it away.

"Thank you, Milo," she said and kissed my cheek. "How are the spicy videos doing?"

"Let's see," I replied as I turned back to the computer

and pulled up Personal Cameras and Sterling's social media accounts.

There were considerably more followers on the social media pages. I furrowed my brow as I saw he'd hit a million followers on some accounts. "Wait... what?" I muttered to myself as I clicked over to Personal Cameras. My heart felt like it seized up with shock. We were in the top spot on the rankings for the entire site. That included career porn stars.

"Are you guys number one?" Emily asked, shock in her voice.

"We... are," I said, my voice hoarse.

"Oh, my god we need to get Sterling in here!" she squealed.

"STERLING!" we both shouted at the same time.

12

Emily

Sterling ran into Milo's room at full speed, looking panicked. Milo gestured to the computer screen displaying the Personal Cameras creator dashboard. It showed their account had almost doubled in subscriptions since they'd last told me the count. Sterling looked at the number and choked.

"What happened?" Sterling gasped.

"I changed your preview video on the site to be a teaser of our first video together mixed with some of your best solo stuff. Then I did some low-key marketing since we've been busy, but it took off. We're viral," Milo explained breathlessly.

"What do you mean, low key marketing?" Sterling asked.

"I posted some pictures we took and edited them with some music. Honestly, I'm talking about the skill level of a fifteen-year-old making a montage of homecoming. I was just messing around to see if anything stuck. And... it stuck,"

Milo explained. "There are fan edits and people posting their predictions and shit."

"We gotta do more!" Sterling exclaimed. "We gotta ride this wave of popularity."

He was right. Their content was the only money we were bringing in to control an entire mafia. "You need to stretch it out more," I interjected. "Do a few blow job videos and then you can have sex on camera."

Milo looked uncomfortable. "We haven't had sex off camera. Why would we do it on camera?"

"Well, you should definitely practice first," I said. Mostly because I wanted to be there for it. But really, Milo's first time needed to be special and private.

It frustrated Milo that we had not taken his virginity yet and he glared at us.

"We can practice first. I'm obviously down for that," Sterling said and rubbed Milo's shoulders.

"I'll fuck you and then I'm going to call it quits on the porn star life. I don't know if I'm comfortable being on camera anymore. It feels too personal," Milo said and looked up at Sterling.

"It is personal when it's both of us, I agree. Wait- no, I'll fuck *you*," Sterling corrected Milo.

Milo made a sound like he didn't agree with Sterling.

"You don't know who would bottom?" I asked. I had never thought about this conversation before. I guessed all men who had sex had to discuss it at some point. They didn't answer, only stared at each other, so I continued. "You could both take turns."

"No," they both said in unison.

"Sterling, go get your box of toys," I said in my Teacher Voice. It felt wrong to use it in this setting, but... it worked.

Sterling was out the door and back in less than thirty seconds. Just enough time for Milo to look at me and ask what I was doing and for me to not answer him. When Sterling came back, he handed it to me and quirked a curious brow.

I opened the black box and dug around until I found what I was looking for and tossed the three items on Milo's unmade bed. Turning, I grinned at them.

"You want to try taking us both?" Sterling asked, his voice low.

"No, you're both trying it out," I said and snapped my fingers and pointed at the two new, still in packaging anal plugs. A bottle of lube sat in the middle and looked like it had never been opened.

"I don't think–" Sterling said, but I cut him a firm look.

"You will both put these plugs in your ass. Now," I said in a firm voice. It was commanding, but it differed from my Teacher Voice. It was huskier and darker. A thrill went through my body when I realized I was capable of a voice so sexual and powerful.

Milo stood up and looked at the two options on the bed. Sterling was watching me with narrowed, challenging eyes. Milo stepped forward to pick one up, but Sterling rushed him to get his choice of toy. I had stepped away, so I didn't see which one they had each picked. One was longer and thinner, and a purple color. The other looked metal and had a black jewel on the flared base. I wasn't sure which one I'd pick. They both looked like they'd be uncomfortable.

Lube and plugs in hand, they made their way to the

bathroom. "Why are you going to the bathroom?" I asked with a pout.

"I don't really want an audience," Sterling muttered.

"Let me watch," I demanded.

"I feel like that's my limit today," Milo said, and Sterling nodded. "I'll do it, but I want to put it in alone this time. You can watch next time if I like it and want to do it again."

"Okay, if you can handle it, come out here with them in," I directed.

They shut the door, and I heard their pants and belts hitting the tiled ground. They didn't speak to each other, and I peeked at the security footage on the screens above Milo's computer. He could have turned it off, but I think I had caught him off guard. The panel dedicated to Milo's bathroom was tiny on the screen and really all I could see were their backs to each other. I stopped watching when I heard a *clunk* and then a chuckle.

"Do you want us clothed?" Sterling asked through the door.

"Naked."

The door opened, and they both came out, cheeks pink with blushes. It was a marvelous sight. My mouth watered, and I thought about what I wanted from them next.

"Lay on the bed. I'll be right back," I said and went into the bathroom. I washed my hands and swished some of Milo's mouthwash. Looking over at the counter, the packaging of both plugs was there. The purple one came with a little remote. There was no battery in it, so I left it on the counter. I wonder which one had the purple plug.

Back in Milo's room, I caught them making out and hard. "Hey," I snapped. "I didn't say you could kiss."

They broke apart.

"Since you two are already hard and ready, touch your-selves," I said. I rolled over the computer chair I'd been in earlier and faced it to the bed. I sat on it and rubbed myself slowly through my leggings.

They were both propped up with pillows, so I could clearly see their faces as they stroked over their own cocks. Almost simultaneously, they spit into their palms. I should have brought the lube in from the bathroom. Their eyes darted from their own cocks to each other's and then to me.

"Tell me what it feels like," I said, my new commanding voice now sounding breathless.

"Full," Sterling said.

"Very full," Milo replied.

"Hmm," I hummed. "I bet you like it. Rock your hips on the bed. Let the plug fuck you."

They followed direction like obedient puppies. I could make them do anything. Last night I had them kill a man for me and today I have them fucking their own asses. There was no limit to my power. To my control over them. I smiled as they both rocked and gyrated their hips on the bed and stroked their cocks. Sterling's head was tipped back as he moaned and Milo was silent but sweating.

I slipped my hand into my leggings and traced my fingers over my clit. It throbbed almost painfully with arousal as I watched them on the bed. Their muscles flexed and their chests heaved as their hips rolled and they gripped their cocks.

Looking at Sterling's box of toys, I saw what looked like a collar type restraint. It was black leather and had silver loops through it. Next to that, I could see a bundle of ropes. I wondered if I could tie them up.

"Hey!" Devon shouted from the stairs. "Come down here. We all need to plan our next move. I can't be the only one working."

Disappointed, I sighed. Milo and Sterling were ignoring Devon. "Stop," I said, thinking of a new idea. "Keep the plugs in, put your clothes on and let's go plan with Devon."

"Stop now?" Milo asked and gestured to his leaking cock.

"Yes," I demanded and stood up. Going into the bathroom, I gathered their clothes. I also slipped the little remote control in my pocket. There were batteries in a drawer in the kitchen.

They were quiet and pissed off as they got dressed and we headed downstairs. I would be sure to make it good for them later if they made it through this meeting with Devon. I could have told Devon to wait until we were finished, but it was exciting and a little bit addicting to flex this newfound power.

13

Milo

We met in the dining room, and Devon already had the big pad of paper and markers on the table. I smiled when I saw the supplies sitting there. Nobody could claim we planned better without Emily. Sterling and I slowly lowered ourselves to sit on the wooden chairs. I kept myself propped on one ass cheek to avoid putting pressure on the plug.

"Alright. That meeting with the gangs didn't go well last night," Devon said.

"No kidding," Sterling grumbled, his cheeks still red and his face in a grimace.

"We have a few options on our next course of action. But we need to be all on the same page," Devon said. "We need to restate our goals. I think after that meeting, some of us changed our minds."

"Not me, I still think we should get out of here," Sterling said irritation clear in his voice.

"Dude, you are not helping. What's up your ass?" Devon spat. I knew he meant it hypothetically, but still I caught a laugh in my throat.

We must have looked guilty enough that Devon groaned and said, "Never mind."

"I'll be right back. We need coffee for this," Emily said and stood up.

"I made some," Devon called out as she went into the kitchen.

Devon wrote on the big paper while Emily was gone. "Option one: Get more money to fully buy out the gangs from Anthony. Take over."

Emily came back in with the pot of coffee and four mugs. She set them out, and we fixed our coffees while Devon stared at us like a teacher waiting for his class to shut up. He tried his best, but nobody did that shit better than Emily.

"Alright, Option two-" Devon started, but I cut him off.

"Kill Anthony," I said.

"And then what?" Devon asked, less cut to his tone than I'd expected. After our late night talk a few weeks ago, he'd been more sympathetic to the idea of killing his father.

"Either take over or disband everything. It doesn't matter," I replied with a shrug.

"So, our motivation to kill him would solely be revenge," Emily clarified.

"Correct," I said with a nod.

Devon wrote on the paper, "Option two: kill Anthony to take over or leave, TBD."

"Option three: Leave. Get the fuck out," Sterling said and

then choked slightly on his coffee as he took a sip like something startled him.

I narrowed my eyes at him. He cleared his throat and avoided eye contact.

Devon wrote the third option on the paper.

"Is there a fourth option?" Devon asked and looked around at us.

Sterling shifted in his seat, and I rested my knee against his. I didn't know what his deal was, but maybe he needed comfort. I mean, I was still painfully rock hard in my pants after being interrupted earlier. The plug in my ass gave just enough pressure that I couldn't get my boner to go down even with talking about horrible shit. But I wasn't shifting around like I had ants in my pants. Sterling wouldn't look at me still.

"I think option four would be to figure out what they were doing with the politicians," Emily said. "Milo and I tracked some of Gregory's finances and we believe he got a deposit of five grand in cash from Anthony as recently as last week. We don't know what he's paying Gregory for, but Gregory seemed to feel guilty about it. He immediately transferred it to an account in his secretary's name and it was withdrawn."

"Why would he do that?" Devon asked, his brow wrinkled.

"I think he thinks he's laundering it?" Emily guessed.

Devon rolled his eyes. "Well, it's convenient for us, at least."

"So, what's the verdict? Should we vote on it?" Emily asked.

Sterling's leg against mine shook. He clenched his jaw tight, and his eyes were staring at the paper of options. Was he in pain? Sure, sitting here with the plug was uncomfortable, but it wasn't painful.

"We should look into the political situation. I've been

watching those other people from the meeting. I haven't been able to get surveillance at all their homes, but their workplaces have it. And I've gotten into some of their bank information. It looks like only one other person is outright receiving money from Anthony and it's a commissioner from a few counties over," I said with a sigh. Truly, I just wanted to kill Anthony and be done with it. "For closure, and so we know all the puzzle pieces. And then we kill Anthony."

Emily nodded. "I agree."

"Should we still be trying to get gangs on our side?" Devon asked. "Are we fully giving up on the family business?"

We all considered this. I knew Sterling was done. Emily was done. And I... I was done, too. But only if I could get my revenge first.

"What do you think, Devon?" Emily asked softly.

Sterling shifted next to me and cleared his throat again. He was visibly sweating now. Was he sick? He wiped his brow with a shaking hand.

"I don't know if I'm ready to give up on it yet," Devon said with a touch of vulnerability. "This is all I know."

"How about we figure out the political side of it? Then we can take out Anthony or buy out the gangs, whichever comes first, and go from there. We can disband or continue the business after we deal with Anthony and we know all the answers to our questions," Emily reasoned. "It's the best of all our options combined."

Sterling groaned in his seat and wiped his brow again. Devon and I looked questioningly at Sterling, but Emily had a look of devious interest. "I, uh, I agree with Emily," Sterling rasped and then took a sip of his coffee with a trembling hand.

"Fine, as long as we get revenge," I said coldly.

"Then it's settled. But in the meantime, we need to remain on our guard," Devon instructed us. "We don't know where Anthony is."

"He hasn't been home since before the meeting. Stephanie packed and left about twenty minutes before he sent in the gang to clear out what he needed. We assume he's operating off cash and gold he had on him, and a burner phone," I said.

"Possibly only some of his gold," Devon amended. "I would think he had to leave most of it behind in his safe."

"Do you think we could get it?" Emily asked. "It would certainly help with buying out the gangs."

Devon raised his eyebrows like he was considering it. "I've thought about it, honestly. But the risks always outweighed the benefits."

"Nobody has been there, and he doesn't have access to the security feeds anymore. Not that he ever used it before, but he can't now," I said. "And we know the codes to get into the safe."

"What if he put up his own surveillance?" Devon asked me.

I scoffed. "Devon, who do you think you're talking to?"

"Alright, fine. I'll think about it. It's still risky," Devon said. "Someone could see me go in there or be camped out waiting to attack."

"Speaking of attacks, are we safe here?" Emily asked and looked out the window.

"There are cameras in every room, and along the property. You know that. There's also some on either end of the road.

Our street is relatively quiet, so I see every car that drives down our road. Then, throughout the wooded property, there are motion detecting cameras. I made a program that uses artificial intelligence to tell me if it's a human or animal that triggered the sensor," I explained.

"Okay, we'd know they were coming. So what?" Emily asked with no bite to her words.

"We'd have enough time to arm ourselves. I've been working on a program that can set off bombs remotely," I said. "There's stuff out there, but I wanted a proprietary software."

"Like booby traps?" Emily asked with a grin. "Are we going to Home Alone the bad guys?"

I shrugged. "If it saves our lives, yeah. There's only four of us and probably a whole lot more of them."

"Sounds expensive," Devon said dryly.

"Are you going to join in their videos to make some more money?" Emily teased Devon.

"Only if you do." Devon gave it right back.

"Okay, well, I'm scheduled for the next video," Emily lied flawlessly. "Better start your manscaping."

Devon approached her slowly and leaned down to whisper in her ear. Molten desire emanated from him as he whispered to her. I couldn't hear what he said, despite craning my neck and leaning forward. Emily's eyes widened and her brows shot up, her mouth forming a little O. Devon's hands traced up her arms to tilt her chin up to him. I grinned as a blush rose to her cheeks. His lips brushed over her jaw and cheek as he moved his hand to wrap around her throat. She swallowed before he gripped her tighter.

I heard a soft buzzing sound, like a phone vibrating in

another room. I felt my pocket where my phone was tucked. Wasn't me. Then Sterling's leg pressed hard against mine as he tipped his head back on the chair. He let out a loud, growling moan and covered his face with his hands. He seemed to be involuntarily rolling his hips and shaking. Through his black t-shirt, I could see his abs contracting over and over like he was orgasming.

Wait.

I let out a bark of laughter and looked at Emily. Devon had backed up from her and was watching Sterling come like he didn't understand what was happening. Emily was grinning like her birthday and Christmas had come on the same day she won the lottery. She slapped a small purple remote onto the table. The buzzing sound continued and was audible between Sterling's gasping, desperate moans.

"Fucking hell, I can't stop coming. Turn it off," Sterling begged. His voice was ruined, and his body was practically convulsing around the plug.

Knowing I could someday make him come like that around my cock almost set me off. But I kept myself in check. I only watched him, drinking in his pleasure that seemed to border on pain. His neck muscles strained, and he breathed through his teeth before letting out another moan. His hands dropped from his face, and he gripped the seat of his chair like he was afraid he was going to fall off. Curling his body in on itself, he continued to rock his hips. His mouth hung open and my urge to shove my dick between his lips was overwhelming.

Emily reached over and pressed a button on the little purple remote and Sterling instantly went lax in the chair like all his muscles had given out. She giggled. The sound was almost eerily menacing while Sterling panted and slowly regained control over his body. He looked up and glared at her from under his brows. It would have been threatening if he wasn't currently made of cooked spaghetti.

"Now I know who took the purple one," she said innocently.

"Can't fucking take anything seriously," Devon snapped and stormed from the room.

Emily flicked the remote, so it skidded in front of Sterling. She stood up and chased after Devon. I wondered again what he'd said to her.

Sterling and I made eye contact. He looked completely spent. Ripples of aftershocks made his breath catch. I smiled. "You're the bottom."

He shook his head, still panting. "No, we'll switch. I want to make you come like this."

"Do it then," I challenged him.

"Are you kidding? I don't think I could walk," Sterling chuckled. "Raincheck."

"Whatever," I grumbled.

14

Emily

Ashamed by my own actions after seeing Devon's reaction, I scraped back my chair and rushed to follow him out of the dining room. His broad shoulders were tight as he walked through the kitchen to the hallway and staircase. His hands were in his pockets as he walked, and I'd never seen him look so uncomfortable. It was my fault.

"Devon, wait!" I called out as I rushed after him.

His long stride outpaced me to the stairs. At a run, I grabbed his arm and spun him around. I'd been moving faster than I'd thought causing him to stumble. His back hit the wall. I caught myself with a hand to the center of his chest. His eyes flashed with something spoke of danger as his head lightly knocked against the wood where the staircase sloped down.

"What do you want?" he said with distaste. I caught the undertones of hurt and confusion in his voice.

"I want to apologize," I said. "I'm sorry. That was inappropriate. You didn't need to see that."

Devon shook his head and huffed out a breath that fanned over my face.

"But... I thought you were okay with us being together?" I asked hesitantly.

"I am. I just... don't need to be intimately aware of when you put a vibrating cock ring on Sterling," Devon said and rolled his eyes.

My mouth snapped shut with an audible click. He had a valid point, but I fought the urge to correct him.

"What was it then?" Devon asked with what seemed like morbid curiosity. Like rubber necking at a car accident.

"A uh, remote controlled vibrating anal plug," I whispered.

Devon wrinkled his entire face with disgust, then his brows went up and he tilted his head to the side like he was considering it. I giggled and stepped back, my hand dropping from his chest. He caught it in his hands and clasped it.

"I'm feeling conflicted, Emily," Devon said and looked down at my hand in his. His fingers were strong and long. His cuticles were slightly frayed like he'd been gnawing on them.

"About what?" I hesitated.

He exhaled slowly through his nose as he gathered himself. "Seeing them happy makes me happy. Seeing them finally give into the tension they'd been dancing around since we were teenagers makes me happy. I feel this as their friend, their brother, their leader. Seeing you get comfortable here, in this life, with us, makes me happy, too. Especially after we almost lost you and Milo. But this was an important planning meeting. And their infallible dedication to you derailed it thoroughly. I understand- *vividly* now how much of a... dominant role you play for them. I've never shared the role of leader over them, and I worry if the time comes, they'd chose your leadership over mine."

His words took me aback. So much so that I stepped away and yanked my hand from his. "Really?" I snapped. "That's what this is about? Your *power* over us?"

"No, Emily-"

"You can't bear the thought of not being in control of everyone around you so much-"

Now it was his turn to cut me off. Quick as lightning, he had me spun around and my back against the wall where his had been moments before. My hair hung over my face and when I gasped, some went into my mouth.

His eyes were dark with anger as he looked over my face. Jaw muscles feathered as he stared down at my shocked expression. "No, listen to me. It's not about power. It's about everyone's safety in moments of weakness. I've trained for this my entire life. Their lives have been *my* responsibility since we took over official roles in the family business over a decade ago. I know how to direct them. I know their strengths and weaknesses. No offence, but you're new here. You may know how to get Sterling to shove a plug up his ass, but you don't know how to reach him when his demons are in control, and he's elbows deep in viscera. You may have Milo on a leash as long as his dick, but you don't know how to direct his incredible intelligence when he hasn't slept in days and is desperate for things to make sense. Emily, I admire your ability to comfort them. To- to love them if that's what this is. But you're not ready to *lead* them. If we were in a dangerous situation, I need to know you all would look to me for direction."

"I- I'm sorry," I said as deep shame and terror settled into my guts. In a way, he was right. I *could* control Sterling and Milo. But only sexually. Right? Sterling had said he loved me before. He also said it to Milo. His attachment to me was more than sexual, it was emotional. And I could exploit that emotional attachment in a second. Devon's fears were astute, but I would lead no one astray intentionally.

His eyes softened, and he stroked my hair away from my face and out of my mouth. He was silent as he caressed my hair and ran his thumb over my bottom lip. Instinctively, I opened my lips to suck his thumb into my mouth, but he pulled away with a warning look and a tilt of his head. I bit my lip and looked up at him from under my lashes. Rejection simmered below the shame of the morning.

"You're a good leader, Devon," I said, my voice raspy with lust and emotion. "I look forward to learning more from you."

"Who said I was going to teach you?" he teased.

"What if I asked nicely?" I pouted at him and asked sweetly.

"Well, go ahead and we'll see," Devon prompted and leaned in further. His breath tickled my skin, and the scent of his cologne filled my lungs.

Silence.

"Go ahead and ask nicely," Devon prompted again, and shoved his hips against mine. His belt buckled pressed into my lower stomach. I swallowed dryly.

"Oh, you meant now? No thanks, I was hoping to go browse a bookstore with an overpriced coffee today," I said brightly.

"Brat," Devon practically snarled as he gave me one more shove and then backed up.

I smiled up at him. "Would you like to come with me?"

"Take Milo. He loves bookstores," Devon said as he smoothed down his shirt.

"Sure, but do you want to come?" I asked again.

Devon looked me over as he thought. "Yes, I'll drive."

"And you'll buy me a coffee," I insisted in the same voice I'd used to get Sterling and Milo to use anal plugs. I wondered if it worked on Devon, too.

Devon quirked an eyebrow, and his jaw muscles feathered again. "What was that?"

"You're going to buy me a coffee," I repeated in the same authoritative and husky voice.

"Does that work on Sterling and Milo?" he asked, his eyes sparkling with humorous interest as he stepped closer again.

"Got them both to put toys up their asses, didn't it?" I challenged him.

Devon tilted his head to the side and slid his tongue over his teeth, that smiling look still in his eyes.

"And you were hoping it would work on me," he said. He was so close to me again I could feel the heat from his body.

I opened my mouth to retort, but his hands moved faster. He shoved two fingers into my mouth and the other hand wrapped around my throat. His hold was tight, and he tilted my chin up. Our noses were almost touching as his fingers slid further to the back of my mouth. I winced and fought a gag at the intrusion.

"The only time I will listen to demands that come from

this mouth is when you're begging me to fuck you. Do you understand me?" he growled in my face.

My eyes watered from fighting back a gag, but I managed a nod.

"Good girl," Devon said and stepped back, removing his hands from me. I had grown hot and needy, so the air that swirled up between us felt cold and unforgiving.

I gasped for air and wiped away my tears.

"I'll buy you a coffee. But not because you asked," Devon said before he disappeared up the stairs.

Being a brat to Devon had been a hobby since I'd first been taken in by these men. Now, I wasn't so sure if it was still fun. It was more embarrassing and degrading when he responded. The dampness between my legs and the awareness that I'd still gotten him to agree to buy me a coffee begged to differ.

An hour later, Devon, Milo, and I were in a little, crammed, multi-level bookstore in a trendy area of the city. They had forced Sterling to stay home to keep watch on the house. Fancy, overpriced coffee in hand, I browsed row after row.

The store was silent other than occasional murmuring and the turning of pages. Devon stood leaning near the door, reading from a book about organized crime in Cleveland. A smirk played at the corner of his mouth.

"Is he reading about himself?" I whispered to Milo, who was intently reading a vintage computer textbook.

He looked up at Devon and snorted. "Sort of. Our names have never been suspected, but some of our... activities have been attributed to others."

I giggled and sipped my mocha.

"Let me know when you're ready to make out in the

basement stacks," Milo said as he plopped down into a worn leather armchair.

I giggled again and finished my coffee. He looked down at the book in his lap, and I studied him. A warm lamp stood next to the chair, and he almost glowed in the yellow light. He placed an ankle over his other knee to create a surface for his book and his azure blue eyes tracked over the pages. His long, unmarred hand hovered over the corner. He looked like a professor. A very sexy professor. I gulped as I watched him lick his lips absently and turn the page. His auburn beard shone almost completely red in the lamplight and his brown hair fell over one eye.

"Now," I rasped.

He looked up suddenly and snapped his book shut. "Say no more," he said and stood, leaving his book on the seat. He took my empty coffee cup and threw it in a nearby trash can before grabbing my hand and weaving us through the stacks to the stairs.

Milo pulled me excitedly down the rickety stairs surrounded by walls decorated with flyers for local events. There was nobody down there, it was mainly nonfiction and textbooks. He pulled me roughly into the computer section and his lips crashed into mine.

As much as I enjoyed Sterling, it was nice to kiss Milo without him there. I knew I could always kick Sterling out, but I wasn't sure how to do that without hurting feelings. Managing two boyfriends at once was a tricky business.

Milo kissed like he was savoring a dessert. His lips and tongue sipped at me gently and reverently. He sighed against my lips and his breath shook like he was trembling with suppressed intensity. My stomach flipped with excitement and desire, and I buried my hands in his hair.

"Tonight," I murmured against his lips.

"Really?" he asked and pulled back. His eyes were alight with excitement as he stroked over my face and hair.

"Really," I assured him.

"Fuck yes," he said and dove back down to my lips.

Distantly, I was aware of footsteps on the stairs, but I didn't care. Milo's hands were delicately tracing over my arms and making me shiver with desire. Whoever was coming downstairs would have a show to accompany their book browsing.

Someone discreetly cleared their throat the next row over, and Milo pulled away from me with a sheepish grin. "Sorry, I got carried away," he whispered and pressed his erection against my stomach.

"Do you guys want to get dinner?" Devon asked, suddenly appearing next to us. I jumped and almost shrieked. He startled Milo as well. "What?" Devon said irritably.

"You scared me," I laughed.

"Boo," Devon said, bored, with his hands in his pockets. "I'm starving. Let's go get dinner."

"Sterling texted me and asked us to bring him home some food," Milo said.

"Of course he did," Devon said.

"Devon's buying us dinner," I said and pulled Milo by the hand towards the stairs.

"You say that like it's not money me and Sterling made," Milo grumbled.

Devon rolled his eyes and followed us up the stairs. I

carried my small stack of romance novels and put the book about crime in Cleveland on top. Milo slid his vintage computer book on the counter next to my stack.

"Who's paying for these books?" Devon asked me as he checked his watch.

"Me. Oh, wait, I never got my paycheck," I said innocently and batted my lashes at Devon.

Devon rolled his eyes again and pulled out his wallet. He quirked an eyebrow at the crime book on top. I fiddled with a button on his shirt and leaned back against the counter. "I want you to point out what parts should have your name on it."

"Trouble," Milo chuckled quietly at me as the young register worker rushed over.

"Milo, I thought you knew everything about computers," I teased him and turned to tap his chosen computer manual.

Devon touched me lightly at about the middle of my back. I recognized he was telling me to shut up. But the words were out.

"It's not my fault if I wasn't born yet," Milo said, and it sounded like he was convincing himself more than answering me.

The girl ringing us up looked at us like we were insane and only spoke to tell us our total. Once Devon had paid her, earning Milo and me some really odd looks, we were out on the blustery street. Early March in Northeast Ohio was still as cold as January. There were very few people on the sidewalk despite it being sunnier than it had been for months. The Vitamin D sunk into my skin and felt like I'd taken party drugs. It was the same every year for most people who lived in a gray and snowy environment. Those first rays of sunlight were like ecstasy. I walked in front of Milo and Devon and kicked each clump of ice and snow as I came across it. There was just something satisfying about seeing it burst into slush and ice under my feet. We were silent as we walked down the sidewalk towards a place that offered sushi and hibachi.

I glimpsed our reflections in the darkened glass of a closed shop. Both men had their hooded eyes glued to my ass as I walked and kicked the snow and ice. Milo had a small smile on his lips and Devon looked like he could kiss me or tear me apart. Probably both, and the order likely didn't matter. I looked more confident than I'd ever felt. The face of the woman reflected in the shop window almost startled me. She was me, but she looked... powerful. She held her shoulders higher and with better posture, her chin lifted, her eyes happier. That woman could kill a man and not get caught. She could help run a mafia. She was unstoppable. That woman looked like she had the men behind her on leashes.

And that was the crux of the whole thing. Being with these men made me feel like I was holding the leash for the Devil's hellhounds. They had killed for me. I had killed for them. They had gone through hell to get me back after I'd been taken. We were bound by blood and guts. I had them and they had me and there was no turning back.

We passed the shop with the darkened windows and approached the restaurant. Devon's phone rang in his pocket. He slid it out and his brow wrinkled as we stopped outside the restaurant for him to answer it. "It says unknown number."

"Then the number is hidden," Milo said and peered down at Devon's phone.

"Like star sixty-seven?" I asked.

"That or something more complex," Milo muttered.

Devon pressed the button to answer it, and he lifted it to his ear. He didn't say anything in greeting. But he didn't need to.

"Hello son," came Anthony's voice.

My stomach dropped and the ice from the sidewalk entered my veins. I reached out for Milo's hand. He gripped it tightly in his while we huddled together to listen.

"I stopped being your son when I found out you killed the parents of the men I consider my brothers," Devon spat.

"You stopped being my son as soon as a fake redhead entered your home and had you thinking about anything other than your duties," Anthony retorted calmly.

"That's false and you know it. Besides, she came into my home at your direct order," Devon said and flashed a sorrowful look down at me.

"One I was looking to rectify with her death, but you intervened," Anthony said.

"And what about Milo? What did he do to deserve it?" Devon growled into the phone.

"He was watching our money and had put a stop to a very important transfer of funds. Funds that were needed for a deal nobody knew about yet. But somehow, he knew enough to cancel the transfer," Anthony said. "He knew too much too soon, and I had to get rid of him."

"Well, you failed," Devon said and looked around us. "They're alive, and your plans have been ruined."

"No, Devon. My plans remain," Anthony said, and Devon whipped around on the street looking around us. "If the distractions are removed, we can reunite the family and continue our legacy."

"You're wrong. The legacy you speak of was founded on murder and betrayal. It's not one I want to continue," Devon said and gestured for us to follow him.

Milo gripped my hand in one and his gun in the other. Devon's gun was also in his hand as we walked back the way we'd come to where Devon had parked. I clumsily took out my gun from its holster. There was nobody else on the street to be frightened by our weapons. Devon nodded to Milo, and he let go of my hand to take up a position behind me as we walked.

"We build success on the blood and bones of the people who stood in our way. You should know this, Devon," Anthony continued.

"And you're in my way," Devon spat. "You can either turn power over to me or we will take it from you."

"You see, that's where you're wrong, son. I'm not in your way. Untrustworthy Milo and disillusioning Emily are," Anthony said. I barely heard him now that we were rushing down the street, but I heard enough.

My heart pounded in my chest and fear curdled the latte in my stomach. But anger overtook every other emotion when I saw the fear flash in Devon's eyes as he looked back at us. I would take Anthony out myself for everything he's put my men through. I clenched the gun in my hand more confidently now and kept my head on a swivel like I'd seen Sterling do.

A shot rang out from an alcove of a closed shop across the street. The brick of the building next to me crumbled. A surprised shriek ripped from my throat before I could swallow it. Devon hung up his phone and pulled me behind him. I clutched the back of his shirt in my hand and aimed my gun towards where the shot had come from. Another shot, louder this time, sounded from behind me. Milo had seen where the shot came from, too. Milo took out the person behind us with ease.

"Milo, get behind me!" Devon bellowed.

"No!" Milo shouted back as another shot was aimed our way.

"They're not aiming at me!" Devon said as he shot off two rounds at the alcove. "Their orders are for you and Emily!"

It wasn't heroism or bravery or a need for justice that led me to step away from Devon and Milo. It was pure rage. Part of it was instinctual animal rage that came when in danger. Fight or flight. I was all fight these days. And part of it was the need to protect Milo and Devon. They'd been through enough, and I wanted it to *stop*.

Running across the street, I blocked out the shouts of Devon and Milo. Closer to the target, I could get a better view of them in the setting sun. He wasn't expecting me to run at him, but he'd seen me run the whole way. His eyes flashed with confusion as he dodged a shot from one of the guys. He was young. Maybe the same age as Tommy. I felt bad for a second before he aimed his gun at me. My gun was already up, and I was close enough for my poor gun skills to be accurate. I fired. He crumpled to the ground.

A hand ripped me back by my sweater and I stumbled into a chest. "What the *fuck* do you think you're doing?" Devon growled in my ear.

"Saving your life," I growled back.

He looked me over desperately, an angry furrow still in his brow. "They were after you two, not me."

Milo forcefully spun me around to face him. His eyes were huge and his breathing was ragged. He held my face in his hands and kissed me hard on the lips. His lips crushed mine. Gone were the gentle, savoring kisses he'd given me earlier.

"That's enough. We have to move," Devon demanded and pulled on my sleeve.

Another shot sounded from somewhere around us. The sound echoed between the buildings and a siren in the distance was getting closer and closer. We had instinctively ducked when the shot was fired, and now Devon was pulling me down the street again. I could see his car about a block away. Surely the shooter was over there. If they knew us, then they likely knew our vehicles.

At a run, Devon led us down the street. Two more shots were fired, and Devon was firing back. I screamed as the asphalt at my feet seemed to explode as a bullet hit it. Milo pushed me forward faster than my feet were moving, and I stumbled into Devon. I gripped the back of his shirt again as I caught myself. I felt the impact before I registered what had happened. Devon had been shot. He gave a wounded, angry shout before the shooter finally came into view, crouching behind our car.

Panic was coursing through me as Milo got a clear shot at our attacker. He shot off three rounds and the man hit the ground. I pushed at Devon now and ripped open the front door of the car and unlocked the back. The key fob in Devon's pocket had unlocked the driver's side door based on his proximity. "Get in! Get in!" the horrified screech ripped from my throat as I pushed Devon into the backseat.

Milo was diving into the driver's seat as I climbed into the back seat over Devon. There was blood all over the shirt on his right shoulder. He groaned as he lay on his back on the beige leather seats. Milo had the car started and moving before another shooter came out of the parking garage. The lights of a police car shone as they sped onto the street behind us. They didn't bother to chase us, as a gunman was visible on the road.

I straddled Devon on the seat and ripped open his shirt. Buttons flew everywhere as I shoved his shirt down his arms and looked at the wound. He hissed through his teeth as the fabric of his shirt separated from the bloody wound. My breath caught in my throat and sounded like a whimper as I saw blood flowing from his shoulder.

"How bad is it?" Milo asked from the front seat, panic audible in his tone. "I think we're being followed; I need to lose them. Can he make it?"

Devon craned his neck to look down at his shoulder. The muscles in his neck strained and he breathed raggedly. I could see his pulse pounding and I considered that a good sign. He prodded at the bloody area with his left hand and winced. He sighed a breath of relief and collapsed back against the seat. "It's just a scrape."

"It's not just a scrape! You scrape your knees on the playground. You don't get scraped with a bullet!" I shrieked as I removed my sweater to press against his wound.

Devon was still panting, but he smiled at me and seemed to laugh. I applied pressure to his gunshot, and he winced and groaned through his smile. A chuckle ended his groan. He had to be delirious. He had to have lost too much blood.

"Milo, hurry, he's lost so much blood. He's like hallucinating or something," I said urgently. My hands shook as I pressed my sweater to his wound.

"Milo, I'm fine," Devon insisted. "Lose them."

"Devon, you're bleeding all over the car!" I insisted.

"Look at the wound now, Emily. It's just a graze," Devon said calmly.

I pulled the soaked sweater from his shoulder and peeked at the wound. It was still bleeding profusely, but I could see the shape of the gash running along the meat of his biceps. The bullet had traveled along the surface of his arm. I sat up with a sigh of immeasurable relief. I was still straddling Devon on the seat, but I didn't care. He was alive and going to be fine.

"They were aiming for your head," Devon clarified quietly.

"How'd they miss? I was literally right there," I said and shook my head in disbelief.

Devon's smile returned. "They didn't."

"What?" I asked and felt at my face. Whole and undamaged.

He reached up and fingered my hair lightly with his bloody left hand. Confused, I looked in the rearview mirror in the front seat. Sure enough, there was a jagged cut through a chunk of my hair. Bile rose in my stomach as I realized how close I had come to dying. I opened the window and puked out of it. Both guys laughed at me. Devon gagged sympathetically while laughing as I barfed out the window of the moving vehicle. They were absolutely deranged.

15

Emily

Milo lost whoever was following us and got us home quickly. I had called Sterling, and he cleared the counter in Devon's bathroom. As soon as we were in the house, Devon barked out orders.

"Sterling, I need the first aid kit from the office. The big one," he ordered, holding his bleeding arm as he stomped up the stairs. "Emily, all the alcohol you can carry. Milo, get Sterling's dumbass ring light."

We followed orders like good little soldiers. I rushed upstairs carrying three bottles of whiskey and the single bottle of vodka that lived in the freezer.

"I'll call Doc," Milo said as he came into the room and finally got a good look at the bullet wound.

"No," Devon said. "Don't bring him in for this. It'll risk him and his family."

"Who's going to stitch you up, then?" Milo argued as he set

up the ring light. The bathroom was bathed in bright light, making it feel like a hospital room.

I opened the first bottle of whiskey and Devon snatched it from my hand. He took two long pulls from the bottle and handed it back to me. "I can do it. My mom taught me embroidery."

"This isn't a throw pillow. This is my flesh, Emily," Devon drawled.

"Okay, then leave it open to fester," I retorted.

"I'm going to stitch it," Devon grumbled as Sterling came in with a big red first aid kit.

"That's fucking sick," Sterling said as he clunked the kit down on the marble counter. I couldn't tell if he meant "gross" or "cool," but it seemed like both.

Devon flicked open the latches on the kit with one bloody hand and without a word to any of us. I hovered, ready to help him, but needing direction. "Devon, what do you need me to do?" I whispered.

"Wash your hands, then thread the needle. I'll get it out," Devon said before clumsily splashing a bottle of isopropyl alcohol over his bloodied hand. Milo helped him rinse his hand with the alcohol and Sterling stood ready with the whiskey.

I followed directions and threaded the needle he handed me. It was curved, and I gagged looking at it. Devon grunted disappointedly after he gagged in echo. "Sorry," I murmured.

"Rinse the cut with alcohol," he directed in an empty voice.

Milo was still holding the alcohol, so he took a breath before pouring it gently over the cut. Devon howled in pain. Tears pricked my eyes in reaction. I dabbed the cut with a roll of paper towels that were in the kit. Devon gently moved me away from him and promptly punched Sterling in the gut with his left arm.

"Oof, what the fuck, dude?" Sterling groaned.

"I feel better. Give me the whiskey," Devon said and held out his hand. Sterling, still bent over, handed him the bottle. Devon chugged from it before Milo took it from him.

"You're going to be too drunk to stitch, suck it up," Milo said, and set the bottle down.

"You suck it up," Devon spat.

"Maybe later if you say 'please.' Stitch it before we have to rinse it again," Milo said.

Devon grunted in acknowledgement before he took off his belt. He put the leather between his teeth and sat on the lid of the toilet. Devon closed his eyes and took a steadying breath before opening them and putting the needle in his skin. The required movement looked like he was scooping his own flesh as he stitched. I used towels to dab at the sweat, tears, and blood that formed as he worked. My own tears stayed put in my lashes as I ground my teeth. Devon screamed and groaned as he worked, stopping only to wipe blood off his hand and needle until he finished and needed help to cut and tie the string. The rest of us had been silent as his flesh slowly closed, only murmuring quiet directions when necessary. When the needle was thrown into a little pan, he slumped back against the toilet and seemed to pass out. Sterling swooped in and picked Devon up bridal style and carried him to the bed right outside the bathroom.

I had come running into Devon's room and hadn't looked around. Knowing Devon was alright allowed me to take in my surroundings. His room was the same as the rest of the bedrooms, though his was decorated with dark wood, emerald greens, and warm lamps. It was very reminiscent of the office downstairs. Two tall bookshelves filled with books stood along one wall. His closet was closed, but I knew it to be full.

Devon groaned in his bed, and Milo came out of the bathroom with bandages. Milo carefully applied bandages and was speaking quietly and lightly to Devon. Devon's eyes were fluttering as he struggled to regain consciousness and listen to Milo. I couldn't hear what Milo was saying, but there was a blush high on Devon's cheekbones. Sterling was sitting on the other side of Devon on the bed, and he was smiling softly at whatever Milo had said.

I felt like I was intruding.

Needing to feel useful, I went to the bathroom and washed blood off the toilet, sink, and floor. There was so much. I would need to make sure Devon ate and drank something soon. Cleaning the trail of blood off the floor as I went, I cleaned until I reached the door we had come in. Both Sterling and Milo had stayed with Devon.

The stove had a bubbling pot of brothy soup on it when Sterling and Milo came down to find me. I smiled at them as I checked the doneness of the vegetables.

"I made Devon some soup. It's not the same as what Doc made us, but it'll help restore his blood," I said.

Sterling nodded solemnly.

"Hey, what's wrong?" I asked him.

"Why is it never me?" he asked, like it had been on the tip of his tongue since we'd gotten home.

"Are you offended nobody is trying to kill you?" Milo snorted.

I shot Milo a look.

"No, well. Sort of, yeah," Sterling said with a sigh. "But it's more like I'm wondering why you two are considered a threat, but I'm not. And I'm angry you two are only ever attacked when I'm not around to protect you."

"Because our attackers know not to try anything when we have our seven-foot tall, three-hundred-pound bodyguard," Milo said.

"I'm six foot four and two sixty-five," Sterling snapped irritably.

"It doesn't matter. What Milo means is that you *are* a threat. A direct threat to their person if they tried anything with you around," I intervened. "It would take a lot more firepower than a couple of gangsters to take you down."

Sterling settled on the seat at the island and seemed to relax a little. Milo came around the counter and tasted the soup. He added more salt and a pat of butter. "He'll need more sodium and fat to get his blood back up. Bring him some of the bread you made the other day. He'll need something to soak up the alcohol."

I nodded to Milo and studied Sterling. His brow was still furrowed as he thought.

"Do you guys just want some freezer pizza for dinner?" I asked, trying to lighten the mood.

"Yeah, I'll make it. While you go spoon feed his royal douchebaggy-ness, Milo can tell me everything that happened today," Sterling directed.

I smiled as I made a tray of soup, bread, coconut water,

and a bar of dark chocolate. I carried it up to Devon's room, where he was lounging back against his headboard with a tablet on his lap. He watched me come in with the tray, his eyes never leaving me as I approached him.

"Thank you," he said and sipped at the coconut water.

"No. Thank *you*," I said, and my voice felt choked. Now that everyone was calm and safe, the adrenaline was wearing thin, leaving me with the realization of how the evening could have gone. I could have been dead. Milo could have been dead. Devon had been shot, but it could have been so much worse.

"Hey," Devon said and tipped my chin up with a finger. "We had our guard down. It had been too long since any word or attack from my father. We relaxed too much. But we learned our lesson, Emily. We're all safe, but we learned."

I nodded, and he caught a tear as it slid down my cheek.

"Thank you for my dinner," Devon said. "Now, go spend time with Milo and Sterling. They'll need... comforting after today's events."

"Do you need any medicine or anything?" I asked him.

"Already taken care of," Devon said and waved me away and picked up his tablet again.

He was acting so nonchalant, and he'd just been shot at by someone hired by his father. I was a mess, and I wasn't the one shot. I couldn't imagine the hurt from knowing the person who wanted to destroy you was your own father. "Devon..." I croaked and reached for his hand.

"I know, Emily," he said tightly. "I'm not ready to talk about it yet." He didn't look at me again.

As I was leaving, he drawled, "Too bad Marie is in hiding. Your hair is a wreck."

I snorted as I left. He wasn't wrong. My roots had grown out in the almost three months I'd been with the guys. Not to mention my hair was singed and cut from the bullet that barely missed my head.

"How much longer until pizza?" I called down from the balcony to the kitchen.

"Box says twenty-two minutes, and I put it in two minutes ago," Sterling called back.

I hurried to shower in my room. There was still blood on me from tending to Devon. I watched it swirl pink down the drain as I scrubbed. Quickly, I washed and shaved, then put my hair up in a wet bun. Dressed in a pair of soft leggings and one of Sterling's sweaters, I met him and Milo downstairs.

Milo's hair was wet, and he was wearing a pair of flannel pajama pants and a zipped black hoodie. I sniffed him as I approached him with a smile on my face. He cringed away from my nose and chuckled. "I love the smell of your soap," I explained as I sat at the barstool next to him.

Sterling slid two plates of pizza at us and glasses of whiskey over ice. "So how was shopping? Get anything cute?" he said sarcastically.

"Oh, no! We must have dropped the bag of books!" I said in between blows of cool air on the hot pizza.

"Nope, I had it in the crook of my arm the whole time. I didn't even notice until I tried to drive and it blocked the gearshift," Milo said and sipped his whiskey.

"He lost his bowels, but not your books," Sterling said proudly.

"I did not!" Milo defended with a laugh.

"Well, no shame because I peed a little," I said and shrugged.

"Okay but, for the record, I did not shit my pants," Milo said and bit into his pizza.

Sterling shook hot sauce over his slice before biting into it. "Today."

Milo glared at Sterling, who gave a challenging look back. I pretended not to notice.

We chatted and ate our pizza. I drank two glasses of whiskey. The nerves of the evening had settled into a more general buzz of anxiety. And the only way I could think to get rid of it was to, well, get buzzed. I had grown accustomed to the guys' preferred alcohol. There was a large wine rack in the pantry I could raid, but whiskey did the job quicker.

Feeling more relaxed and ready to fulfill my promise to Milo, I told the guys I was going to the bathroom. Upstairs, I gathered the rope from Sterling's room and rolled one of Milo's computer chairs across the hall to my room. I made my bed nicely, lit a few candles, put on some lingerie, and texted Sterling to come up to my room.

He came in with a confused expression on his face that cleared when he saw me standing with the rope. I had chosen a soft gray cotton and lace lingerie set and hoped it looked sweet and welcoming. Milo's first time was going to be perfect.

"Whatcha doin'?" Sterling asked as he took me standing in lingerie with bondage ropes.

"I'm about to deflower Milo," I said. "Sit, I have promises to fulfill."

Sterling practically jumped into the seat and put his hands behind his back. I wound the rope around his wrists behind the chair and giggled as he showed how easily he could get out. I scolded him and moved to text Milo.

"Wait, go to Dev's room. Find one of his old man cardigans and wear those stupid blue light blocking glasses Milo got for you," Sterling directed. "And let me pull down some of your hair."

He pulled his hands out of the ropes with ease again, and I huffed in annoyance. He gave me a sheepish, boyish grin before he pulled down little pieces of my hair from my bun.

"He'll probably pull your hair out of the bun and take the glasses off your face before anything happens," Sterling explained. "I've been well acquainted with that man's fantasies since puberty."

"Thank you. Now, please, kindly re-bondage yourself." I pointed to his assigned seat as I rushed out to Devon's room.

He was still on his tablet but looked drowsier when I knocked lightly and entered. His eyes widened when I entered. "Can I borrow a cardigan?" I asked him brightly. "I promise I'll wash it before I return it."

There was a pause, like he needed to re-listen to what I'd said in his brain. "Sure, yeah. Any of them."

"Thank you!" I said and opened his closet.

A bright light came on automatically and I blinked rapidly to adjust to the assault. His closet was organized by clothing type and then color. Shoes were lined up on clean, velour lined shelving and ties were displayed on a rack. As psychotic as his closet was, it was easy to find his cardigans. He had many. I chose one that was black and knitted, with leather patches on the elbows and big wooden buttons. I imagined on Devon it would look like Villain Mr. Rogers, but on me it would look cute and bookish. Apparently, that was Milo's type.

"I promise I'll return it clean!" I said as I rushed from Devon's room and closed the door behind me.

Sterling was tied in the chair when I returned. "Devon asleep?"

"No, he's still up on his tablet," I said and slipped the cardigan on.

Sterling snorted and raised his eyebrows.

"What?" I asked and located the blue light blocking glasses.

"You went in there like that? You're lucky he's injured and almost knocked out with pain pills," Sterling explained and looked me up and down.

I realized with a flash of heat I had only been wearing a lacy bra and a thong when I'd gone into Devon's room. Embarrassment washed over me. Being comfortable around most men in the house didn't mean everyone was okay with me being in my underwear.

With no further discussion on my particular brand of humiliation with Devon, I texted Milo. "Can you come help me with my phone? It's not charging when I plug it in." I read aloud to Sterling.

"Is the other end plugged into the wall?" Milo shot back immediately.

"Yes. Come here," I replied.

"Turn it off and on again," Milo said almost instantly.

Sterling laughed when I read it out.

"Milo. Come. Here. Now," I said finally and tossed my phone down on the dresser.

I sat on the bed, facing the door, and spread my legs a little. Sterling rolled in the computer chair to get a better angle. A few moments later, an annoyed looking Milo came into my room looking like he'd rather take the phone back than provide tech support. His eyes instantly flicked from Sterling in the chair, to me on the bed, to the candles around the room. A grin slowly grew on his face, and he approached me slowly.

"I promised you that day I'd take your virginity with Sterling tied up in the room. I wanted it to be special, so I made you wait. But today showed me that as soon as we let our guard down and try to be normal, there will always be a threat. The life we have doesn't care about special days," I said in a voice just above a whisper. "Milo, take off your clothes."

16

Milo

I understood instantly there was no need to troubleshoot Emily's phone when I saw Sterling tied up in my desk chair. I saw him first and then my eyes settled on her. Reclining back on her hands on the bed, she looked like every nerdy guy's dream. She wore a black cardigan and glasses, her breasts pushed up to show cleavage above the knitwear and her legs were crossed before her. Candlelight flickered over her face, making her look like smooth marble.

She was right when she said there was no such thing as a normal day in our lives. I understood then that she'd been waiting for a time to make this special. But there were no sentimental or special days anymore. We were at war. Now was not the time to think about that. Not when I had a woman like this in front of me.

I smiled at her as I unzipped my hoodie. The sound was loud in the room. She bit her lip and looked at my body like it was something she wanted to devour. It instantly aroused me, tenting my pajama pants. From my left, Sterling let out a sigh of relief. I didn't look at him. We'd have our own first time. This was Emily's.

She moved back on the bed towards the pillows, and I followed her onto the bed, keeping my face near hers. I felt like I was prowling after my prey. Her blue eyes were dilated and filled with a look of trust and desire. I'd never had someone look at me like that. I never wanted to forget that expression on her face. She smiled when I started unbuttoning her cardigan. It smelled faintly like cedar and spice, and I realized this was one of Devon's sweaters. I stooped to sniff the fabric at the collar.

She laughed. "It's Devon's, I borrowed it."

"Take it off. I want you to smell like you, not him," I said and practically ripped it from her body.

"Sterling said–"

I cut her off with a kiss before pulling back to growl, "Shut up about other men." I kissed her again, hungry and shaking with a feral desire.

Sex and intimacy were... distorted in my life. I'd seen my uncle parade woman after woman through our house growing up. There was always a strange woman at home. There'd been countless naked women in our pool, our kitchen, our den, and wandering the house like it wasn't a fucked up family home. I never saw the same woman twice. He encouraged me to do the same and had even told the women he'd slept with to seduce me once I'd graduated high school. Seeing sex and intimacy so tainted and impersonal made me vow to myself from a very early age to make sure it was meaningful for me.

I never wanted to wait for marriage, but I didn't want sex to be transactional.

Emily was unlike any woman I'd known in my life. She was soft and hard at the same time. She respected me and wanted me and wanted to provide for me. Emily had killed to save me, and I had killed to save her. She would go to the ends of the world to protect me, and I would do the same and more for her.

With the cardigan on the floor, I got a better view of her body. She was soft and feminine and all mine tonight. Her panties and bra were a pale gray lace and looked almost angelic in the flickering candlelight. I kissed her stomach, and she giggled, tipping her head back. Slowly, I slipped the straps of her bra off her shoulders.

Sure, I'd seen her naked. Tasted her. Made her come, even. But tonight was different. Tonight, she was mine entirely differently.

She reached back and unclasped her bra before I could struggle with it. I watched, rapt, as her breasts fell and rested, full and supple, against her skin. "You're so beautiful, Emily," I whispered.

Her cheeks turned pink, and she looked up at me through her lashes. "I would look prettier with you inside me."

I nodded. "I figured that went without saying," I joked in a serious tone.

She snorted softly and pushed down my pajama pants. I wasn't wearing any underwear. I desperately needed clean laundry. So, I was now bare before her. She stared at my body with wide eyes.

"You've seen me before," I chuckled.

"Yeah, but now I have to fit it all inside me," she said with quiet apprehension.

"You can do it. I know you can. Show me how well you can take it," I murmured to her and carefully removed the glasses from her face. I folded them carefully and set them on the nightstand.

Sterling moaned from his seat near the foot of the bed. "Dirty talk to her some more. I like it."

Emily and I smiled at each other for a second before I pulled her panties down her legs. I kissed her thighs as I moved. Once her panties were off, I hopped off the bed to shove them in Sterling's mouth. He winked at me, and I couldn't help but smirk at him before returning to Emily.

She was reclined on the mattress and giggling at Sterling. I took in the sight of her naked before me. I wanted to savor this moment. Her hair was up in a bun and loose tendrils fell like a tease around her face and neck. Kneeling before her, I gently removed the tie from her hair and let it fall in damp curls around her shoulders. The smell of her lavender and vanilla shampoo surrounded us and overtook the beeswax scent of the candles.

Kissing my way down her body, I anticipated tasting her again. When I finally got there, I settled on my stomach on the bed and looked at her. I could see her arousal gathering on her skin and I teased her with a gentle lick. Long, light, and very slow.

"M-Milo." Her thighs shook as she gave a breathy moan.

All mine.

With my name as my cue, I stopped holding back. I licked and sucked her pussy. I gripped her thighs so tight I was sure

I'd be leaving bruises on her skin. She didn't seem to mind as she cried out and writhed against my mouth. My eyes stayed on her face as she gave in to the pleasure. It didn't take long before she was coming against my tongue. I ate her through it, not letting up until her tremors stopped and she was gasping for breath with her pussy fluttering on my tongue. She tugged on my hair and gave a high-pitched squeal when I lightly nipped at her swollen clit.

I pulled away and wiped my mouth with my hand as I sat up. I kneeled on the bed before her and gestured for her to get up. "Get it wet before I fuck you." My voice was hoarse and deep, and I almost shocked myself with the audible need.

She offered no argument and shot to her hands and knees before me. My cock was almost aching for her. Emily took me into her mouth slowly, sucking me as she went. Her mouth was hot and wet and the best thing I'd ever felt so far. I knew there were better things to come, so I didn't let her suck me long. With a stroke of her wild hair, I gestured for her to pull off of me.

"Lie back, I want to do this vanilla the first time," I said, my voice still ruined. I thought I'd be embarrassed to admit I'd wanted missionary sex for the first time. But Emily didn't condescend to me. She didn't laugh. She obediently got on her back below the pillows and let her knees fall apart.

Settling between her legs, I paused. This was the moment I'd guarded so fiercely most of my life. So much so that I'd built it up to be some sort of momentous, magical moment in my mind. I knew it was silly. I knew it was over the top. It was a vagina, not fucking Narnia.

I slid the head of my cock over her wetness and had the

almost uncontrollable urge to slam into her. To sheath myself entirely in her. But I stopped. I was a grown man who'd waited over thirty years. I could control my urge to be aggressive. A shiver went through me.

Just as I was about to push into her, I heard the thump and then clatter of Sterling scooting in the desk chair. I glared back at him, but he only winked again, his mouth stuffed with panties. His heels thumped the floor, and the wheels clattered across the floor four times before he settled into his position next to the bed. His knees touching the mattress and his body leaned forward, so he was only a few inches from our bodies. I shoved his face back wordlessly.

Emily giggled beneath me, and I couldn't help but smile down at her.

She looked up at me and while we weren't speaking words, a lot was being communicated. I knew by the look in her eyes she loved me. I hoped my expression said the same thing because I didn't think I could speak coherent language anymore. The urge to claim, to mark, to *breed* was loud in my body.

Pushing the lightest bit, I felt her body open to envelop me. I was so close to her I could see the tightening around her eyes when I entered her. The fluttering of her lashes as she gasped. The cooling saliva she'd left on my cock made my skin feel cold, so pushing into her body felt like liquid heat. It was a tight fit, and she hissed as the head of my cock stretched her. Every neuron in my brain was firing on full power as I slowly sunk into her. My eyes closed, and I rested my forehead in the crook of her neck. My breath was panting and hot as it reflected on my face.

She ran her fingers over my back lightly, raising goose-bumps on my skin. "You're so big," she whisper moaned.

"That's only half of me," I said in a choked, whimpering voice.

"Just slam into me," she whispered. The need in her voice short circuited my spinal cord.

"Nmh, nmh!" Sterling gave a quick, muffled sound of disapproval.

I glanced at him to see him with wide eyes and shaking his head.

"I'll go slow for you, baby," I cooed breathlessly.

Emily pouted but her eyes were still tensed with pain. "Fuck me, Milo. Now."

I looked back over at Sterling to see him watching her proudly. His eyes flicked up to mine and he shook his head slowly. He was right, though. If I slammed into Emily, I would hurt her. And I definitely did not want our first time to be remembered as painful.

It felt achingly, desperately, impossibly long before my hips met hers. It felt so long and yet not long enough as I fought the urge ripping through my brain to *fuck*.

"See? I knew you could do it. I knew you could take me. I knew you'd be the perfect fit," I whispered down at her. "So proud of you. So perfect."

She rolled her hips beneath me, and I looked into her smiling eyes. They were no longer tight with the tension of discomfort.

"Let me do it," I said.

I pulled almost all the way out of her and slammed back in. At the impact, she tilted her head back and cried out. I could have come right there, but I was determined to make it last over two minutes at least. Repeating the action, I became addicted to the way her inner walls fluttered when I bottomed out and my skin smacked hers.

She was panting, and her legs shook on either side of me as I circled my hips to slam home again. I knew she was about to come. I glanced at Sterling to make sure he was watching, and he nodded enthusiastically. He mumbled something around the panties and mimed with his hips the circle movement I'd just done. I took that as him coaching me.

Rolling my hips the same way had her practically screaming beneath me before I felt her clenching. The pressure around my cock was unbelievable. Wet and pulsating and perfect. It had me almost blacking out. I heard my voice give a growling moan before I lost my thin string of control. I fucked into her almost cruelly, but I couldn't stop. She didn't ask me to stop, either. She screamed my name and clung to my sweating skin as her pussy gripped me almost rhythmically. My body didn't feel tired with the effort of fucking her. All of my nerve endings focused on my cock.

She was sweating and panting beneath me as her orgasm waned. Her hands were all over my body and she pulled me into her with her legs. "You look so beautiful like this," I growled in an unfamiliar, lust crazed voice. "You look amazing stuffed full of my cock."

She could only give a moan in response, but her legs tightened around my waist even more.

I felt myself press into her hard and deep. As hard and deep as I could go as my balls emptied. I came with a groaning shout. I had never come so hard as that, and I never wanted to leave the feeling. It felt like I could live inside her.

When I became aware of my body again, I had collapsed half on Emily and half on the bed. She was reaching over to stroke my hair, but stopped and gasped.

I shot up, thinking I had hurt her, but saw Sterling leaned over the bed and his mouth on her pussy. The panties that had been in his mouth were gone. The ropes were still loosely around his wrists as he licked her pussy. He moaned as she cried out.

"Give him one more for me," I whispered in her ear. "Let him see and taste how good I fucked you."

She whimpered and let him devour our combined come from her pussy. When she came with a jagged cry, he pulled away, licking his lips.

"I always wondered what you two would taste like together," Sterling rasped. "Fucking cake."

Nuzzling into Emily's sweaty neck, I chuckled. She giggled too as her post orgasmic tremors kept her body soft and warm against mine.

Sterling undid his ties.

"Where'd my panties go?" Emily asked sleepily.

"He swallowed them," I said without looking.

"Sterling, I'll have to call a vet. I don't think Devon or Doc could help us," Emily scolded.

Sterling laughed. "No, I spit them out, dumbasses. Now, if you'll excuse me, I think I'm going to make some solo content for my porno page."

"Let me know when you're ready to upload," I murmured and yawned.

"No, we're going to get in the shower, fuck again, and then finish our night with more whiskey and snacks in bed," Emily said. "Love you, Sterling. Have a good night." She waved at him and blew him a kiss before snuggling into my chest.

Sterling froze where he stood. Eyes wide, mouth open.

I looked at Sterling with an expression that said, "Oh my god?!"

Sterling pointed at Emily, drew a heart on his chest with his fingers, and then pointed at himself.

I nodded, smiling hugely.

He rolled his eyes back, bit his lip, and gripped his cock through his pants as he stepped backwards to the door.

I chuckled as he left the room.

"I love you, too, Milo. I hope you know," she said as soon as the door had shut.

My heart felt like it was about to thump out of my chest. "I- I love you, Emily," I sputtered. I meant it. It just felt really big to say. But also, really small because it was so simple to comprehend. I loved this woman. The same as I loved the man who'd just left. They were it for me. They were the ones I'd chosen to base the rest of my life around.

17

Emily

I was dozing on Milo's chest, reveling in the smell of his soap and sweat. His bare chest rose and fell beneath my cheek. I had fallen asleep tracing my fingers over his skin freckle to freckle like a numbered dot to dot coloring page. We had round two in the shower and a sleepy, slow round three before falling asleep in each other's arms and the tangled sheets. I was about to drift into a deeper sleep when I heard a distant alarm sound. I opened my eyes, thinking it was already morning and one of the guys had an alarm set. But it was still pitch dark. I blinked and looked around the room. My phone was on the nightstand, and it read three in the morning. An alarm blared, closer and louder this time, somewhere near Milo's pants on my floor.

He jerked awake under me and scrambled around, looking for his phone. "Fuck, fuck, fuck," he chanted with a panicked tone in his sleep gruff voice.

"What is it?" I asked and sat up in bed.

"An alarm," he grumbled.

"I gathered."

"Fucking hell. A perimeter alarm," he shot back.

I scrambled up and to my dresser to pull on a pair of jeans and a camisole. If we had company, I didn't want to be caught with my pants down. Literally. I didn't take the time for a bra or socks, just shoved my body into my clothes.

"Sterling! Devon!" Milo shouted as he pulled his flannel pajama pants back on. He flung open the door as I pulled Devon's cardigan over my camisole and followed him. Milo ran across the hall to his room and looked over the security cameras with eyes flashing with panic. "Get Sterling! Now! Tell him it's the street and woods."

I turned on my heel and ran to Sterling's room. He was asleep on his stomach when I burst through the door. He sat up and had a handgun in his hand in a second. "It's me!" I shrieked.

"Sorry, Bambi," he grunted, as he lowered his gun and placed it on his nightstand.

"Dev! Dev, wake up! Devon!" Milo shouted down the hall as more alarms went off.

"Oh, fuck!" Sterling said as he jumped out of bed and pulled on clothes.

"Street and woods!" I said quickly before running out of his room. I headed to Devon's room, but Milo was already there.

"Milo, help me dress," Devon said to Milo. His tone was scared and vulnerable. I wanted to help him, but I needed to get back to Milo's security feed.

I heard them shouting and running around while I stayed

in Milo's room, eyes on the screens. There were at least twenty men carrying guns in the woods and on the street. My hands shook with fear as I watched them get closer and closer. My breath caught in my throat, and I felt like I was going to be sick.

Sterling bounded into the room, carrying a large gun. He set it on Milo's mattress and pulled more guns out from under the bed. "Bambi, we have to get you somewhere safe. I want you down in the surgery. Barricade yourself in and don't answer anyone other than us. Only come out when it's quiet or we come and get you."

"No, I'm not leaving you guys to fight alone. No way," I insisted, ignoring the audible shake to my voice.

"Emily, you have to hide. This is going to be ugly," Sterling said and gripped my arms. His steel-gray eyes were wide and fearful. All the color had drained from his face after glancing at the security footage.

"Dev! Get to the gun case before they cut power!" Milo shouted before coming into the room.

"Emily," he addressed me. "Get in my closet. It has a lock on the inside."

"No!" I insisted.

"Are you kidding? You're not an experienced fighter," Milo said, tearing his eyes away from the computer screens.

"I can hold my own and you know it," I insisted and crossed my trembling arms over my chest.

"Please," Sterling begged quietly. His voice was a whisper, but still audible over the alarms.

"I'm not leaving you," I insisted again.

"We don't have time," Milo groaned. "Go get a gun from Devon."

Sprinting down the stairs with knees as wobbly as a fawn's, I made my way to the office. Devon spun around as I entered and didn't even blink in surprise that it was me and not one of the other guys. He handed me the gun I'd used before. Paint it pink and bedazzle it. It was basically mine now. Devon kneeled and strapped knives to my thighs like usual, albeit quicker.

"They're coming after me, aren't they?" I asked in a choked whisper. "They want me dead so you can rejoin your father."

Devon swallowed and looked up at me from where he was still kneeling. He said nothing and his eyes were dark and angry.

"I can leave. Disappear again. I don't want you guys to get hurt because of me," I continued, my voice strained and cracked.

He stood up sharply and looked down at me, brow furrowed and expression furious. "No," was all he said in a deep and rumbling voice. It seemed like he was going to say more. He took in a breath like he was going to speak, but was interrupted by Milo coming in.

"Here, take these radios," he said and set them on the desk with a clunk.

"Walkie Talkie? Like kids at a sleepover?" I asked, looking at them.

"Yeah, if they have a cell phone signal jammer, our phones are useless. It'll block a traditional two-way radio signal, too. But these are satellite ones," Milo explained as he emptied the guns and ammo cases into three boxes. "I happen to know

Anthony has a jammer since I was the one who provided it to him."

He turned around and accidentally bumped the door to the gun case shut behind him, leaving three guns still on their shelf. Almost as the door shut with a click, the power went out. We stood silently in the dark room for a second.

"Hey, remember that time three years ago when I said a gun case that required electricity to open was a bad upgrade?" Milo spat sarcastically.

"Shut up," Devon ground out.

Lights flickered on again and I heard a faint beeping from somewhere in the house.

"The battery back ups on my computer will keep the security feeds up. The generators are running half of our lights, the cameras, and my explosives," Milo said.

"Should we call the police? We're super outnumbered," I said nervously. My throat was dry and scratchy.

"If we're all down, you call them," Devon said quietly in the mostly silent room.

My tongue soured in my mouth, and I fought a gag. I cleared my throat instead.

Sterling shouted from upstairs, "Let's go! They're about three minutes out on foot!"

Milo handed Devon one box of guns and ammo and they picked up long guns I assumed to be rifles from the desk. Guns, ammo, and radios in hand, we joined Sterling upstairs. I stood in front of the security feeds while all three guys set up their places on the floor of their balconies. I was in Milo's room, and I watched as he checked his scope. His and Devon's room faced the front of the house, and Sterling was along the back, watching the woods.

"Keep your radios open to the group channel," Milo said. "Emily, give us heads up when guys show up in the second and third rows."

Staring at the screens, I figured out Milo's order of operations. There were three screens that all had twelve video feeds displayed. The top row of four feeds on each screen were the furthest cameras from the house. When guys disappeared from the top row, they came into focus on the second, and presumably the third would be next.

"Second screen for the woods," I said into the radio.

"Sterling, close your eyes," Milo said, and I heard his voice echo through the radio.

An explosion sounded from the back of the house. I saw it happen on the screen. It sounded like fireworks and not like a bomb. Likely, the neighborhood wouldn't think much of the sound. The screen was white with light for a moment before the black and white night vision cameras adjusted back to the darkness. I could see bodies on the ground. Some were dead, and some were injured and no longer moving towards the house. The ones who were able were dragging the injured back the way they came.

"What the fuck was that?" Sterling asked, his voice breaking in shock.

"I've only been telling you about the explosives I have set up for weeks, Sterling. Do you not listen when I speak?" Milo asked.

"Sometimes. What were you wearing when you told me about them?" Sterling asked.

"Settle down on the chatter," Devon instructed. "We need to be able to hear Emily's directions."

"Second screen for the front. They're climbing the fence in the driveway. Fifteen men," I said. My voice was cold, unfeeling, and even. My stomach was roiling with unease, but I had a job to do to keep me and my men safe.

"Dev, close your eyes," Milo said before one of the approaching men landed on his feet on the inside of the driveway gate. The man turned and watched his comrades make it over before they all lifted their weapons and made their way toward the house. A few steps in and the screen went white for a second and a *pop* sound echoed from the front yard. Three more went off soon after.

They were shrapnel bombs and the men that lay on the ground nearest to the explosions had been torn apart. Many more were injured. Again, the ones who could fall back did.

"There were only four," Milo said.

"Any more out back?" Sterling asked.

"No, I only had the one so far," Milo grumbled disappointedly.

"That's alright, my trigger finger is getting antsy," Sterling said brightly.

"Why aren't they all turning back?" I asked. "If half of their men just got blown up, then why aren't they leaving?"

"The price on our heads must be worth the risk," Devon replied dryly. "We're still outnumbered."

"Some *are* leaving," Milo said, watching through his scope. "The ones that continue are our marks, Devon."

"Got it," Devon said. "Fire a warning shot. Let them know we're awake."

Milo shot his gun, and I was startled at the sound. He was on his stomach and aiming out over the grass. "They're running at us. Open fire," he breathed into the radio.

I watched as his shoulder jerked back from the rapid recoil of the gun. His shoulders tensed as he regained his position. I was sure the recoil from a gun like that would have me thrown across the room.

Looking back at the security feeds, I saw a familiar face come into focus. His eyes were wide and fearful as he was running along the garage. He was alone, but Tommy was here. I paused. Was he coming to help? I hadn't seen him in about a week since he had dropped by to check in with Devon. I lost sight of him on the camera and nobody else was near the garage.

"Sterling, there's a guy coming out of the woods. That's the third camera," I said, focusing my attention back on my job.

"Got him," Sterling said, and I heard the shot.

"Emily, any other visuals?" Milo asked, as I heard Devon's gunfire.

"Just the guys you can see out front. Sterling, there's a few more in the woods. It looks like they're arguing about if they should continue or turn back," I informed them.

"Any more Home Alone booby traps?" Devon asked.

"No," Milo grunted.

A few more shots rang out, and I watched a man drop in the front yard. The cameras remained unchanged as the guys shot the attackers that filtered into their view. I stood, leaning my hands on the desk, unmoving, as I watched intently. Seeing it on the screens and not in front of my face felt like a removal. A disassociation from the horrors on the property.

Logically, I knew the front yard was covered in blood and bodies and my men could be shot at any moment. But I felt removed enough that my stomach settled from a boiling anxiety to a simmering unease.

My eyes caught on someone using their phone flashlight to tumble through the woods in the backyard. It took a moment before more men came into focus on that same line of cameras. "Sterling," I said uneasily. "There's- oh, god- like twenty men in the woods. First camera."

"How many in the front?" Devon asked.

"I don't see any more right now," I replied.

"I'll move to Emily's balcony," Devon said.

"Is it still bolted shut?" I asked.

"Fuck," Devon muttered.

"No, I undid it," Milo said. "Does nobody notice anything I do around this house?"

"Put on Emily's maid cos-" Sterling said.

"Alright, alright," Devon interrupted with a grumble. "I'll pack up here. We should have had a gun set up on her balcony to begin with."

"You're right. An unattended high-powered weapon with a cache of ammunition during an attack would have been a great idea," Milo snarked as he fired off a few shots.

Something cold pressed against the base of my skull. "Devon?"

In the reflection of a dark, unused monitor, I saw a face. It was not Devon behind me.

18

Milo

A scream ripped from Emily had me whipping around and getting up off the floor. My eyes locked on Tommy and where he had a gun pressed to the back of Emily's head. My stomach went rancid, and my body locked up for a moment before I grabbed my pistol. Tommy shifted so his back was against the wall near the door and Emily's body blocked his. He was taller than she was, but not by much. I couldn't get a clear shot.

"Tommy, put the gun down," I said as calmly as I could. I knew my voice had carried through the open radio channel.

My hearing slowly returned to me after completely washing out in my surge of adrenaline and fear. I could hear the pops of Devon and Sterling's guns and the shots being returned to them. Devon and Sterling were both shouting into their radios, and I could hear their voices echoing through the hall. I couldn't make out their words. All of my focus was on Emily and Tommy in front of me.

"I'm sorry, but he has my grandma," Tommy half sobbed, half growled desperately. "I hesitated for this job, and he picked up my grandma."

I didn't know a lot about Tommy, but I knew his grandma had raised him most of his life. She was a good woman and owned a restaurant that ran a soup kitchen on Sundays. I'd set up internet and security for her place. My heart sank and joined the decay in my stomach. To save the woman I loved, I was going to have to kill someone who didn't deserve it.

Before anyone said anything else, Sterling and Devon swung into the room. Both had their guns raised and their eyes wide and assessing. The house was now unmanned and unprotected at all angles. I glanced at the security feeds briefly. If I could have been any more panic ridden, I'd have screamed and pissed myself. As it was, I was too angry for fear creeping in anymore that it had.

Of course, just hours after losing my virginity to the woman I loved, someone held her at gunpoint. *Of fucking course.*

But no way.

I wasn't going to allow this to happen. I looked at Sterling and Devon, where their eyes were wide with horror. Devon's hands shook on his gun, and Sterling's jaw clenched so hard I was sure his teeth would crumble.

"Hey Tommy, put the gun down and we'll help you. We'll get her back. Please, Tommy," Devon was saying in what he had clearly hoped to be a soothing tone but shook like he was seconds away from begging.

"Tommy, no," Emily squeaked around the forearm that was crushing her neck.

"I have to. He wants you gone. He thinks everything is your fault. That you corrupted them," Tommy said, his voice tight like he wanted to cry.

"Let's pretend," Emily tried. "Let's pretend you killed me. I'll disappear and you'll get your grandma back."

Devon shifted at her words. He made eye contact with her tearful blue gaze. He looked ruined. Defeated. I didn't understand that look. But I understood Emily was not only mine. She was his, too. And Sterling's.

We had different ideas about our futures in the business or out of the business. We had different ideas for leadership. But we had the same love and devotion to Emily. The woman who was reaching for the knives strapped to her thigh without attracting Tommy's notice.

"He's deranged. He won't stop until Emily and Milo are dead," Tommy said and looked at me. "You've got him all fucked up."

"You haven't seen deranged yet," Sterling snarled. His voice was so cold and brutal that even my blood iced over. "If you don't drop the gun-"

Pounding footsteps on the stairs grabbed everyone's attention. I hadn't been looking at the cameras within the house and now I saw multiple men on the stairs, in the office, and coming through the kitchen door.

The footsteps were enough to take some of Tommy's attention away from Emily, and she pulled her arm up and stabbed backwards at him. She got him in the gut with a cry of anguish and effort. It wasn't a disabling wound yet, but it shocked him and moved him enough I could get a clean shot at his head. I took it without a moment of hesitation.

Sterling and Devon shot down the hallway, and Emily collapsed against my desk with a cry of relief. I rushed to her and held her against me, my hand in her hair and my lips on the sweaty skin of her forehead. The relief I felt holding her was visceral and short-lived.

"Milo," she said and steadied herself. "They're in the house."

"I know," I ground out and looked at the screen. "They've spread out throughout the house. Two more on the stairs."

Emily bent and reclaimed her knife from Tommy's stomach. With shaking hands, she wiped it on her pant leg and holstered it. She looked up at me and breathed out deeply, like she was settling herself. I watched her closely. She was regaining her strength and determination. My heart rose from the corrosion in my stomach for only a moment as I admired her. She was amazing and I could never express it to her sufficiently. I was an intelligent person. A genius, actually. But there weren't enough words in my vocabulary to express what I felt when I saw her stand up and wipe her bloody knife on her jeans. Or when she took a deep, steadying breath before readying herself to kill again to protect me.

"We need to cut them off at the doors," Devon demanded. "We can't let them continue to get inside our walls."

"C-could they be planting bombs?" Emily asked. Her voice shook, but she was doing her best to sound strong.

Her question snapped me back into the moment. "I don't think so," I blurted. They could have been planting bombs but getting her into a panic wouldn't help anyone.

"Three more on the stairs," I murmured so my voice didn't carry to the attackers.

"I see them," Sterling breathed as he peeked around the door frame.

"You go left, I go right," Devon whispered as they both readied themselves. "One... two...three."

They both leaned around the doorframe and shot at the men as they stepped up the last stair. Once the stairs were clear, they pulled back into the room.

"Emily, get in Milo's closet," Sterling said.

"We're not having this fight again," she said stubbornly. "I'm coming with you."

Devon rolled his eyes. "I'll take point. You guys block her."

I grabbed my tablet. It had a cell card in it and could still watch our security feeds if they weren't using blockers. It seemed that they weren't, likely thinking they'd have us overrun faster than we could call for help. One glance at our cameras and I could see we were almost entirely overtaken. It was hard to tell how many men there were, but it seemed like they had us massively outnumbered.

Sticking together with our guns reloaded and raised, we made our way to the stairs. There was a man at the front door, stepping in with his gun raised. He was looking into the kitchen and didn't see us above him. Sterling was closest and took him out without leaning over the railing.

Some men coming into the house were slow and stealthy, while others came in at a run and shot at any shadow. I wondered if Anthony held family members over more of his gangs or if it was purely a money grab. Judging by the amount of people attacking, he had mobilized every one of his loyal gangs. Some of these people we had met with recently. They hadn't been able to promise not to kill us, and I hadn't expected to see that come to fruition so soon.

We were silent as we crept down the stairs, all of us mindful of the stair that creaked. My body buzzed with awareness. I knew every sound of this house. The way every room felt in the darkness. A light was above the sink in the kitchen, the only light in the room that was run by the generator.

I closed and locked the front door before anyone else could enter. I had installed a metal bar that could drop into place around the door frame for extra protection, and I slid it into place now. Although it couldn't stop a car, it could stop men from breaking in the door. Our front door had been replaced a few years ago with some regular maintenance, and we had chosen a door with a metal core within the wood. Tonight, it had been unlocked and opened from the inside. The sliding door in the kitchen was shattered and had been the first entrance for the attackers. Sterling and Devon both took out men coming in before they had seen us.

"We need to secure the other doors," Devon said as we hid ourselves in the formal living room we never used.

"I'll clear the rest of this floor before I head to the office floor," Sterling said.

"I can check the kitchen," Emily said and rose from her crouching position.

"No, you watch our backs in case anyone is in here while we keep this door secured," Devon told her in a sharp tone.

She nodded and didn't argue with him. Likely because he gave her a task and didn't try to hide her away like Sterling and I had tried to do. It was a wonder she wasn't already sleeping with him. He seemed to understand her better than we did.

I shook my head and turned back to my task as a man crept over the glass of the sliding door. His boots crunched in the broken glass as he whipped around, looking for his target. Devon had a better shot, and he took it. It was clean. Sterling took this as the opportunity to rush out of the living room to check the hearth room. He had his radio still, and he breathed "Clear" into the receiver as he left.

"Milo, move to the other side of the door," Devon directed.

I followed orders immediately and glanced outside as I went. I could see slowly approaching flashlights and vague shadows. It seemed like they were slowing down their attacks and were hoping to give up and leave with their lives. Emily remained near Devon but faced the other direction. I looked back to check on her in the dim light a few times. I didn't hear anyone within the house, and Sterling was checking the office and den before moving to the basement. So, I wasn't worried about her safety.

She proved me wrong when two men entered the kitchen from the den. Sterling must have missed them, or they had come in before Sterling could clear the floor. He hadn't said anything yet, so I had assumed he was still looking. Emily shot four bullets to take them both out. We'd need to work on her aim under pressure later. As both men crumpled to the floor, I raised my radio to my mouth. My heart sloshed in the acid of my stomach. "Sterling, where are you?"

"Basement. I thought I heard someone down here after I shut the side door," Sterling's voice crackled through the radio. Relief coursed through me like a cool breeze. "By the way, those metal bars over the doors are bad ass, Milo."

"Thanks," I whispered into the radio as another attacker stepped through the remains of the glass door.

I took him out, his body landing with a gross thud almost directly on top of the one Devon had killed. This was getting ridiculous. Anthony had to be offering more than money to these people. There was no way they were fighting this hard just for fucking money. He had Tommy's grandma, and I didn't put it past him to have someone each of these people loved. Wives, children, husbands, girlfriends, boyfriends. It had to be serious.

I felt bad for them for a moment and a moment only. We had tried to get them to work with us. We had tried to tell them about Anthony's corruption and psychopathic tendencies. We had tried to get them to our side. But they had all chosen money. Well, look where that got them.

Fuckers.

I heard shouts come from the backyard and I checked my dimmed tablet on the floor next to me. The remaining men were retreating. I watched as every one of the men, not dead and dying on our lawn, were picked up on the street by vans and SUVs.

"It looks like they're all leaving," I said to the group. "Let me check every camera, to be sure."

I scrolled through each screen on my tablet, taking a minute to really be sure. I saw us crouching in the kitchen and Sterling spinning and finding the camera in the office. When he located it, he shoved down his sweatpants and helicoptered his dick, two guns still in his hands, and raised above his head.

"Nice, I screen recorded that," I said dryly as I scrolled on through the camera feeds.

"Ew, nuh-uh. I'm covered in blood," Sterling said through the radio. His voice echoed as he came closer in the house.

"Alright, we need to get the power back on, board up this door, and call for a cleanup," Devon said as we all relaxed our defensive postures.

"Are you sure they're gone?" Emily asked, her voice still shaking.

"For now," I said with a sigh.

Devon shot me a look that nonverbally reminded me to use social skills, and I realized I was supposed to console her.

"Sorry," I said. "I mean, they're not likely to come back to-night. They're going to assess their damages and losses before they regroup."

Emily seemed to relax only in the slightest.

"Emily, can you please make us some coffee? It's going to be a long night. Or... morning, I guess," Devon said, again giving her a job to do. "I'll make the call for cleanup."

"Milo and I will board up the door," Sterling volunteered us and gestured for me to follow him.

I placed the tablet on the kitchen island, ignoring the blood spatter, and kept the security feeds on the screen for Emily to look at if she wanted. I wanted her to know she was safe with us.

19

Emily

They were gone, and the house was cleared. *They were gone, and the house was cleared.* I had to keep repeating it and reminding myself as I swept up the glass from the back door. The shaking in my hands had not abated, and I was doing a terrible job cleaning up the glass from around the multiple dead bodies and blood on the floor. I felt exposed standing in front of the space used as an entrance for our attackers and raw with emotion.

"We'll pay it. Tell me how much," Devon said into his phone as he leaned back against the kitchen island. His eyes watched me as I swept, but his brows furrowed at whatever the person said on the other line. "Fucking ridiculous, you know that, Sonny?"

He snapped his fingers a few times to get my attention, and I looked up with a raised eyebrow. He pointed to a spot I'd missed next to a dead man's head. I shot him a glare, and he had the audacity to smile at me in return. The lights flickered on, and a few appliances chimed in the quiet house. The beep of Milo's battery backups and the whirring of the generator ceased immediately. I blinked as my eyes adjusted.

Devon winced and moved to dim some lights as he listened to Sonny. I could hear Sterling and Milo cheering from wherever they were. I was finishing up sweeping when Sterling and Milo came in carrying sheets of plywood and a tool set. The coffee pot had been plugged into an outlet run by the generator before the power came back on, and it beeped that it was finished brewing. I poured mugs for us all. Devon set up a time and cost for clean-up and mostly watched Sterling and Milo work.

I felt my heart rate decrease as I watched them work, their muscles tensing and sweat dripping down their collars. I crossed my legs and watched them work, the ache between my thighs reminding me of the hours of pleasure I'd had with Milo before the attack. He'd been gentle, but damn, was that man big. The aching pain grounded me. It reminded me of where I was and who I was with. It detached me from the what-ifs and the fear. With a long breath in and out, I clutched my coffee to my chest.

Milo and Sterling turned around as they finished. They were talking about plywood. They said something about it being good enough until they could get a replacement when the stores opened. But I was too occupied staring at their bodies to listen much. The bodies that had shielded me to protect me. And I had killed again to protect them.

"Hey," Milo said, his voice soft as tipped my chin up to him.

"Hm?" I hummed. I was barely in this universe.

"You okay?" he asked me.

I took me a moment to unstick my tongue from the roof of my mouth.

"Bambi," Sterling said as he approached me and stood next to Milo. His voice was concerned and deep.

"I'm alright," I said and swallowed. "That was just... scary."

Milo stroked over my hair and then pulled his hand back and wiped it on his shirt. His nostrils flared with repressed disgust. I reached a hand up to my hair and Sterling tried to stop me, but I was quicker this time. My hand came back streaked with sticky, drying blood. Not my blood, I was pretty sure.

I gagged. Both Sterling and Milo's eyes flicked up to Devon behind me in unison and then back at me. "Oh my god," I said with a trembling jaw. "That's not my blood."

"Not your brain matter, either," Milo said and delicately picked a bloody chunk out of my hair near my neck. Sterling elbowed Milo to scold him.

I gagged harder, covering my mouth. Sterling swooped in and picked me up, taking me into the half-bathroom attached to the kitchen near the pantry. I heard Devon shouting to get me out of there, his voice rasping from his own gags. I would have found it funny if I wasn't about to lose my stomach.

Sterling held back my bloody and apparently brain covered hair as I vomited. He smoothed a hand over my back soothingly until I was finished. "Wanna go take a shower while the cleaners are here?"

"Yeah," I whispered as I flushed the toilet.

"Can I come, too?" Milo asked from outside the closed bathroom door.

"You've come enough tonight," Sterling scolded, but his eyes sparkled with amusement.

"Fuck you," Milo laughed.

When Devon saw me as I came out of the bathroom, he looked me over quickly before looking back down at his phone. "You guys go get cleaned up. I'll stay with Sonny's crew."

I was about to pass him on my way out of the kitchen when I caught sight of the bright red blood on his arm. I gasped. "Devon! Your arm!"

He looked down at it. "Yeah, I think I bust open a few of my stitches."

"I'll help you," I said and moved to push up his sleeve.

He pulled it from my reach. "Emily, get cleaned up and stop shaking and then I'll let you near me."

"You're going to bleed to death!" I insisted and made to reach for him again.

"No, I pulled the stitches early in the attack and this is all the blood that came from it. It's not that bad," he countered.

A man entered the room, and I jumped in shock. It was Sonny who'd I'd seen when he came for Matthew's body. Devon ran a hand from my shoulder to my wrist to soothe me, making sure I was alright before he turned around to greet Sonny.

"Let's go get cleaned up," Milo said behind me.

"Devon," Sonny greeted. "You know I don't want it to be like this. But your father, he offered me a lot more than our usual fare to ignore your calls."

"And I offered you a lot more than that to ignore his call to ignore our call," Devon snarked in return.

My blood boiled again. "Listen here, Sonny," I said in a sharp tone and approached him. I jabbed a finger into his chest. "The bodies you're picking up are the bodies of men and women who were offered the chance to be on our side. We offered them our allegiance. As you can see, they didn't take our deal. You have the same two choices: work with us, or against us. Let's make good choices, Sonny. Good choices."

Sonny watched me go as Milo and Sterling steered me away and up the stairs. Sonny asked Devon, "Who's the prissy broad?" I heard Devon make some sort of excuse or an explanation for my behavior. I wasn't sure which one. But what I said needed to be said. I wasn't wrong. We had that meeting with the gang leaders and told them what was going on, and they still worked with Anthony. I didn't care if he was holding a family member hostage to get them to fight for him. He hadn't been when we met with them. They had a choice, and they clearly chose wrong. And if what I heard from Devon's phone call with Sonny earlier was any indication, he was on the same path. Someone had to let him know his options.

Sterling and Milo accompanied me to my bathroom. They were mouthing words behind my back. From behind me, I could hear their mouths moving and brief gusts of breath when they got animated. I didn't care what they were saying. All I wanted was a scalding hot shower and at least two shots of whiskey.

I stripped in the bathroom and turned the water on so hot the bathroom steamed up. I threw in a eucalyptus and mint shower fizz I'd had Devon buy when we all had the sniffles a few weeks ago. None of us was sick now, but I wanted something to sear the scent of blood and death from my nose.

"If you're not getting in with me, bring me some whiskey," I said as I stepped into the scalding water. I hissed a breath through my teeth.

When I turned around, it was only Milo in the room. He was undressing and piling his bloody clothes on top of mine with a lip curled in disgust. When he stepped into the shower, he yelped at the temperature. I was already violently scrubbing my hair with shampoo, and I smiled as he inched around the edge of the shower to get to the knob. I took his blood-spattered glasses off his face with my soapy hands and rubbed the lenses. He adjusted the temperature of the water before ducking his head under the stream. We wordlessly scrubbed our hair and skin for some time. I washed my hair at least three times before he stopped me and slicked some conditioner through the strands.

Sterling had come back in to drop off a bottle of whiskey before he left again. Milo and I sipped from the bottle, careful not to drop it with our soapy hands.

"We need to get guard dogs," I mumbled as I rinsed out the conditioner.

"Why? We have Sterling," Milo half heartedly joked.

"They'd bark if someone was on the property," I explained.

"Again: why? We have Sterling," Milo chuckled.

"Milo," I sighed.

He put some of my conditioner in his hands and sniffed it before shrugging and putting it in his hair. "The dogs would get shot," he finally replied. "We have cameras and movement alarms. We don't need dogs."

"Then we need... we need... more bombs or something,"

I said, and the frayed edges of my nerves caused my voice to crack.

Milo exhaled long and slow. "Emily."

"We need more defenses. We need better doors and windows."

"Emily."

"They were in our house, Milo!" I was practically shrieking.

"I know."

"He had a gun to my head."

"I know."

"They were here to kill us."

"I know."

"They could have hurt you."

"I know."

"THEY GOT IN OUR HOUSE!"

I was screaming and was sure there were tears on my already wet face. Milo gripped me by the shoulders under the stream of the shower.

"I know," he whispered one last time before clutching me to him. I felt safer knowing he was there with me. But I was very aware of all the people brought in by Sonny. There were still strangers in our house.

"I can't stop shaking," I said into his chest. Water ran down my temples and dripped off my nose.

"Me neither," Milo said against my head. "I feel like an alarm is going to go off at any moment."

We stood clutching each other for a few more minutes before the water cooled. I turned the water off and Milo got our towels. I sipped the whiskey again with the bottle clutched in my wrinkled fingertips. Sterling leaned in the doorway, his hands on his hips and his brows furrowed.

"Both of you. Come to my room," he demanded.

"Why?" I asked him.

"Because you two need to relax," he said gruffly.

"We're relaxed. We just had a shower," Milo said and rolled his eyes.

"Get. The. Fuck. In my room," Sterling said, his voice dark and unforgiving.

I looked from Sterling to Milo and back again a few times while they glared at each other. Milo's lip tipped up in a smirk. "Fine," Milo snapped. "Emily, leave your towel here."

Sterling grinned. It wasn't a friendly grin. It was one that promised agony and pleasure. My stomach gave a flutter when I realized what was happening. Sterling reached behind him and came back with two sets of leather wrist cuffs connected with leather braiding. Biting my lip, I set down the whiskey bottle and dropped my towel.

20

Emily

"Check the hall. Make sure nobody's out there," I demanded of Sterling as he finished putting the leather cuffs on Milo. The leather against my skin was buttery soft but stiff enough I couldn't rip out of the cuffs. Even the braided leather strap that connected my cuffs behind me was soft as it rubbed against the skin of my ass.

Sterling hesitated a second before obeying. He was trying to be all dominant and here I was, ordering him around. Milo and I followed him into my room while he opened the door. He greeted someone, checked in on the man's sports betting hobby, and then kindly asked him to clear the hall for a minute.

"You almost had us parading naked in front of other men," I scoffed as I heard a door shut in the hall.

"Yeah, I didn't realize you were into sharing with *strangers*," Milo added sarcastically.

Sterling glared at us both as he ushered us down the hall to his room. Once the door shut and locked behind us, he pushed at the center of our backs until we were both bent over his bed. I turned my face to look at Milo, and he was smirking at me. I couldn't help but grin back at him. Sterling always knew what we needed, even if we didn't.

The first watery rays of dawn were illuminating the room, and I sighed as my body relaxed. Sterling was rustling behind us, like he was getting something out of his toy box. I heard the strike of a match and Milo lifted his head to look at what Sterling was doing. "Candles," Milo mouthed to me.

"Ooh, so romantic," I whispered and giggled at Milo.

Milo's eyes flashed like I'd said something stupid, but he didn't have time to respond. Sterling was standing over him now. "Milo?" he asked.

"Yes, please," Milo rasped.

Sterling hummed in approval and dripped some massage oil from a bottle onto Milo's skin. He rubbed it, and the smell of jasmine and vanilla filled the room. The only sound was the smooth slide of Sterling's hands on Milo's body. He covered Milo's back, shoulders, and ass with the fragrant oil. "Milo, did you lose your virginity yesterday?"

"I did," Milo said and gasped. Sterling had poured candle wax on Milo's oiled skin.

I watched as the black wax dripped down and hardened along the grooves of his ribcage. It hardened and then crackled apart slightly as he panted. His eyes were closed, and his face relaxed like it was pleasurable. I couldn't imagine being burned with wax would feel good at all. I shifted nervously, my arms beginning to ache behind me.

"Did you make her come?" Sterling asked, his voice rumbling and deep.

"I did," Milo whispered and ground his hips against the mattress.

Sterling dripped more wax on Milo's back. It puddled at the base of his spine, in the dimples above his ass. Sterling swore under his breath as Milo shivered.

"Did you use that big cock on our girl? Did you make her drip with your come for hours?" Sterling rasped.

"I did," Milo sighed.

Sterling dripped wax on the globes of Milo's ass and watched intently as it dripped. I swallowed and rubbed my thighs together. It did nothing to help me. I ached with anticipation and need. My pussy clenched desperately around nothing as I watched them together with every bit of my attention.

"Am I next to fuck you?" Sterling asked almost breathlessly.

"Fuck yes," Milo moaned as Sterling dripped more wax on him.

"Good boy," Sterling said and then looked at me.

My heart stuttered and my stomach fluttered. "Sterling," I whispered and looked at the wax.

He smiled serenely. "It's low heat wax, Bambi. It won't burn you. Do you want to try it?"

Low heat wax? I'd never heard of it, but Milo didn't seem to be hurt. "Yes," I replied.

Sterling's smile turned animal as he set the candle down and picked up the oil.

"C-can I ask what the oil is for?" I stutter, not wanting to ruin the scene with silly questions.

"It makes the wax easier to remove, and it doesn't grab any hair," Sterling said as he rubbed the oil into my skin. It was cool when he poured it on my skin, and I felt my muscles feather in reaction. As he rubbed it over my back, shoulders, and ass, it warmed to match my body temperature.

I looked into Milo's eyes as Sterling picked up the candle. He gave me a hooded, lazy smile like the wax was a hot stone massage and we were in a fancy resort and not cuffed and bent over a bed with our asses in the air.

"Did you deflower Milo yesterday?" Sterling asked me.

The term "deflowering" made it sound... immature. What Milo and I had experienced wasn't a "deflowering," it was much bigger than that. It cemented our connection physically. In a way that outshone our education and intelligence and ability to express ourselves verbally. It had been so much bigger than just a deflowering. But, for the sake of keeping the mood, I said, "I fucked his brains out."

Milo snorted a laugh.

Heat seared into my back, and I gasped. It wasn't so hot that it burned, but the water had dripped from my wet hair and made my skin cool. I shivered in response to the change in temperature and arched my back. Sterling pushed my hips down and caught a drip of wax that had been on its way to my hairline.

"Did you let him come in your pussy?" Sterling rasped.

"Yes," I whimpered in anticipation of more wax.

The wax met my skin, and I felt it drip down my sides in a heated tickle. I shivered again. Something about him painting my body had my core pulsating. The dimmed light, the sunrise creeping through the trees, the jasmine and vanilla scented oil, the strain of my arms behind my back, and the heat of the wax on my naked skin had me almost dripping with need. Sterling let out a long, low humming growl when he saw I was clenching my thighs. He slid a finger up from where my thighs met to my pussy. I cried out at his featherlight touch.

"Not yet," he drawled. More wax met my skin, and I moaned as it dripped down my ass.

Milo was watching me, and it occurred to me Sterling was juggling both of us and I'd never gotten his full attention during a scene. We'd been mostly vanilla since that first time when he tied me and Milo up. "Sterling, we can do this more often," I whispered.

An eyebrow arched at me. "Wax play?"

"Yeah, but this... in general," I said.

"Do you mean kink?" he asked and blew out the candle.

"Yeah," I said and shrugged. "We've only done it one time and we've been doing normal stuff the other times."

Sterling sighed. "The fact you called it 'normal' means you're not into this."

"No!" I insisted quickly. "No, I just don't know what else to call it. Vanilla? Un-kinked?"

A smirk creased the corner of his mouth. "Mrs. Suburban Housewife *likes* to be tied up and fucked."

I glared. It was useless to seem threatening as I was still face down, ass up, bound, and covered in wax. "I'm not married anymore and I'm not a suburban housewife," I snapped.

"Struck a nerve, Sterling," Milo said.

"I see that," Sterling said with that smirk still in place. "Do you two remember your safe word?"

"Devon's polka dotted underwear," Milo and I said in unison.

"Good job," Sterling said and smacked us both on the ass. "Kneel on the bed. I'm going to tie you both up the right way."

Milo and I obeyed silently and quickly. Sterling had us wait while he gathered the ropes and turned on music. It was the same haunting, melancholic metal as last time. He lit the same incense as the last time, but I now knew it to be Palo Santo and rose. I wasn't sure if this was how he set the scene, or if he was simply trying to recreate the space from our first time like this. Perhaps both. I inhaled deeply and leaned into Milo's body. He kissed the top of my head.

We were both covered in wax still, so I wondered how Sterling would use the ropes without ruining them. I said nothing because I didn't want to get spanked at the moment. Sterling set the bundles of ropes before us and then kneeled on the bed behind us.

"Bend over the ropes. Both of you. Face down, ass up," Sterling ordered.

I leaned over and mostly fell onto my face. Milo's descent was considerably more controlled. Sterling ran his hands over the wax on Milo's back before slowly peeling the black wax. I saw Sterling's eyes light with delight as he continued to peel a large sheet of wax, much like the protective coating on new electronics. It broke as it got to Milo's lower back. "If you didn't have a hairy ass, I could have gotten it off in one go," Sterling pouted.

"I do not have a hairy ass!" Milo insisted.

Smack. "No talking," Sterling growled before returning to

his low murmur. "No, you have like peach fuzz... on your peach."

I didn't see Milo roll his eyes, but I knew he did it.

Sterling waved the enormous piece of wax at us before tossing it to the bed. "There's little bits here and there, but I'll get them off later." He turned to me, and I smiled through my messy hair and wiggled my butt at him. The wax near my hairline was difficult to get off, and I felt the scrape of something flat and cold against my skin. When it was off my neck, Sterling got a good grip on the wax and peeled most of it off my back. I had been wigglier than Milo, so there were streaks in every which way. It didn't take long for most of the wax to be removed from me and Milo, leaving flecks and drops strewn over our skin like freckles.

"Hmm, you both did so good at waiting and getting cleaned up." Sterling's rasp bordered on a growl now.

My eyes had fluttered shut in relaxation as he removed the wax, and they shot open in shock when his tongue swiped over my core. Clit to opening and dipping in. I gasped at the warmth and startling pleasure. He gripped my ass as he ate me like a man starved. Trembling and crying out, I was on the edge of coming. Jolts of pleasure coursed through my body, leaving me flushed and beginning to sweat. He pulled away. I whimpered.

Directly, he dove to Milo. He gripped Milo's ass now as he devoured him with the same fervor as he'd consumed me. Milo let out a startled yelp that toed the line of shriek. Sterling's eyes slanted in a smile at Milo's reaction. As far as I was aware, they'd not done this yet. I felt honored to be a part of that first. I watched as Milo's hips bucked like he was fucking the air. Having mercy, Sterling reached for Milo's cock and stroked it. Milo was moaning and panting seconds later. His skin bloomed with a flush and his back arched as he fucked Sterling's hand while he ate his ass.

Sterling moved away from Milo just as abruptly as he had moved away from me. Milo groaned and swore under his ragged breath. Sterling tugged the leather cuffs off my wrists and my arms fell limply to my sides. He lifted me back to a kneeling position and started tying me with the bundle of smooth, red rope. The ropes were warm, likely from my body leaning over them. The warmth and pressure as he bound me had my brain going fuzzy. For a moment, I thought it was from lack of oxygen, but he hadn't gotten to my chest yet. That fuzziness met the need that coursed from between my legs, and I felt drunker than the whiskey had made me.

I tilted my head back with my eyes closed as Sterling wound the rope around my chest and torso, keeping my hands bound behind me. The pressure of the bind wasn't intense, I could easily breathe and nothing was painful, but the unyielding hold woven by strong, tattooed hands was just what I needed.

"There you go, Bambi," Sterling murmured before moving to Milo and tying him up similarly.

I would never tell, but I saw Sterling consulting his phone for the proper steps for tying up a male submissive. With a serene smile, I waited. Milo's head bowed forward with his eyes closed, and I wondered if he felt the same as I did.

"Bambi, look at his muscles in these ropes," Sterling whispered reverently.

I was already staring at his smooth skin and where his

muscles strained against the ropes. I nodded and swallowed. Milo huffed a laugh and flexed his muscles where he could in the binds. He looked truly amazing in the ropes. The dark color contrasted with his pale skin where it slightly bubbled over the ropes when his muscles were relaxed.

Sterling wordlessly moved to kneel on the bed in front of us. He reached out and stroked both of us. His fingers slowly drifted between my legs, and I shook, waiting for him to get where I needed him. I was practically dripping. He closed his eyes, tipped his head back, and let out a sigh like our pleasure was his pleasure. When he finally graced his fingers over my clit, I cried out. He chuckled and did it again. And again. Until I was at the top of my orgasm. Then he stopped and continued working on Milo, who wasn't far behind me. The air where his hand had been was cold. My teeth ground together in my frustration.

Milo was swaying on his knees, his head tipped back and mouth open. His glasses were askew on his face, but his eyes were closed, anyway. A small stream of morning sunlight streaked through the gap in the curtains and illuminated his face. It made his beard almost glow and sparkle ginger as he rocked his body. He let out a hoarse moan and his eyes shut harder. Sterling removed his hands from Milo's cock.

"Fuck you," Milo groaned.

Sterling had been about to get off the bed, but he jumped back on to spank Milo's ass. I didn't mind Milo getting in trouble. I liked the way his ass bounced and turned pink.

"Close your eyes," Sterling said in a quiet but demanding voice.

I obeyed and a soft slip of fabric covered my eyes. I peeked one open to see nothing but blackness. Not even a peek of light at the bottom. Once he'd tied Milo's blindfold, I tried to guess where he was in the room. I could practically feel him stalking around the bed, looking at us.

We were powerless to him. Our lives and bodies were in his hands, and he was prowling the room like an animal. A predator. Devon had once told me Sterling had a hard time letting go of his aggression and violence once he got started with it. That he was the only one who knew how to calm the rage that burned in Sterling. It was a power I wanted to share, sure, but I really wanted the rage. I wanted it to burn me with him. I wanted the power to stop it, but I wanted the power to choose to let it eat me alive.

"You both have the most perfect... unblemished skin," Sterling said. He was in front of us now. Standing at the foot of the bed. "No tattoos, no piercings. A perfect canvas."

Milo scoffed, and I felt him move beside me. His leg hair tickled my skin where our legs were pressed together on the mattress. His biceps knocked into my shoulder.

"What is it, Milo?" Sterling asked in a tone that suggested Milo was about to get in trouble.

"We both are covered in recent scars," Milo replied.

"Hmm, but those can fade. I think we need something more permanent," Sterling replied and prowled the room again.

"You better not pierce my dick," Milo warned.

Smack!

Milo hissed in a breath, and I pouted.

"What's the lip for, Bambi?" Sterling asked.

"I like when I can see you spank Milo. I like it when his

butt cheek bounces and turns pink," I said with my voice raspy, like I'd been smoking.

Both guys chuckled.

"Me, too," Sterling admitted. "I'll let you watch another time."

Sterling moved around us again, and I lost track of where he was in the room. I turned my head to see if I might hear him breathing or moving. The not knowing had my fight-or-flight instinct starting up. The anxiety of knowing he was in the room but not what he was doing or planning had my heart pounding. Suddenly, something cold and hard was pressed against the skin under my breast. It slid to the other and I involuntarily whimpered. I didn't want my nipples pierced. I tucked my lips into my mouth to prevent myself from speaking or crying.

"I'm not piercing you," Sterling said softly. "I'm just going to give you some pretty scars."

I swallowed nervously.

"Do you trust me?" he asked.

I wanted to yell "*Obviously*! Or I wouldn't be tied up and blindfolded!" Instead, I only nodded.

"Good girl," he crooned before there was a quick slice under my left breast and I felt the hot trickle of blood down my stomach to my legs. I cried out in shock and pain. I felt Sterling wipe some blood before it went to my pussy. Then his mouth was on my clit. He must have been laying on the bed in front of me. I spread my legs despite the burning feeling just below my breast. The mixture of pleasure and pain was a heady one. In the darkness of the blindfold, colors swirled behind my eyes like an oil spill as I arched and writhed. I was vaguely aware of my keening voice as I reached the precipice of the orgasm that had been wrenched from my grasp twice now. He pulled away again and left me dripping with arousal. I felt it course down my thighs as my abdomen clenched and ached with unmet need. He could read my body so precisely that he had stopped touching me when I was one stroke, one lick, away from detonating.

He must have had a hand on Milo while he was licking me, because Milo was moaning when I became aware of my surroundings. There was a movement next to me and then I felt Milo jerk, and he hissed a breath through his teeth. He growled out his pain while Sterling praised him. "Good boy. You held so still for me."

Sterling's mouth was back on my clit and it was two strokes until I was at the edge again. I anticipated him cutting off my orgasm, so I did my best to keep quiet and still. There was nothing more I wanted than to come at that moment. I would have agreed to anything that man asked of me if I got to come. I felt hot tears on my face under my blindfold. Crying seemed like the opposite thing Sterling would want to see right now, so I sniffed and did my best to control them.

"Oh," he crooned. It was a taunting threat and not a comfort. It was dark and smoky and promised more pain. "I've got another scar to make. You can handle it. You can do it. I know you can do it. Can I cut you one more time?"

I swallowed down the sob that was caught in my throat. The cut he already had done barely hurt anymore. Like it wasn't even there. Like the impatient pain between my legs and in my lower abdomen had overtaken most other sensations. I tugged at my ropes experimentally. I wanted out. Not for escape, but to take control and climb on top of Sterling to take what I wanted. "Do it and then fuck me," I said in a voice so unlike my own. My thighs were shaking with the effort of remaining upright in a kneeling position on the mattress. I was running out of patience.

Both men groaned softly.

Sterling gave one long suck to my clit, and I shrieked. Almost immediately after, there was a slice under my right breast and that same hot trickle of blood down my body. All the fight I'd had coursing through my body disappeared. A fuzzy, black space replaced it. It felt like floating. Like bliss. It felt like a post orgasmic high, but without the orgasm. My arms and legs had been tired from their position, but now felt like I was swimming in cotton. My body swayed.

I heard Milo cry out in pleasure and then end in a growl of pain. He was breathing a stream of curses to Sterling, earning him yet another sharp spank. Sterling gripped my hair in his fist, making the wet and tangled strands pull, and yanked my head down and over on the bed. My forehead knocked into Milo's hip, and he gasped at the impact.

"Finish him while I fuck you," Sterling instructed me before kneeling behind me, my hair in his fist.

My arms were bound behind me, so his hold on my hair was the only thing keeping me from face planting on the mattress. Sterling's cock slammed into me as I had opened my mouth for Milo. He must have done it intentionally. We all groaned in unison. He repeated the hard thrust until I gagged on Milo and pulled off, gasping for air.

"Fuck, Emily, I'm gonna-" Milo breathed.

I hummed my consent, and he gave two shaking, slow

thrusts before he erupted in my mouth. A deep, ragged, needy, but relieved moan tore from Milo. I swallowed him down as much as I could, but I was sluggish and wholly focused on Sterling's cock in my pussy. Sterling's pace behind me kicked up, and he reached around to rub my clit in little circles. His thrusts were loud and smacking.

The colors behind my eyes that looked like an oil spill brightened to stars and blinded me. All sensation narrowed to my core, silent, frozen, and poised to burst. And when the bubble of sensation did burst, it sent embers of that fire I'd wanted from Sterling throughout my body. It burned away the anger I'd been holding onto all evening. It burned away the fear that kept my adrenaline pumping. And it burned away the last shred of possibility that my life could ever go back to the way I'd lived a year ago.

I was vaguely aware of Sterling shouting out his release through the roaring in my ears from my orgasm. When I fully came back to my senses, my arms and chest were unbound, and my eyes were uncovered. My skin prickled where the ropes had been, and I felt sticky where blood had dripped down my stomach. I blinked my eyes open and saw a smiling Milo. His eyes were hooded, and his smile relaxed as he panted. Sterling was tracing his fingers over the lines from the ropes, and I heard him chuckle breathlessly.

"You did so good. Both of you," he said.

"Thank you," I replied sleepily.

Milo leaned over me and kissed Sterling gently before laying back on the bed. I stretched like a cat. My muscles were stiff from holding the same position.

"Do we need stitches?" I asked, remembering the cuts he'd

made on us. I didn't feel them anymore and figured they must have not been deep. It felt like a lot of blood when it happened.

"So many stitches," Sterling said in a sarcastic tone.

Milo and I both jumped up to sit and looked at our bodies. There was wax poured down undamaged skin. "You dick!" Milo shouted.

Sterling laughed. "Did you actually think I was going to cut you?"

Milo and I were both silent and staring at him.

"You both were going to *let* me *cut* you?" Sterling's eyes bulged and his mouth gaped.

I shrugged. "Yeah, I mean, it was pretty hot."

Sterling went from shocked to cocky as he strutted into his bathroom. He helped us get cleaned up, remove the wax, and apply aloe to our heat pink skin before we switched to Milo's room to sleep. "We're going to run out of clean places to sleep," I giggled and yawned as we climbed under the covers.

"I never said my bed was clean," Milo said as he curled around my back.

Sterling only paused a second before shaking his head. "I don't even care. I'm so tired."

I rested my head on his chest, and he wrapped an arm around me to reach Milo. Despite the events of the night, I felt safe. And not because of the many surveillance camera feeds on the wall above us. It was because of the men who had taken my body to the limits and were now holding me like I was precious. Like I was worth protecting

21

Milo

"Milo, Sterling," a whispered voice woke me with a start. I was still wrapped around Emily's back, her soft body cradled in mine and her head rested on Sterling's chest. "Can one of you guys come be with the door company?"

"The what?" Sterling mumbled.

"The people I hired to replace the sliding door," Devon said, his voice laced with irritation.

"Oh, shit! Yeah, sorry man," Sterling said and carefully slid out from under Emily.

Devon must have been awake this entire time, and he was injured. Emily had wanted to help clean up his wound, but we had distracted her. I also slid out of the bed to join Sterling and Devon. "Did you get any sleep?" I asked him as I pulled on a pair of jeans.

"No," Devon snapped. "Sonny's guys left about an hour

ago. I called the window and door repair place, and now I'm waking you guys up so I can sleep."

"Got it," Sterling said with a note of guilt.

"How is she?" Devon asked and nodded to Emily.

"She's alright. Had a bit of a freak out about the house not being safe anymore, but she calmed down," I explained and picked up my laptop.

Devon nodded, still looking at Emily.

"She might freak out if she wakes up alone. You should climb in there with her," Sterling said as he stretched.

"I'm not sleeping in this bed," Devon said with a curled lip and a wrinkled nose.

I snorted.

"I'll carry her to your room. She's out cold and won't even notice," Sterling chuckled. He scooped Emily up before Devon could protest, and they were both out the door.

On the security cameras, I saw the door company's van pull up to the driveway gate. An app on my phone sent me the alert, and I pressed the button to open the gate. I had enough time to get downstairs, stow a handgun in my waistband, and get to the front door before they rang the doorbell.

There were four men who showed no signs of recognition when I opened the door right as the first man was reaching for the doorbell. I welcomed them in to get started and sign the paperwork. None of them were armed beyond their tool belts and likely did not know who we were. I only relaxed slightly as I showed them the broken sliding door.

"This looks like someone tried to break in," one guy said with concern.

"Yeah, they made off with some of my wife's jewelry," I lied smoothly and ruffled the hair at the back of my head.

Sterling bound down the stairs and met me in the kitchen. "Did you make coffee?" He nodded and smiled at the door repairmen, but his eyes resettled on me.

"Not yet. I was showing them the broken door," I said, and the men turned to each other to discuss their plan of action.

Sterling made coffee while I made toast. We remained mostly quiet while the men worked, and we had breakfast. It was nearly two in the afternoon, but it had been a long night. I blushed thinking about it.

"What are you thinking about?" Sterling asked in a low, teasing voice.

"I'm thinking about what you said to me," I whispered and continued to work on my laptop. I was monitoring Marie's emails and credit card activity. She'd made no purchases on her card since she went into hiding, but her emails said she was online shopping for baby clothes at a little shop in upstate New York. She was pretty good at hiding her whereabouts, but I was better.

"Which part?" Sterling prodded.

"The part where you said you're next," I admitted.

"Drink your coffee," he said and lifted my mug to my lips.

"Why?" I asked him, flinching away from the mug that had bounced off my front teeth.

"I need your energy and strength up. Drink your coffee and eat your toast," he demanded.

I fought the yawn that threatened to break free. "The door guys are here."

"Not all day," Sterling reasoned and refilled his mug. "They're halfway done already."

It turned out they had been halfway through the steps, but not time wise. It was close to five in the evening when they finished up. We'd had a new door put in a few years ago, and the one we'd chosen then was still in stock now. The replacement was quicker than I'd expected. They instructed us to avoid using the door for the night while the caulk died, but the job went seamless.

A seamless job.

It was almost a foreign concept in the computer world. There was always something holding up a project. Whether it was a hardware failure, a server upgrade, a software upgrade, or an incompatibility, there was always something. Trouble-shooting was half the job, no matter how much of a genius I was. I knew replacing doors wasn't typically a seamless job. We'd just been the dumbasses to get a new door broken a few years after installation. But the job was helping people and their homes. Helping families. Those men put in a solid day's work doing something visibly constructive and then went home to normal homes and families. I couldn't help but be jealous.

Once the men had left with their payment, Sterling was pulling me upstairs. Despite being tired, I followed obediently. Part of me wanted to wait to experience sex with Sterling. I had waited so long and denied my feelings for him for most of my life that I was afraid to take that ultimate step with him. There was no going back after that. He pulled me down the hall to his room. There was no sound coming from Devon's room, so I assumed he and Emily were still asleep.

Sterling shut the door behind us, and his mouth was on mine, my back pressed against the door. It was reminiscent of our first kiss on New Year. I smiled into the kiss before I deepened it. His hands shook as he lifted my shirt over my head. He tasted like fresh coffee and warm, buttery toast.

"Are you nervous?" I asked him.

He swallowed. "Yeah, sort of. I don't want to hurt you."

"Shocking."

"You know what I mean," he huffed. "I don't want to *really* hurt you and have to call Doc. I don't want to explain why your asshole is broken."

"Ew, okay. Let's not... talk about that. Let's do it the right way," I said and lifted his shirt over his head.

We kissed slowly while we removed our pants and boxers. His tongue swiped against mine possessively, and I sighed into the kiss. The first crush I ever had on a guy was Sterling, and it came soon after my first crush on a girl. He and I had a strong bond and relationship before the attraction came. Our emotional connection probably played as much into my rejection of meaningless sexual relations as much as seeing my uncle flaunt them did. Kissing him now, knowing what we were about to do, felt like my sexuality had come full circle. While Emily was a very real and very important part of our relationship, she was new to our lives. There had always been me and Sterling.

Sterling walked us until my legs hit the side of his bed. I sat down and looked at his cock. It was hard and a bead of pre-come sat on the tip. I stooped to lick it. He groaned low in his throat. Sterling stroked back my hair while I sucked and licked him slowly and adoringly. His piercing dragged in my mouth and knocked into my teeth a few times and I wondered how it would feel inside me. I should have asked Emily about it.

"Stop, let me get you ready for me," Sterling rasped and rummaged in his nightstand for a bottle of lube. I scooted back on the bed and opened my legs. I wasn't sure of the best way to go about it for the first time. Maybe not missionary, I wanted some control. It wasn't that I didn't trust Sterling. I trusted him with my life. But I wasn't sure how much communicating I'd be able to do and wanted to be able to pull away if I needed to.

Sterling opened the bottle and shook the rest of the contents down like a ketchup bottle while I flipped over on all fours. He looked up and his eyebrows rose in shock. "Oh, like that?"

"I... feel like I'm more... open this way," I said, and a slight rise in my tone made it sound like a question.

Sterling smiled. When he smiled genuinely like that, I was reminded of our childhoods together. Not in a creepy way, but in a way that made me feel at ease. I *knew* Sterling, and he *knew* me. There was nobody else I would want to do this with. My heart stumbled and took on a gallop as he climbed on the bed behind me, his eyes on my ass. His pupils were so wide they almost overtook the silvery gray of his irises as he lowered himself. Peering over my shoulder, our eyes connected as he licked me. My eyes rolled back in pleasure, and I hung my head and panted. It was unlike anything I'd ever experienced, and I had almost exploded out of my skin when he'd done it while I was tied up last night. His tongue probed into me, and I jerked forward. A shameful flush crept up my chest and I closed my eyes.

"You're fucking amazing, Milo," Sterling said, his voice growling and hungry. "Don't pull away from me. I want every part of you."

I returned to my original position, and he repeated his probing. He hummed against my skin and gripped my ass cheeks in his big hands. I shook off my remaining knots of apprehension and surrendered. He was a grown man and wouldn't do anything he didn't want to.

The cap of the lube snapping was loud in the quiet room, and I listened as it spluttered. He warmed the lube in his hand with a hot breath, like he was trying to fog up a window. I smiled at his consideration and looked over my shoulder.

"I'm glad you're presenting to me like this. I want to see every bit of me that goes into that tight fucking asshole of yours," he said, his voice just above a whisper. He looked back down at my ass and I felt the warm pressure of his index finger as it slowly slid into me. It burned and stretched and didn't feel good at all. Regret washed over me. I had liked the plug fine enough, but maybe I couldn't enjo-

Oh fuck.

Sterling had turned his wrist so his finger could curl toward the front of my body as he slid in. I changed my mind. I could enjoy this. Sweat broke out along my back and I was panting like I'd run a marathon.

"This is barely one finger, baby," Sterling chuckled softly.

"Two," I demanded breathlessly.

He used more lube and pressed his middle finger in next to

his index. Slowly. Painfully slow until he was to his knuckles. "Fuck," he swore under his breath. "So fucking tight."

I breathed through my teeth, trying not to come with just two fingers in me. He pumped them out and back in and curled his fingers against my prostate. I couldn't help the sound that came out of me. Half whimper and half growling moan. It was animalistic and needy. He chuckled breathlessly and scissored his fingers a few times and turned his hand around, stretching me. I looked down to my weeping cock and saw him pour more lube onto his hand, dripping the clear liquid all over his bed in his haste. He plunged his fingers back into me and it felt like relief. A slick glide replaced the burning stretch.

"Did you know you can come more times and longer with a prostate orgasm?" Sterling whispered huskily as he slowly inserted a third finger.

My moan was like a sob, and I rested my sweaty forehead on my arms. I did know that fact. But verbal communication was limited in my current state. I was impressed and turned on that Sterling had done research, though.

"When I came at the table with the plug, I didn't know that yet," he chuckled, almost conversationally. The tightness in his voice was barely audible as he held himself back. "I already come a lot, so with a prostate orgasm I had to straight up throw away those pants. There was no saving them. It looked like I'd pissed myself."

"It's. Called. Milking," I said between gasps.

"That's disgusting. Can we call it something less like a cow?" Sterling cringed. "Like, um, ass blasting. Or butt nut."

I laughed, and he swore. "Fuck, when you laughed, your ass squeezed me so hard."

"Then shut up and fuck me," I said, my voice strangled.

"Since you asked so nicely," Sterling said sarcastically and removed his fingers.

I watched down my body as he sat up and poured lube on his hard cock. I watched as he jacked himself off for a few seconds and then lined himself up. With a gulp of anticipation, I lifted my head back up and made eye contact with him. He was open mouth breathing and the corner of his mouth lifted in a smile before he looked back down to make sure he was lined up. I felt the warm, plush tip of his cock and the hard metal of his piercing meet my skin and I tried not to shake with anticipation. He noticed the vibration of my body and smoothed his hands over my back and around my hips.

"You ready?" he asked in a whisper, his eyes locked back on mine.

"Are you?" I asked.

He swallowed and nodded. "Yeah, I'm ready."

"Then do it," I encouraged. "But go slow."

Sterling nodded again and pressed against my ass. I watched his abs and pecs jump as he moved. His mouth fell open again and his eyes were fixed on his cock. He pushed into me and I hissed a breath at the burn. It was more intense now, even with the lube than it was with his fingers. I concentrated on relaxing. "Push out a little," he coached hoarsely.

I did, and he was able to get the head of his cock in me. "Good boy."

The burn was insane as he gently and slowly pushed into me, but faded once his head was past. I felt sweat slide down my back and the trembling was unavoidable. Sterling was in me. Almost all the way, judging by how long he'd been pushing. Sterling. My best friend. Who I'd been crushing on most of my life.

"Fuck, you feel so good," he groaned. His voice shook like he was barely restraining himself from fucking me hard and fast. I wanted it.

I wanted it very badly.

"Wait, wait, wait," he soothed in a tight voice. I had unconsciously pushed back towards him to make him move faster.

My head felt dizzy, and the room felt unbearably hot. I thought maybe I was about to pass out from the burn and the pleasure when I felt the skin of his hips meet my ass and thighs. He was fully seated in me. Or, rather, I was fully seated on him. I put my head down on my forearms to rest.

We took a moment to breathe and adjust. I felt his cock jump in me, and I gasped. "Holy shit."

"Good?" he asked.

"It's so much," I said.

"I bet. I don't know how I'll ever take you," Sterling said, and his hips moved the slightest bit like he couldn't help it.

"Slowly, probably," I replied.

"Can I move now? It's almost unbearable to be in you and not fucking you," Sterling growled.

"Yeah," I said and nodded against my arms.

He rolled his hips and let out a rumbling moan. He swore in a steady stream as he pulled almost all the way out and slid back in. The movement was gentle for a few strokes before he slammed into me with enough force I reached out to the headboard to brace myself.

"Wait, yeah. Put your fucking hands on the headboard," he said and pulled out of me completely. I felt exposed and raw without him in me, but I knee walked so I could brace my hands on the top of the black dented metal headboard.

Sterling was pushing back into me seconds later and his piercing dragged across my prostate at this angle. I cried out and gripped the metal until I was white knuckling it. "Such a greedy ass," Sterling grunted as he fucked me harder and faster. His hips were meeting my sweaty thighs and ass with a dull smacking sound. His hands gripped my hips hard, his thumbs pressing so hard into my back I was sure to have oval bruises.

With every drag over my prostate, I was practically whimpering. I hadn't even been aware of the sound until I looked down and my voice echoed against the headboard. Getting closer and closer to coming, I reached one arm back to pull his mouth down to mine. It was an awkward angle, our teeth clacking and breath gasping. The kiss was clumsy and devolved into us panting into each other's mouth with our lips occasionally touching. I didn't care. I was nearing an explosion without even touching my cock. Sterling's eyes screwed shut and his hips stuttered in their rhythm as he neared his own climax. "Come for me, baby," he panted. "I'm going to fucking fill you."

Seeing him ruined like this was mesmerizing. His sweaty forehead, blown pupils, and open mouth as he fucked *me* senseless was what sent me over the edge. That damned piercing smashing my prostate had me coming all over his bed. It felt like it lasted forever. My vision blurred and my body collapsed, only held up by his hands and his cock.

He roared as he came, his forehead pressed against my shoulder. I felt the warmth of his come filling me to where it came out on the last few thrusts. The sound was filthy and erotic. I felt like I could come again and again.

Sterling and I fell onto the bed on our stomachs with him still inside me. I dreaded him pulling out, not just for the lack of his cock in me, but because of the mess that was sure to come. He pulled out of me with a grunt and I felt the warmth of some of his come leak out of me. Without a word, he roughly flipped me on my back and kissed me hard. I had fallen into my own come and was now covered with both of our releases. While we kissed, he brought his hand down to my ass and curled two fingers in, finding my prostate quickly. I cried out, long and growling, as he brought me to a second orgasm quickly. My come came out hard and fast and painted the side of his face and neck while he kissed me. He chuckled into the kiss. With a numb and shaking arm, I reached up and swiped it from his face. He looked at my hand in just enough time for me to shove my come covered fingers in his mouth. Dutifully, he cleaned them, keeping eye contact the entire time.

"Do you think you can come the normal way now?" he asked and looked down at my still hard cock.

"Absolutely," I said breathlessly.

Sterling dove and took my cock in his mouth. He sucked hard and bobbed his head, swirling his tongue around the head. I grabbed his hair and pulled him onto me hard. I felt him gag around me\], and I grinned down at him. His eyes watered and streamed. I realized I wanted him gagging and weeping and drooling over my cock for the rest of my life.

He gagged a second time and then I felt myself gain access to his throat. His hands gripped my thighs as I fucked his face. My orgasm came quick and hard, and I felt him swallow me down. The tight squeeze of his swallows sent me to orbit. He pulled off me with a wet gasp for breath and a fit of coughs before laying down next to me.

"I can't feel my limbs," I slurred.

"Can you feel your ass?" he asked, his voice scratchy but concerned.

I thought about it for a second. "I can't feel my entire body."

He chuckled and coughed again. "Maybe that's for the best. Fuck, Milo. That was so fucking amazing. You did so well. You took all of me."

"Well," I said, still slurring in my exhaustion. "I love all of you."

"I love all of you, too. Especially the freckle above your ass crack," Sterling said and kissed my neck.

I gave a sleepy chuckle. The freckle was news to me.

"Can I run you a bath?" he asked.

"I'm not a girl. I'm not going to get a UTI," I scoffed.

"No, but you are filled and covered with come," he explained and poked at a streak of drying come on my stomach.

"I didn't research what to do after you fill me," I said and yawned.

"Pretty sure you like... shit it out," Sterling said and reached for his phone. He opened a web browser and typed something I couldn't read. My glasses had come off at some point. "Yup, you push it out."

"Gross," I chuckled.

Sterling shrugged and got up for the bathroom. I heard the bath start and dozed off with a smile.

22

Emily

I slept deeply. That kind of sleep where waking up feels like reentering Earth's atmosphere. I gasped awake in complete darkness. A weight was propped on my side, and I panicked in that sleep confused way. I took a deep breath to steady myself and got a lungful of a spicy, woodsy scent. Devon's cologne.

"Shh," soothed a sleepy male voice behind me. Their breath ghosted on the back of my neck.

The weight on my side moved, and I realized it was an arm. The slight crinkling shuffle of cotton and paper, like bandages, was what clued me fully into the fact that I was curled up in bed with Devon. "Devon?"

"Yeah?" he asked in a sleep thick voice.

"What's going on?" I asked and sat up. The room was completely dark, and I didn't know his room well enough to reach over to turn on a light.

"Sleep," he responded. "It's three in the morning."

"I slept forever!"

He yawned, and I heard him scrub his hand over his face. "You had a long couple of days."

"Please, turn on a light," I said, my voice more begging than I'd intended.

I felt him move in the bed, pulling the blankets with him. A bedside lamp flicked on and I blinked to adjust. I was wearing the shirt I'd borrowed from Milo over a pair of brief panties I'd put on after my shower. Reaching down to cover myself with a blush, I looked around. We were in Devon's room, in Devon's bed, and I was curled up with a shirtless *Devon*. "I'm sorry."

"What for?" he asked and cleared the sleep from his throat.

"For- for being in your bed," I stuttered.

He gave a tired smile. "I wasn't exactly going to sleep in Sterling's bed after what I heard happening in there."

My blush deepened and my eyes settled on his bandage over his arm. "Oh, I was supposed to help you clean up!"

He shook his head. "I didn't tear any stitches. I had just moved around too much. There's nothing to clean up."

"Are you sure?" I asked.

"I'm sure. You took care of them when they needed it," he said. His amber eyes were a warm brown in the soft light of the room.

I scoffed. "I don't think I took care of anyone. I'm pretty sure I had a meltdown."

Devon shook his head and sat up more. He grabbed my hand. "No, you gave them something else to focus on.

Something else to do. I didn't have to talk the demons out of Sterling and Milo *slept*. You helped."

I winced. "Yeah, but you were alone."

Devon smiled again. This time a small, sad smile. "I'm used to it."

"Oh, Devon," I sighed and rested my forehead on his chest. "I feel horrible I was someone who left you alone. Please, don't let me do that again."

Devon considered me for a moment before exhaling and stroking my hair. We were silent for a few moments, and I wondered if he'd fallen asleep sitting up, his hand in my hair. "So, you're not going to run away from us?" he asked.

"No," I said. "I don't think I could ever leave you three now."

He pressed his mouth on my hair. Like he wanted to kiss me, but couldn't bring himself to do it.

"Devon?"

"Hm?"

"Are Sterling and Milo here?"

"I don't think they left. I left them to oversee the door repair," he murmured.

"After Sonny's crew and the door repair, that's got to be expensive," I groaned and sat back to look up at him.

"Very," he said ruefully.

"Gotta get those guys to make more videos," I joked half-heartedly.

"I was thinking of contributing," Devon said.

"Oh?" My eyes bugged out. It had been a source of jokes in the house that Devon would participate, I never thought he'd actually be willing.

"Yeah, I have an idea of how I can help," Devon said with a nod.

"With one of them, or both of them?" I asked and cleared the excitement from my throat.

"Myself."

"A solo video on Sterling's channel?"

"No! Oh god, Emily!" He laughed.

"Then what?" I joined in his laughter.

"My dad has a safe of gold bullion and cash. I can get into it," he explained and lounged back on the pillows. The move extended his lean body in the bed, and I couldn't help my eyes from tracing the lines of his body. The hair on his chest tapered off at his abs and then a trail continued from his navel to below the low-slung black pajama pants.

I tore my eyes from his body and back to his face. "I've heard about this gold. But how can you get it if it's in his house?"

"He hasn't been there since the meeting where he killed Matthew. Milo was the one who set up the security to begin with. I know enough to get in," Devon explained and yawned again.

"Are you sure?"

"Yes. I have a password into the safe and a key," Devon said. "I did grow up there."

"Won't he find out?" I asked and fidgeted with the hem of my t-shirt.

"Not unless he goes in there himself," Devon said confidently.

"What about the security system? Won't he get some sort of alert or alarm?" I asked.

"I can turn it off."

"And you think you're doing this alone?" I asked, my eyes narrowing.

"I will be. Don't talk to Sterling or Milo about it. They'll get involved and too many people going in would be harder to hide. I don't know if he has people staged outside, so I want to go alone," Devon said sternly.

"No."

"Yes."

"No, I'm going with you. I just told you I would never leave you alone again," I insisted.

He glared at me. "You're not coming with me. I'm doing this alone and that's it."

"If you don't let me go, I'll tell Sterling and Milo," I said and crossed my arms over my chest. "Make a good choice, Devon."

"Fuck," he groaned and covered his face with his hands. "Now is not the time to be a brat."

I grinned triumphantly.

"Fine, you can come," he grumbled. "We'll still hide it from the guys. I can't have them coming along or shutting it down."

"When?" I asked him.

"Tomorrow night when they go to sleep," Devon said. "As long as everything is clear all day, we'll go. Now, go back to sleep."

"I'm not sleepy."

"Go... watch a movie or something," he said and rolled over in the bed and pulled the blankets up to his chin.

"I don't want to be alone," I said with a huff.

"Well, I'm sleeping. Make sure your activity can be done silently and in the dark," he grumbled.

The day was spent quietly. Milo worked on the security system upgrades, Sterling carried materials for Milo to and from the house, and Devon spent most of his time in the office. I worked out, took a long bath, and then spent the rest of the day watching movies. Intentionally, I kept away from Sterling and Milo. I was afraid I'd let it slip I was going to break into Anthony's house with Devon. I wasn't a poor liar, but I didn't have any excuses for leaving the house with Devon. They didn't seem to notice I was avoiding them. Everyone was busy with tasks.

I did, however, notice the way Milo and Sterling looked at each other over breakfast. Sterling's eyes blazed with desire when he looked at Milo, who blushed and gave the look right back. It had me biting back a grin and pinching both of them under the table.

That night, I feigned period cramps and went to my room early. Devon had nodded to me over dinner to say our plan was on. I was dressed and ready when there was a soft knock on my door close to midnight. I peeked out to see Devon leaning against my door frame. He was wearing black pants and a black button-up, matching my black jeans and black sweater. He looked shocked to see me dressed and ready.

"Ready to do some breaking and entering?" I asked as I slipped out of my room.

"Shh," he shushed me as he ushered me down the hall. I was carrying my black boots in one hand and slid my phone into my back pocket with the other.

Once we were in the garage, he spoke. "We have ten minutes to get off the property and down the street. I disabled Milo's security system temporarily, and it starts back up in ten minutes."

"You can do that?" I asked as we got into a black sedan I'd never been in before.

"I've watched Milo do it a million times on jobs," Devon said and started the engine.

"That's impressive," I said and buckled.

"Thank you. I made it a mission to be a leader who understood the jobs of his people," Devon explained as we crept down the driveway without headlights.

Once on the road, Devon put his phone on the dash. "We'll see if they notice and call us. This should be a quick job. An hour tops with travel time. I checked, and they were asleep, so we should be good."

"You checked? That's brave," I giggled.

"I waited until the bed stopped hitting the wall and the moaning was done," Devon said. His tone suggested it disgusted him, but a smile played on his lips.

"Aw, I missed out," I pouted.

Devon rolled his eyes.

It wasn't a long drive to Anthony's house. We drove past once to look for lights on or men stationed, but saw nothing. We parked about a block down the road and crept up to the side of the house. My heart raced in my chest despite seeing no threats. Devon gripped my hand in his to keep me close in the dark. I was thankful, as there were limited streetlights, and the moon was mostly hidden by late winter clouds.

The house was still and dark as we crept around the

landscaping. The grass was wet with the melting snow, and we squished along until we reached the back door of the house. Devon used a house key from his pocket to open the door. A beep sounded for an alarm system and Devon peered around the back door before opening it fully. I looked at Stephanie's gazebo and tea garden with a sad pang in my chest. It was still well maintained and perfect looking, though empty without the chairs and heater and blankets. I had been so excited to be accepted by the women of this family, and now it was all torn to the ground. I swallowed a sad sigh as I followed Devon into the kitchen where he unarmed the security system.

Milo was monitoring the cameras in this house as well, but I didn't think he'd talked about any motion detection alerts here. He'd also said he'd revoked Anthony's access to view the cameras remotely. I felt safe in the assumption we weren't being watched on a camera, but there was still the threat of someone being inside.

It didn't seem like anyone was there as we crept through the kitchen. My hand was sweaty in Devon's as we moved through the huge, dark house. I had only been here once, but I remembered it to be lavishly decorated in a modern art déco style. I tried to regulate my breathing, but I was practically hyperventilating with my anxiety. Each time we moved to a new room or hallway we froze to listen for someone else. Blood pounded in my ears, and I couldn't tell if I'd gone deaf or if there was simply no sound in the house.

"Stairs," Devon breathed as the toes of my shoes scuffed the bottom step.

We climbed the stairs, and Devon halted us. I held my breath and listened as hard as I could. He leaned down to me and whispered, "The last time I was on these stairs, I had just been told you were dead."

I squeezed his hand in mine. I didn't know what to say, so I raised his hand to my lips and pressed a gentle kiss there. He let out a soft exhale, like he'd needed reassurance that I was there.

He tugged my hand along and we continued to the top of the stairs. We stopped to listen again and heard no sign of movement. It was darkest in this hallway, and I relied entirely on Devon's guidance. He'd grown up in this house and knew it well. We made our way to a room down the hall, and Devon ran his hand along the wall to find the doorknob. Once located, he quietly opened the door. There was no sound other than the soft creak of the door. We paused, and he entered first, waiting for any sign of a person guarding the safe. He came back and felt around for my hand in the dark. In the room, we crossed to the other side. I bumped into what seemed like a chair and it skidded against the wood floor.

Devon swung back around and gripped my waist to settle me. I hadn't been about to fall, but I appreciated the touch. "I'm okay. Sorry," I breathed.

"Please be careful," he whispered back. He let go of my hand and I believed us to be near a bookshelf. I breathed the smell of book glue, paper, and leather. Devon ran his hands over something on the shelf or wall. I couldn't tell. There was a muffled beeping sound and green lighting illuminated his face from a keypad on the wall. It had been hidden behind a family picture. Little Devon and Sterling smiled up at me from the picture that was swung to the side. Devon put a finger over the little speaker the beeps emanated from to stifle the shrill sound. He pressed a six-digit password into the keypad and a framed painting of a mountain clicked open next to him. I smiled widely. It was exactly what I'd hoped a secret safe in a mafia boss' home to look like.

"You're joking!" I whispered and clapped quietly.

"Stop, Emily," Devon chuckled under his breath.

Devon opened the painting the rest of the way and stepped in. A small light was inside, and I saw him hunch over slightly to enter through the painting before he stood to full height again. I followed him eagerly. It was a small space, about the size of a closet, and I whipped my head around to take it all in. I couldn't fit in the safe with him comfortably, so I remained with one foot in and one out as I looked around. There were black bags on metal shelves, and I peeked in a close by one to see it was cash. I gulped audibly, and Devon smirked back at me.

"This is easier to carry," he whispered and showed me a piece of gold in what looked like a small glass case.

"Wait, that's it?" I asked with a small pout.

"It's worth almost twenty thousand dollars," he snapped and shook his head.

"I was expecting something the size of a brick. That's barely the size of a deck of cards," I explained.

"This isn't a cartoon," he scoffed and put a few of the bars into a black duffel bag.

"Are we taking it all?" I asked.

"No, I don't want my dad to come in here tomorrow and see too much missing and attack us again. I want this to fly under the radar as much as possible," he explained.

"I can carry-" I started, but stopped when I heard a sound.

Devon's head snapped over to me, eyes fearful and wide. My heart dropped through the soles of my shoes and I froze as solid as the gold bars. We waited, staring at each other until I heard the unmistakable sound of a door closing. Devon looked sorrowful for a moment before he closed his eyes briefly. He pulled me into the safe with him, reached out to flip down the keypad picture, and then pulled the safe door closed. When the door closed, the soft light went out like a refrigerator light.

We were pressed front to front between the shelving of the safe. The safe door had closed us off to the sound of whoever was in the house. It was painfully quiet, and I was close enough I could hear Devon's heart pounding in his chest. It matched my own and his breath puffed against my forehead. He awkwardly reached a hand to his gun holster and took out his gun and flipped off the safety as quietly as he could. The sound of him preparing his gun in the silence was as loud as him firing a shot.

I couldn't help my shaking and I rested my head on his chest, gripping his shirt at his sides with my fists. He smoothed my hair with his free hand. I was so terribly scared. Again. I couldn't count the times I'd been scared like this in the past few months with these men. I'd never experienced a fear of this bone drying level before I met Devon, Sterling, and Milo. But I'd also never felt the relief of safety like I felt with them, either. It had to be a yin and yang situation. The safety I'd had in my life before them couldn't have been appreciated without knowing danger. And now, clutching the man before me, I realized even in situations where I was fearful and in danger, I felt a sense of relief that he was there. Because he would protect me.

My heart swelled and clenched painfully in my chest as I looked up to where I knew his face to be. I felt his muscles in his chest move and he leaned down to whisper, "What?"

With him close, I took the opportunity to press my lips to his. It was so dark I couldn't tell where he was. I missed and kissed his chin. A surprised gasp left his lips, and I used the sound as a guide to find him. Now my lips met his in a hurried, trembling peck. His lips were soft beneath mine. My heart gave an extra thump in between my panic at the current of electricity that coursed through me. Lust and electricity buzzed in my veins like a beehive.

The hand that had been stroking my hair came around and cupped my jaw lightly as he pulled away. "Stop, Emily."

"Why? I never got to kiss you," I breathed back.

He rested his face against mine, cheek to cheek. I felt his eyelashes move when he blinked in the darkness. His exhale warmed the side of my neck, and I itched with the need to kiss him. We were pressed so close, but yet not close enough. I could have moved to the side, further into the safe, and not been quite so cramped. But I wanted to stay close to him. I liked the press of our bodies. I liked the heat of him. I liked I could feel the jump of his cock as he hardened against me. Standing on tiptoes, I leaned to kiss his neck and ground my body against his.

He let out a whispered groan and stilled me. "Please, Emily."

"If we're about to die, I'd like to go out wrapped around you," I whispered back.

"We're not ab-"

The door to the safe clicked open, and the light turned on above our heads. I blinked to adjust and cut my scream off at my throat.

"FUCKING HELL!" Devon swore loudly.

Sterling and Milo stood outside the safe looking dreadfully angry. Relief so palpable I swore I could hold it in my hands filled the safe.

"What are you two doing?" Sterling snapped at us.

"Contributing," I retorted as my heart stuttered on its way back to a normal rate.

"I almost *shot* you!" Devon scolded.

"Thank you for *not* doing that," Milo drawled.

"Why didn't you tell us you were robbing Anthony?" Sterling asked.

"I didn't want all of us to draw attention," Devon explained.

"So, you took *Emily*?" Milo asked and wrinkled his nose.

"Hey!" I shouted, offended.

"I just meant you're inexperienced," Milo defended.

"She forced my hand," Devon grumbled.

"How'd you know where we were?" I asked, changing the subject.

"Oh, my god," Milo groaned and scrubbed a hand over his face. "If it was complex tech that caught you, then I wouldn't care. But it was the same Air Tags that saved our lives a couple of months ago. I have them set to notify me if any of you leave the house. It's just embarrassing at this point. I'm embarrassed."

"It doesn't matter," Devon interjected. "We have cash and gold now. We have more options to plan with. Let's get home."

"Can we stop for Taco Bell on the way? Pass me some of that cash. Running after your dumb asses got me hungry for some fourth meal," Sterling said, slinging an arm over my shoulder as we headed for the stairs.

Devon made a sound of disapproval behind us as he closed the safe. Milo flicked on his phone flashlight, keeping the light towards the floor so as not to attract attention through the windows. I looked back to make sure Devon was behind us and locked eyes with him in the dim light. His expression was hard to read in the darkness, but I thought it looked regretful and maybe a little sad. I gave him a small smile because despite my embarrassment from his rejection earlier, we had succeeded in our mission.

The exit from the house was considerably less stressful. We had a duffle bag of cash and gold bars, and I had my three grumpy men beside me.

23

✧

Milo

A late morning saw us sitting in the office with a box of donuts and coffees. As an apology for going behind our backs, Devon had gotten us breakfast from a place that sold seven-dollar donuts and ten-dollar coffees as if it wasn't made with the same ingredients as Dunkin' Donuts. I understood and respected his gesture, though. However ridiculous it was that he thought I'd forgive him over food.

Sterling sat across the room chewing a chocolate donut with a peanut butter frosting and a coco pebbles sprinkle with his eyes closed and a smile on his lips. He sighed and moaned and sipped the coffee. Okay, *some* people can forgive atrocities and betrayals over expensive carbohydrates and caffeine.

Emily was happily sniffing markers in front of the big white paper pad she had smoothed out and propped on a chair. I wondered if she missed being a teacher and felt a pang of sadness in my chest. I rubbed it and took a sip of my own hot coffee, hoping to replace the stab of sadness with the warmth of boutique light roasted Hawaiian peaberry coffee. Fuck, it was excellent coffee.

"Alright, let's get started," Devon said and brushed invisible crumbs from his shirt.

"The last time we had a planning meeting-" Emily started and flipped back a page to Devon's written options from a few days ago.

"I came so hard at the table I had to throw away a pair of pants," Sterling interrupted.

"Yes, I remember," Emily said and looked at Sterling with hooded, lustful eyes.

Devon huffed in annoyance. "New house rule: no orgasms while we're discussing business."

"Sure thing, *boss*," Sterling challenged.

"Anyway, the last time we had a meeting, we had these four options," Emily said and gestured to the paper. "One: get more money and buy out gangs to take over. Two: Kill Anthony to take over or leave. Three: Leave. Get out of family business."

Sterling interrupted her to sing the JoJo song loudly and off tune, "Leave. Get Out. It's the end of you and me."

"Sterling, I am talking, and you have interrupted me twice. If there is a third interruption, I'll have to ask you to sit in the hall," Emily said in her Teacher Voice.

Devon smirked at her proudly. I sipped my delicious coffee to hide my smile. Sterling adjusted his cock in his pants. "Fuck, Devon. Why did you make that new rule?"

"Option four was to figure out what he's doing with the

politicians and Gregory," Emily continued. A frown etched into her features as she looked at the paper. "Did we do any of it?"

"No, we've been distracted. That meeting was barely three days ago, and we were shot at in the street, had a major attack at our home, and stole gold. Well, technically, it's the first step for option one," Devon reasoned.

"But our plan was to go with option four, right?" Emily asked and cocked her head to the side.

"Before we could come up with a plan, we were rudely interrupted by a-" Devon started.

"A butt nut. An Ass Blast," Sterling interrupted.

"Sterling, that's three interruptions. Please stand in the hall," Emily said coolly and turned away from us to flip the page to a clean one. I saw her biting her lip to hold in a laugh in the reflection on a glass picture frame.

Devon and I exchanged amused glances while Sterling grabbed another donut and his coffee and sat in the hallway. He could still see and hear the meeting and would likely never stop interrupting.

"Okay, I think we need to start over with our planning now that things have changed," Emily said and wrote "Option One" on the board.

"Option one," I said, eager to be a good student. "Kill Anthony."

She wrote it down.

"Option two," she said as she wrote. "Turn in Anthony to the authorities."

"Remember, we'd be implicated in many of his crimes," Devon said.

"Right," she said and drew a squiggly line through that option.

"I could use some jail time, though," Sterling said with a dramatic yawn from the hall. "Three hots, a cot, and a whole lotta cock sounds great after the week we've had."

"Sterling!" Emily scolded with a laugh. I chuckled and even Devon laughed with us.

"What? It's been fucking insane!" Sterling defended his statement with a laugh of his own.

"Option three: force him to give us control," Devon said loudly to get us back on track.

Emily wrote it down.

"Option four: buy his gang allegiances and take over?" Emily asked. "Is that different from option three?"

"Yeah, because three could be done with violence and four is just business," Devon replied.

"So, what are we thinking?" Emily asked after finishing writing on the paper. "Our options have been similar this entire time. We've not made a whole lot of progress."

"Option one. Anthony needs to pay for what he's done to our families and what he continues to do to us," I grumbled.

Emily put a star next to option one.

"Ditto. And then we get the hell out of here," Sterling said from the hall.

Emily glanced at Devon before adding another star next to option one.

Devon leaned back in his chair and stared at the ceiling. "I'm having difficulty... accepting the idea of killing my father."

I nodded. I understood his reaction. Really, I did logically understand killing his father would be difficult for him. But it didn't have to be Devon. I could do it easily. Sterling could do it. Hell, I'm pretty sure Emily would do it.

"That means you're at, what, option four? Taking control?" Emily asked.

"Yeah, four. No violence. But I'd agree to option three, with violence, if necessary," Devon said and shifted in his seat. Emily marked a star next to four.

I rolled my eyes, and he saw.

"Milo, I'm not entirely counting it out. I need to know I've given him the chance," Devon said, his voice quiet and almost begging.

"I understand, Devon. I get it. It's hard for me to think someone that has taken so much from me and continues to take from me is out there. Alive and well," I replied, maintaining eye contact.

"Let's give that a try," Sterling said with an exhale. "Let him beg like a bitch for mercy, though."

Devon smirked. "I expect nothing less."

"How do we do this?" Emily asked and flipped the page. "How do we get to him to take control?"

"We use the money and the gold to buy some gang allegiances. Ask them to get us information about where he's living and working," Devon explained.

"Do we just go up to a gang leader and hand them cash?" Emily asked and looked confusedly at us.

"We know where the gangs hide out. They likely haven't changed their entire operations just because Anthony said not to talk to us. They were all established before we came along and wormed our way in," Sterling said. "We find some gang members and ask for a meeting."

"That's the easiest part of the plan. It's like fishing in a stocked pond," I said and drained the last of my coffee.

"Tonight?" Emily asked.

Devon nodded. "I can have the gold converted to cash tonight. I already know some buyers."

"Tonight, it is then," Emily said and capped the marker she was holding.

Later, we piled into Devon's SUV and headed towards one of the gang's headquarters. We'd chosen to seek out members of the River Blades. They were a high production gang out of the Flats. They dealt with pretty much everything we had within the business. Drugs, guns, protection, and some laundering. They'd never given us issues with inventory or earnings and had always shown an ability to get shit done. Finding a few of their members was, like I'd said, the easiest part of the plan. They even greeted us when we pulled up.

"You guys busy? Or could you come for a few drinks with us down the road?" Devon said with a friendly smirk at the two of them from the driver's side window.

David, one member, looked down the road. "It's been real slow tonight. I've already seen the regulars I'd expected." He shrugged at the other man, who I only knew as "Knuckles." Knuckles shrugged back and they approached the car.

"We can meet you at the bar on the corner," David said and pointed after slapping hands with Sterling in the passenger's seat across Devon.

We'd kept the windows up in the back with me and Emily

since there was a hit out for us. I rolled my side down. "Will it be a problem for you if we're here?"

David and Knuckles ducked their heads to look in the car. Recognition and understanding lit their eyes. "Not a problem at all."

I felt Emily relax some of her tension next to me. I stroked her knee soothingly. Devon drove us to park outside the hole in the wall bar. While the Flats was where a lot of Cleveland's nightlife was located, this was off the beaten path.

Inside the bar, the four of us doubled the occupancy. We slid into a long, sticky table while Sterling ordered us beers. David and Knuckles came in and greeted the old bartender by his first name. Devon and I kept Emily between us, using our shoulders to keep her mostly hidden in case David and Knuckles decided the bounty was worth it.

"So, this is the famous woman who corrupted the minds of the mafia's leaders," David said with a mischievous grin as Sterling set down beers for each of us.

"They were corrupted when I found them," Emily giggled.

"You know that's not what Anthony says," David said and gestured with his beer bottle.

"Anthony killed our parents, killed Matthew right in front of us, and has tried to have us killed multiple times," I informed him.

"I know. It's fucked up," David said with a respectful nod. Knuckles raised his glass.

"I'm not going to ask where he is until I pay you and meet with your leader," Devon said. "I understand there's money involved, and I'm prepared to negotiate."

"Good," David said and drained his beer. "Because that son of a bitch has us doing some dirty shit."

Knuckles pulled out his phone and typed out a text. "I've called in Randy." I almost jumped when he spoke for the first time.

Randy was the leader of the River Blades had been at the meeting we'd held. He'd denied us then, but now we were ready to pay him and his people.

We had a few more beers until Randy showed up. It didn't take him long to get there. He looked tired and nervous. Something I'd never seen of him before. He sat in a chair at the end of the table, and we ordered him a beer. "You boys do not know the grief that devil of a man has caused me."

"Randy, we understand it's been difficult. It's been hard for us as well. We've been attacked nearly every day and have no support in the streets," Devon said.

"No, you've got that twisted. You've got support in the streets. We just can't say a single thing on it," Randy said and scrubbed a hand over his face. His eye caught on the bartender, who was pretending not to listen to our conversation. His other patrons had left soon after we'd arrived, leaving only us and him. "Hey, you been paid to keep your mouth shut?"

The bartender shook his head despite having been five hundred dollars richer after Sterling had slipped him money. Devon slid more cash over to the bartender and he waved sheepishly before going into a back room.

"What does he have you doing?" I asked. "He doesn't have you ambushing us in our home, does he?"

Randy looked at me for a long moment. "No offense, Milo, but I've got mouths to feed and men to pay."

"I'm ready to give you twenty grand right now to work with us," Devon said and dipped his chin down in a mock bow to Randy.

Randy sat back in his seat and crossed his arms. "He's got me tied up with blackmail. It's not only me, either. He's got something big over Prospect Kings and East Side Warriors. I heard he's got men's family members locked away and everything."

"Can you tell us what he has you doing?" Sterling asked as he twirled his empty beer bottle in the condensation on the sticky table.

"He's got us setting up... pipelines, for lack of a better word, for human trafficking, man. It's sick," Randy said and looked over at Emily. "He's got politicians in on it and everything."

I'd had my suspicions he was setting this up again. The signs had been there ever since Giovanni and Taz were killed and that deal fell through. But Anthony had always said he'd never deal in skin. We didn't even allow our gangs to run prostitution rings. They offered protection to the girls and often worked side by side with them, but never had our family business worked in the sex industry. The business had been bleeding money for a few years, prompting Anthony and Matthew to consider the merger with Giovanni and Taz. That I could wrap my head around logically. But after Giovanni and Taz were killed, I expected Anthony to drop the idea.

"Is he blackmailing them, too?" Emily asked. Her voice sounded like her throat was dry despite her empty beer before her.

"Some of them. Others it's money and others it's threats," Randy said. "I don't know the details of who each of them are, but I know they're politicians and police and shit. Listen, I have daughters. We can't have any more of that shit in our city. It's bad enough as it is. I would do this work for free if I didn't have to pay my guys."

"I'll pay you, but I'll need you to play double agent for a little while," Devon said. "We have no intention of picking up where Anthony left off and taking over trafficking. We're only trying to stop him."

"I get it. He's been after your asses, too," Randy said and gestured to me and Emily.

"Do you know where he's living and working?" I asked.

"No, we've only met at our headquarters or a random business in town," Randy said with the shake of his head.

"Do you think you can get me that information?" I continued.

"It might take me a bit to do it without seeming suspicious," Randy said. "But you have us."

"Thank you, Randy. You too, David and Knuckles," Devon said and gestured to Emily.

She happily pulled her purse from her lap and slid it over the table to Devon. Devon pulled out the money he'd promised Randy and put it on the table before him. We shook hands and exchanged small talk before heading out to Devon's car.

As soon as the doors were shut and we were encased in the silence of Devon's car, Emily spoke up. "He's back on the human trafficking bullshit?"

"He's got to go," Sterling said.

Devon nodded before letting his head fall back against his seat. "It's looking more and more like that's the direction we're heading."

2 4

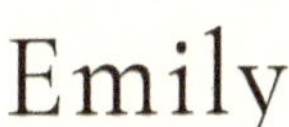

Emily

Devon and Sterling went to meet with another gang while Milo and I stayed home. It had been about a week since we'd met with Randy, David, and Knuckles. Randy checked in with Devon a few times with no news, but to reassure Devon that they were still working for us. The gang Devon and Sterling were meeting with today was known for their violence, so Devon had felt it best that we didn't taunt them with the bounty that was on Milo and me. Instead, I paced while Milo typed on his laptop. He had a furrow in his brow, and I stopped to smooth it with my fingers. He smirked but kept his eyes on his screen.

"I'm so anxious. Distract me," I said and flopped down next to him on the couch.

"You can watch a movie," Milo muttered.

"I don't want to," I pouted.

Milo looked at me like he was annoyed for a moment before

it visibly occurred to him I meant for us to fool around. "Let me finish this line of code before I forget my place," he said and typed faster than I'd thought to be humanly possible.

I stood in front of him and unzipped my hooded sweatshirt. Underneath I was wearing an emerald green lacy bralette. "Are you done yet?" I asked him.

He huffed a laugh but kept typing.

Pushed my leggings down and revealed matching lace panties.

"Fucking hell," he mumbled and threw his laptop on the couch next to him.

I giggled and climbed onto his lap. I kissed him slowly, savoring his soft sighs and roaming hands. We stayed there, touching and kissing for a deliciously long time. He'd been hard beneath my hips for a long time, but neither of us made a move to go further. It felt good to make out on the couch for a while, but I grew needy and frustrated.

"Touch me," I sighed into the kiss and directed his hand to my lace covered pussy.

When his fingers grazed over me, over the soaked lace, we both sucked in a hiss. "Oh, wow," he crooned. "Is this all for me?"

"For you," I replied. I closed my eyes and moaned as he ran his fingertips over me again.

He brought his hand up to his mouth and licked his fingers. He moaned before returning his hand to my pussy.

"Please," I begged, as he ran his fingers lightly over my drenched panties again. I gave a shiver of anticipation.

He chuckled and slid his fingers under the lace, skating

around where I needed him most. I growled in frustration. "Milo, fucking touch me or I'm going to scream."

Milo barked out a laugh, his head tipped back on the couch. I desperately tried to ride his hand, but he kept pulling away. Not feeling like I wanted to be teased anymore, I gripped his hair and pulled him down on the couch. He winced at the pain of the tug but adjusted so he was lying on his back on the couch. He smirked up at me before his face became a seat. I straddled his shoulders and plopped down. My knees bumped into his glasses, and I removed them.

I felt him laugh against my skin before his tongue laved me from opening to clit. He licked and sucked until I was trembling and coming. I heard him curse and his voice vibrated against my skin. "More," I demanded through grit teeth. "Again."

His hand joined his tongue, and he speared two fingers inside me. I was just about to come again when I heard a buzz on Milo's phone. It wasn't an alarm, so I wasn't worried. I ignored it and continued to rock on Milo's face. My second orgasm was just about to pour over me when Devon and Sterling entered the room.

I stopped riding Milo's face with a gasp. Sterling grinned widely and rushed to us, clothes and shoes dropping to the ground. I was beyond happy to see them alive and back in one piece. Wait, was Devon staying? I greeted Sterling with a kiss and looked to find Devon leaning against the wall. Exactly in the space where I'd seen him get a blow job from a random blonde on New Year's Eve. He crossed his arms over his chest, and he watched with a furrowed brow.

"Let him fucking watch," Sterling breathed in my ear. "But

if he walks over here, are you okay with it?" I nodded up at Sterling and his face split into a grin. "That's my girl."

Milo resumed his work on my pussy and my second orgasm climbed quickly, returning to the height it was at moments before. Sterling kissed me and gripped my neck tight. I saw stars as I came, groaning loud and long.

Sterling picked me up from Milo's face and shoved me to my knees on the ground to suck his cock. I took him into my mouth, still shivering with aftershocks from my climax. He thrust into my mouth hard and fast. My eyes streamed, and I gagged on the intrusion. His piercing clacked against my teeth, and I tugged it with my tongue.

I heard a movement behind me, and Milo's clothes dropped to the floor. "Fuck," Sterling swore. "I want it to be my turn, Milo. While I'm in her."

"Okay, we need to go upstairs. I don't have lube down here," Milo said. I didn't know what they'd meant, but Milo's tone was excited.

"You coming along, freak?" Sterling asked Devon.

Devon only glared at him in response.

Sterling laughed and picked me up and slung me over his shoulder. It was exactly the same way he'd carried me when they had drugged me and kidnapped me all those months ago. This time I spanked and pinched him on his bare ass while he carried me up the stairs.

In Sterling's room, he threw me down on the bed. He strode to his dresser where his box of toys rested. Milo sat on the bed next to me with a grin. Devon entered the room and sat on the floor near the door, his back against the wall.

His legs stretched out in front of him. He watched pensively and silently.

"While you were sleeping after the attack, Sterling took my other virginity," Milo said with a smile.

"Oh, Milo!" I gasped happily. "I thought something had changed between you two!"

Milo smiled and his eyes settled on Sterling's back as he rustled through his black box. "It was better than I'd thought it would be."

"I want to watch sometime," I said and kissed Milo's shoulder.

"Well, Sterling just asked me to fuck him while he's in you," Milo clarified their earlier exchange.

"Holy shit," I whispered as a new flood of arousal slicked between my thighs.

"I haven't fucked him yet, so we'll have to go slow," Milo informed me.

Sterling chose that moment to turn around, holding what looked like a bundle of leather straps. His face was dark, and his eyes flamed with desire as he looked at me and Milo. "Emily, sit in the middle of the bed."

I obeyed instantly, watching him approach me. He tapped my thighs until I opened up for him. I watched his hard, pierced cock jump as he looked at me. "These need to come off," he said and ripped my lace panties right off me. My skin burned where the lace had cut into my skin before tearing away. More gently, he unclasped my bra and slid it down my arms. I watched with a dry mouth as he wrapped the leather around my left thigh and fastened it like a belt. The leather was slightly padded and felt soft. He wrapped the long strap around the back of my shoulders and down to my right thigh where the end looped around and fastened like a belt there, too. My breathing kicked up when I realized I couldn't put my legs down. He shortened the sides before they reached behind my shoulders so that I was curled up and even more open. I could lay flat on my back, but my legs were curled up in front of me. It would have been humiliating if I were with anyone other than these two men.

Suddenly, I remembered Devon was in the room. My head snapped over to see him still sitting near the door. He sat with one knee bent and one leg extended on the floor. His posture looked relaxed, but his expression revealed the opposite of relaxed. He looked like he was not enjoying being there. His brow was furrowed, his glaring eyes focused on where Sterling was gently caressing my pussy.

"I love watching you get wetter and wetter," Sterling said. His voice was gruff and deep and sent jolts of arousal to my core. "Your body knows what it needs to take me. It was made to be fucked like this by me. Absolutely beautiful."

"Bend over," Milo said from behind Sterling. I hadn't noticed him get up, but he was holding a new bottle of lube and looking feral. His glasses had been lost downstairs, and he was naked with messy hair and a wild expression.

Sterling positioned himself over me, his cock sliding against my open, wet pussy. He groaned and slid up and down in the wetness for a moment before he kissed me and entered me. I moaned deep in my throat as he kissed me. He reached so deep inside me I felt him painfully knock into my cervix. I hissed, and he reached up to grab a pillow. He pulled out of me and lifted me up to slide the pillow under my ass. When he entered me again, it was at a different angle that put more pressure on my g spot.

I gasped at the sensation just as Sterling gulped and swore.

"That's good. Just keep fucking her," Milo said over Sterling's shoulder.

Sterling shuddered and sighed, his eyes fluttering closed. I grinned up at him as his face and neck flushed with pleasure under his tattoos. His hips stilled with an intrusion. I looked down to see Milo's knees behind Sterling's and a flash of his hand as he moved.

"I could blow just like this," Sterling said, still not moving.

I giggled and rolled my hips. He groaned and opened his gray eyes. They were almost entirely blown black with his arousal.

Sterling slowly thrust into me a few times while Milo prepared him. His cock pulsed inside me like he was coming, but I didn't feel the warmth of come. He didn't pull out of me throughout Milo's ministrations, and his body sagged slightly under the weight of his pleasure.

"I think you're ready for me," Milo said in a hoarse whisper.

Anyone being ready to take Milo's length in their ass was likely impossible. I tensed as I watched the lube being practically poured all over the sheets as Milo covered himself. Sterling hissed in a breath and his eyes screwed shut as Milo pressed into him. I knew he was pushing because Sterling's body rocked forward over mine.

Sterling breathed in shattered gasps and sharp exhales after holding his breath as Milo pushed into him. Milo was breathing slowly. His exhales were a softly growled "Ah" sound. The sound of their combined breathing was erotic music to me, and I felt like I could have come just from the sound.

The muscles in my pussy fluttered around Sterling, and his lips tipped up slightly in a smile. "She likes this, Milo. She's so fucking wet for us."

Milo gave a strained, choked chuckle before peering down at me over Sterling's shoulder. His face loosened in an expression of pleasure, and he looked down at where they were connected. "Fuck, I'm all the way in. Breathe for a minute. Adjust to me."

Sterling did as he was told, his arms shaking on either side of me. I kissed one of his tattooed forearms where the veins bulged under his skin. With my head turned, I caught sight of Devon. He had a hand down the front of his unfastened jeans and his jaw was slack as he watched us. If it was possible, I was sure I was even wetter.

"Wait, shit. This angle has you pressing that spot and I'm-oh, fuck!" Sterling said and his cock pulsed with his orgasm inside me. I felt the heat of his pleasure within me and felt the space where our bodies met grow wet.

Unable to help himself, he rocked his body into mine and back into Milo's. My arousal at the sight of them together had kept me at the top of an orgasm and the clumsy, stuttered thrusts had me tumbling over the edge.

"Fucking hell," Sterling growled, the corded muscles of his neck stood out in the shadows of the room. "I've never- oh. My. God."

Milo chuckled breathlessly, and I realized Sterling's thrusts were actually Milo's because he picked up the pace. Sterling gave a moan that had his voice cracking. I felt more warmth bloom in my core and I wondered if he'd come again.

Sterling was sweating. It dripped from his forehead, down his chest, and into the patch of hair below his belly button. Our skin slid smoothly, responding to Milo's thrusts. Sterling slid a hand between us and gathered our combined come on his fingertips, trailing it over my body and up to my mouth.

"Open. Suck," Sterling demanded.

I obeyed and the salty taste of us invaded my mouth as he shoved his fingers over my tongue and to my throat. I gagged once, but he kept a hold on my mouth. He quietly praised my throat and my mouth. I saw him glance at Devon, and I wondered what he had been trying to accomplish. Was he trying to get Devon to join and take my mouth? Saliva pooled at the thought.

"It's like I'm fucking both of you," Milo grunted.

"No kidding," Sterling exhaled.

I looked over to Devon and witnessed him tip his head back against the wall and his chest rise and fall quickly. His eyes locked on mine and a fire roared there. Despite the physical connection with the men above me, I also felt connected to him. I held up three fingers to say that I felt like I was fucking all three of them. Sterling kissed my fingertips and looked at Devon. With most of Sterling's fingers in my mouth while watching Devon, I shattered. Devon's eyes never left mine as his breathing hitched and a visible wet patch bloomed on the front of his jeans.

Another explosion of warmth in my core. But the clenching of my own muscles during my orgasm had me pushing some of his come out. Everything felt wet, and the sound was beyond vulgar. Milo gave a shout and thrusted deep and hard. Sterling winced only slightly in the glow of his pleasure as he removed his hand from my mouth to hold himself upright.

Milo collapsed onto Sterling's back. Sterling was typically strong enough to hold Milo's weight with no issue, but now his arms shook with effort. Milo sat up and pulled out of Sterling with a curse. When Milo was laying down next to me, he kissed me deeply and breathlessly.

"I feel like I can come again," Sterling whispered. He leaned back and unbuckled the cuffs around my thighs. My body uncurled with a few pops of my spine and hips. "Ride me. Let me see it all pour out of you."

He rolled us over and I got on top with shaking legs. His cock brushed against my g spot and as I rocked on him, my clit sent zaps of pleasure through me. He groaned as my core clenched. He lifted me by my hips until his cock was out of me and he watched as come dripped from me. "Baby, that's so hot," he rasped.

"It's all yours," I whispered.

"What about this pussy? Does it belong to me, too?" he asked.

"It belongs to all of you," I said without thinking.

Milo grinned sleepily and slid a hand between us, his thumb rubbing circles on my clit.

"I'm so close. Baby, I'm going to need you to come on my cock," Sterling groaned. "Milo, do you see this? Is it not the most beautiful thing you've ever seen? Watch my come just pour out of her." He pulled out of me again and I felt the rush of liquid.

"If I wasn't paralyzed, I would be hard again," Milo said and kissed Sterling's sweaty shoulder.

"Let me ride," I whined.

Sterling swore and took his hands from my hips. He ran his hands through his sweaty black hair as I rode him hard and fast. His hair stuck up at all angles. I ignored the burn of my muscles and bounced on him until I saw stars again. I propped my hands against his thighs behind me as I writhed and came. Sterling's torso curled up like he was doing a crunch as he came. His abs contracted and released over and over as he came and came inside me. Milo helped me lift off Sterling, and I opened my eyes. I must have blacked out because I opened my eyes to see Devon bent over and watching come drip from my pussy. Milo, my back to his front, held me up. He wrapped one of his arms around my ribs and the other hand was spreading my pussy open for Devon's inspection.

Seeing Devon watch the come drip from me had my core giving a small fluttering clench. More dripped from me, and Devon stood to his full height. His expression was unreadable and dark. He was almost glaring at me. He gripped my face in his hand. "You're a fucking come slut," he growled. "You *love* dripping with come, don't you."

I blinked my agreement up at him. His lip curled in a snarl as he shoved away from me. He put his hand down his opened, wet jeans. He was quick to shove his wet fingers into my eager mouth. I was too weak to speak to tell him how badly I wanted him. How much I wished he'd been in my mouth earlier. Instead, I sucked hard on his come covered fingers and moaned enthusiastically. I swirled my tongue over his salty fingers and watched his eyes flutter. "You like that, don't you?" he snarled and pulled his fingers free with a wet pop.

"Yes," I breathed.

Devon stared at me for a moment before spinning and leaving the room. He closed the door behind him, and the room felt stiflingly quiet. My body deflated in Milo's arms, and he helped me nestle between him and Sterling.

"Am I alive?" Sterling muttered next to me.

Milo reached over me to pinch Sterling's nipple. He yelped.

"Yup, still alive," Milo answered with a yawn.

"Bambi, you've been taking your birth control, right?" Sterling asked.

"Yeah," I replied. "I've been on the pill before. I know how it works."

"Good, because if you weren't, there'd be no way you wouldn't be pregnant after all that," Sterling said and lazily traced invisible patterns on my arm.

"There's no sperm in prostate ejaculate," Milo muttered, mostly asleep.

"No kidding," Sterling said, sounding impressed.

"Is that why there was so much?" I asked. "Because you were coming with your butt?"

We all giggled at my words. Living with men will do that to a girl.

"Yeah, even Milo can soak the sheets," Sterling said.

"There's going to be so much laundry in this house," I sighed.

"Speaking of laundry, do you think Devon's going to keep those jeans?" Sterling asked.

We devolved into laughter, making two-thirds of us leak

come. A long, hot shower was a desperate need. And a new set of sheets.

25

Emily

Over a lunch of leftover Chinese takeout, Devon got a phone call. It had been two weeks since Sterling and Devon had gotten a second gang to work with us. It had cost almost all the money from the gold and stolen cash to get two gangs on our side, but it was worth it.

Devon held his phone with his chin and shoulder as he wrote on a napkin. "You saw him go in? They came out, but he stayed?" Devon turned the napkin towards Milo.

Milo immediately grabbed his laptop from the island and brought it to the dining table. He opened it and began typing. Sterling and I watched and listened. Sterling cracked his knuckles while he watched Devon intently.

"Thank you, Randy. I'll let you know if we need backup," Devon said. "Let me know when the girls are on spring break. I'll send over some stylists, and they can have princess makeovers."

I smiled as Devon used his leadership skills and charisma to maintain his relationship with Randy. Sterling and Milo were impatient for information and gestured for him to hurry. Devon rolled his eyes at them and turned away as he finished his call with some small talk.

"Anthony's been living in an apartment on the East side," Devon said after he hung up. "Randy saw him go in last night with a couple of guys. They came out, but Anthony didn't until this morning."

"The apartment is leased to a name I don't recognize. Do you know it?" Milo asked and turned his laptop.

"No, I bet it's a new gang member we don't know," Devon said and waved it off.

"Probably, but I'm going to look into it," Milo said, and typed furiously fast on his laptop.

"Can you get surveillance on the building?" Devon asked.

"Might be tricky. That's not an area with a lot of cameras," Milo muttered as he worked.

"Could we get one of Randy's guys to set up a camera outside?" Sterling asked.

"Yeah, right," I joked. "As if Milo would trust anyone with his expensive equipment."

Milo smirked but didn't look at me. "I don't use very expensive equipment outside this home. Stuff gets destroyed too often."

"I bet it's complicated to set up still," I shrugged.

"Well, actually I use-" Milo started.

"What a cause for celebration!" Sterling was so loud next to me, I jumped. "Oh, happy day!" He jumped up and reached out to shake my hand. He shook my entire arm in an exagger-ated handshake.

"Welcome to the family, Emily," Devon said and gave me the same overly enthusiastic handshake across the table. A wide grin was on his lips and a teasing expression in his eyes.

"What a joy it is!" Sterling said in the same loud, expressive voice. He shook my hand again and my shoulder almost ached with it.

I looked at Milo, who was red in the face above his beard and his lips were pursed. He shook his head and kept his eyes on his computer.

"What?" I asked with an awkward laugh.

"You got Well, Actually-ed by Milo. You're officially one of us," Sterling explained in his normal tone of voice.

I giggled and squeezed Milo's knee under the table. "Mansplained?" I asked.

"Milo-splained. We are all subject to it," Devon said.

"Shut the hell up," Milo groaned.

"No, I love it," I said and squeezed his leg again. "I love that he's smart and wants to educate us."

"Only a teacher would say that," Sterling laughed. "It drives us non-teachers crazy."

"Milo can educate me any day," I said and winked at him.

"Let's get back on track," Devon said and sat back down at the table and took a huge bite of orange chicken. "Milo, can you set up some sort of surveillance by tonight?"

"Yes," Milo grumbled.

"Sterling, I have an ammo order waiting for pickup," Devon directed. "Emily. Can you please do some laundry? I've not worn underwear in a week."

"Sick," Sterling said with a disgusted look.

"Why do I have to do the laundry?" I asked and folded my arms over my chest. It irritated me I was being reduced to someone who cleaned for them again. Hadn't I proven my worth?

"Because they're busy and I've been doing it for months," Devon shot back.

"If you've been doing it for months, why do you not have any underwear?" I spat back.

"I can't keep up with it. Can you please at least wash us some outfits for tonight? With underwear?" Devon asked, his voice softer since he knew he had to ask nicely.

"Is there any other job I can do? Like help pack up the weapons in the car?" I asked.

"Emily, I'm not insulting you by giving you this task," Devon insisted. "I know you've been on this kick of boycotting all household tasks to prove you're one of the guys. But this isn't an insult. It's a task that needs to be done if we're planning a confrontation or attack."

I sighed and sat back in my seat, not looking at Devon. I didn't like his tone.

"You can pout all you want. But please, the laundry," Devon said quietly.

Milo cleared his throat. "Emily, I also have not had clean underwear for a while."

I rolled my eyes and got up from the table, my chair scraping on the admittedly dirty floor. "Leave what you want washed on the floor outside your door."

Devon's phone rang again a few hours later. I was in the basement, grumpily doing laundry, when I heard it ring in the office. Leaving my task, I hurried upstairs to listen.

"What time?" Devon was asking the person on the phone. Devon's wide eyes shot to me as I entered the room. "You're fucking kidding! Okay. No, we'll go in alone. But can you have a few guys around in case it gets ugly? I don't want anyone of your guys getting involved unless it's an emergency."

He was silent as he listened and gestured for me to sit in a chair. I leaned on the desk next to him instead. I looked at the new address he'd written. It had to be close to the warehouse we'd used when we met with all the gang leaders.

"Right now? What channel?" Devon asked, sounding startled. He rummaged around him, opening drawers and closing them. He was moving quickly and didn't tell me what he was looking for. I was about to move so he could get to the drawers behind me, but he pulled me onto his lap faster than I could move. I landed clumsily, and the chair creaked beneath us. "Do you think it's a move of Anthony's or unrelated? No, I know, I'm just getting your views on it."

Devon located a remote control and pressed the power button. The dusty TV on the wall blinked on and he quickly pressed buttons to get to a local news station. My heart caught in my chest like needles had pierced it through. My parents and Gregory were on the news. A picture of me, taken in my classroom, wearing my Mrs. Frizzle Halloween costume, was displayed in the corner.

"Thank you again, Randy. I'll talk to you soon," Devon said as my shaking hands wrestled with him to take the remote and turn up the volume.

Devon hung up and turned it up so I could hear my mom's pleading, tearful voice. "-would never disappear without telling us where she went. We know she was taken, and we might know who. I plead with you to send my baby home."

My skin crawled with discomfort. Seeing my mom so upset had two drastically different emotions rising within me. Disgust that it took close to sixteen weeks for her to feel grief after she had shown me so little respect and care before I'd left. And a painful longing to make her the smiling, soft-spoken woman I'd known my whole life again.

She stepped away from the microphone and into my father's embrace. Gregory rubbed her shoulder and nodded solemnly to my dad before he stepped up to the podium.

"We've received information about my wife's disappearance that point to her being kidnapped. The individuals named are no strangers to law enforcement in the area, so I know they will be found. I have full confidence my wife will be returned to our family safe and sound. Her students have shared with me artwork and cards depicting their hopes that their beloved teacher comes home safe," Gregory said with his perfect public speaking voice. He held up a child's drawing depicting a brown-haired stick figure standing on the circular carpet we used for story time and holding what was likely a book.

I choked on my breath, fighting down an angry sob.

Gregory stepped back from the podium and an aged cop took his place, looking severe. "In the case of Emily Ambrose, we have named Sterling Hawthorne and Milo Holden as prime suspects in her disappearance. She was last seen with both men getting into a van in Cleveland. We presume these suspects are armed and highly dangerous." Side by side pictures of Sterling and Milo were displayed next to mine. Theirs looked like old mugshots. These had to be at least ten-year-old pictures. "If they are seen, we encourage you to call 911 and not to engage with them. Please call this our tip line if you see them. A reward of two hundred thousand dollars has been arranged for Mrs. Ambrose's return. Thank you."

The news station moved to a weather report, and Devon turned the TV off. I was frozen. The rage within my body had melted and re-solidified my bones into lava rock. My blood felt fizzy as it rushed through me.

"Hey," I heard Sterling's voice through Devon's phone right behind me. "I'm leaving the-"

"Get home now. Skip your other stops," Devon said, his voice quiet but demanding.

"What happened?" Sterling asked quickly. He sounded worried. "I'm fifteen minutes out. Is she okay? What happened?"

"Don't make any stops. Do you have a hat? Put it on. Glasses. Anything," Devon said.

"Milo has a spare in my car. Where's Milo?" Sterling asked, his voice harsh.

"I'm calling him next," Devon said. "Get home, don't look at anyone as you drive. Fast." Devon hung up.

I still hadn't moved. It wasn't until Devon massaged the back of my sweating neck that I came back into my body. I felt him move as he lifted his phone back up to his ear.

"Yeah," Milo grumbled as a greeting. It sounded like he put Devon on speaker phone and was a few feet from the device.

"Drop what you're doing. Get home now. Don't look at

anyone, don't talk to anyone. Try to avoid being seen. Wear a hat, sunglasses, whatever you can do," Devon demanded.

"Fuck. Why?" Something clattered to the ground on Milo's side and his voice got closer to the phone.

"Just get home. Now," Devon said before hanging up.

I took a gasping inhale and stood from Devon's lap. The air felt choking. Too heavy. I wanted to scream. My hands balled into fists, and I screamed through my teeth. "This is all his fault! *He* got himself into shady deals! *He* got me kidnapped to be used as fucking blackmail or- or bait, or collateral or *whatever*. It's *his* fault I left him to begin with! And my parents!" I choked on another sob and bent over, hands on my knees. "My parents sided with him! I could have been sleeping in my old childhood room, teaching my students, saving up for my own house. No! I had to be alone and desperate to leave."

"Emily," Devon said, and I whirled around to see him standing just behind me. His voice was soft, almost gentle, but still commanding.

"I wouldn't have been kidnapped a second time and held hostage, tortured, almost *fucking killed* if it weren't for them! Then shot at in the street, then attacked in my new home! Or- or have two bounties on my head! Devon, it's *all his fault*!" I was screaming. Hysterical even. Tears and snot were all over my face. "Oh, my god! Sterling and Milo are out there!"

I'd heard his phone calls. I knew what he was doing. But the gravity of Sterling and Milo being out there after their faces were displayed across the local news, as wanted criminals had hit me like a brick.

Devon gripped my biceps hard. "Emily!" He said my name louder, more insistently. His eyes were calculating and worried as he looked me over. He looked at me like I was a bomb and he had to cut the right wire to diffuse me. "Please," he begged.

A well of anger rose again. My parents knew I'd divorced Gregory. They knew what he'd done to me and yet they were up there with him as if he was their son. They had to know this was their fault, too. They were all pawns in Anthony's game, I realized with clarity. That's what Devon had said to Randy before they hung up. He'd asked Randy if he thought it was a "move of Anthony's."

I screamed my anger through my teeth again. This time it ended with a wrenching sob that took the rest of my breath from me. I couldn't get my chest to let go of the contracting sob, and I was sure I'd be turning blue.

"Emily," Devon growled and gripped me by my throat, tipping my head up like he was clearing my airway or making me look into his eyes. Maybe both. He twisted his hand into my hair at the back of my head and clenched. He spun me and walked me to lean against the mahogany desk. "Emily, breathe. Come on. It hurts, I know, baby."

My chest let go of its aching, contracting sob and I finally sucked in a wet breath. Devon shook me slightly. "Another." I obeyed. "Good girl."

He gripped my hair and held my throat until I'd taken five breaths. He let go of my hair and thumbed away my tears on one side before cradling my face. Devon swallowed as he looked over my face, his expression was unreadable. My heart still felt seized with anger and a deeply penetrating sadness, but that hot and steely rage had unclenched its fists. My hands fluttered up to his arms.

"I've got you," he murmured as my fingers curled into the fabric of his shirt.

I closed my eyes against the flow of tears.

"Uh-uh," he said and gave me another gentle shake. "Eyes on me."

I opened my eyes but could only make out the blurry shape of him. Blinking away the tears, I focused on being able to see his beautiful honey-colored eyes. He was watching me so intently. Like he was studying me. Like he was looking behind every wall in my soul to parts even I had never looked at too closely. I peered up at him, watching him watch me.

"There you are," he said in a soft whisper. Barely above a breath. His shoulders relaxed, but his hands never left me. He said it in a way that had me wondering if he meant my rage and sadness had loosened and I seemed myself again or something else.

Before I could answer, Sterling came running into the office. "What's going on?" I startled, but Devon didn't. He glanced at the clock on the wall behind the desk.

"Seven minutes? You said you were fifteen minutes out?" Devon said and slowly let go of me.

"Yeah, if I followed traffic laws," Sterling said and approached us, his eyes wary. "Why is our girl in a chokehold?"

"Sit down, let's wait for Milo," Devon said and gave me one nod before going behind the desk to the computer. "I'll find the footage while we wait. In the meantime, I believe Emily needs some- uh, gentle care."

He'd given Sterling a loaded look and Sterling pulled me to sit on his lap. "Why do you look like someone died and why do you need aftercare?" Sterling whispered to me.

I shook my head. I didn't know what to say without him seeing the press conference. Sterling ran his fingers through my hair, untangling what Devon had knotted. Both men were silent and tense other than Devon typing on the computer. Sterling kissed my shoulder and neck and I turned into him and cuddled on his chest. He wrapped his arms around me in a tight embrace. I breathed in his scent with my nose pressed into his tattooed neck. He smelled like soap, coffee, and a little of sweat. I closed my eyes and breathed, anxiously awaiting Milo's arrival.

"Okay, I'm here and my phone is blowing up. Please tell me before I read it," Milo droned as he entered the office. I hadn't heard him come into the house. Milo's eyes fell on me, curled up and likely tear stained in Sterling's lap, and then jumped to Devon at the computer. I reached out for his hand, thankful to see him. His hand was warm around mine as he squeezed me.

"Watch this and then I have more news," Devon said, and pressed play.

Sterling stood up from the chair and went to take my hand to pull me to watch the computer screen, but I let go. I shook my head and sat back down. I didn't need to see it again.

"What the fuck?" Sterling asked as he watched my ex-husband and parents take the stage.

I wanted to rage all over again, but I knew it was no use. My body felt exhausted from it. Devon watched me the whole time, his eyes calculating and concerned.

"'Highly dangerous?'" Sterling quoted as the video ended. "Nice."

"It's not funny, Sterling," I snapped.

He looked at me, shocked. "I know, Bambi. I only-"

"There's more," Devon interrupted. "Randy had called me just as that garbage was on the TV to let me know Anthony's having a meeting tonight with a few people. He gave me the location because Randy's guys are part of the security. Randy's going to pull his guys out as soon as we get there, but there will be guys from the Prospect Kings working security, too. He said Anthony has them shutting down the entire street."

"Where?" Milo asked.

"A warehouse a block from where we had the meeting with the leaders," Devon said.

"Too close," Sterling said.

"I know," Devon said and raised his brows.

"Are we going?" Milo asked. "Is today the day?"

Devon looked at me. His expression again unreadable as he studied me. I refused to turn away from his gaze. "Yes."

"Change of plans, then. Good thing I got most of our ammo," Sterling said with a clap of his hands.

"Emily, I'm sorry the press conference happened. I had no clue it was coming," Milo said, his eyes on me. He looked concerned for me but also confused why it was so upsetting. I didn't blame him for not understanding. I hadn't exactly spoken to them regarding my feelings about Gregory and my parents. It felt like talking about an ex to a current boyfriend. And while that was true, it also confronted my feelings about being kidnapped by them. I had changed my mind about living with these men, but my feelings about my initial kidnapping had not changed.

I shrugged and swallowed. "I'm not upset with you guys. It was just... weird seeing that." I glanced at Devon, who lifted his chin and pursed his lips like he realized I was hiding my breakdown from Sterling and Milo. "I'm going to go shower," murmuring, I left them to finalize the plan. All I knew was I was going with them no matter what. I wanted to be there when they confronted Anthony.

Stepping into a scorching hot shower, I reveled in the heat. I washed my hair, letting the water turn my skin a deep pink. The water was so hot it was forging. It forged my bones into iron and ate away at what was left of me.

I used to love lunch duty as a teacher. Most of my colleagues hated the rotation of duty, but I enjoyed it. My kindergarteners would eat their lunches while talking with their friends and swinging their little feet. They consumed meals packed with love or provided with care from the school. That consumption of love and care would leave behind art in the form of sandwich crusts, straw wrappers, crumbs, and jam covered notes from Mommy. They ate the good parts and left the bad parts to be cleaned up. Now, it felt like was happening to me. My anger and rage at the injustice and mistreatment in my life was eating away at the good parts of me and leaving all the bad.

I used to love lunch duty as a teacher, and now I was a killer.

26

Emily

The feeble warmth of the spring day had gone completely when we were gearing up to confront Anthony. Parked a street over from where the deranged mobster was, Milo monitored all the surveillance cameras he could access in the area. Since we'd had a meeting at a building a block from Anthony's building, Milo already knew where the access points were.

We waited in silence, watching our surroundings until we had word of Anthony's arrival. Devon got a text just as Milo said, "I see a car being allowed through the roadblock."

"It's Anthony," Devon said, checking for his text from Randy. "Once he's in the building, Randy's guys will leave. Give them a few minutes and then we have half of the security out."

My heart pounded hard in my chest with anticipation. This was it. Whatever came after this confrontation was a mystery. But I needed this one obstacle dealt with before I could even think about talking to my family or feeling secure in my new home. The van smelled like gun polish and laundry detergent, and I breathed deeply to steady myself.

"Wait, a second car," Milo said, just before Devon's phone vibrated.

"It's whoever he's meeting with. Randy didn't get a look at the car and the person who let them through wasn't one of his," Devon said. "We'll give them a few minutes to clear out."

We waited, practically holding our breath, for Randy's guys to get texts and slip out behind buildings and down alleys. Some of them were visible in the security footage, but not all. Some seemed to make excuses to the other gang members if they were close enough, and a few left without speaking to anyone.

"Wait," Milo muttered and showed me his tablet.

It was my car. License plate frame about being a teacher and everything. Well, it *was* my car before I had to hand the keys over to Gregory. My heart pounded in my throat now, rather than my chest, and I felt like I was about to be sick.

Gregory and Clara, the secretary he'd cheated on me with, stepped out of my car. My vision went white, and my ears rang like there'd been an explosion. It was like my brain short-circuited instead of feeling the level of rage and betrayal that was warranted. I felt nothing. I gripped the handle of a gun I wasn't meant to use. I was supposed to sit and wait in the van like a good little getaway driver. Instead, I pushed open the back doors of the van and slung the huge gun over my shoulder. I felt one guy reach for me and miss, and all three of them shouted my name as I hopped out of the van.

"Fucking hell, at least let me help you," Sterling swore as

he caught up to me. He gently tugged the gun out of my hand and got it ready. He loaded the gun and clicked off the safety for me like a parent loading a toddler's Nerf gun. "Safety's off. Don't shoot us."

"You can't be out here!" Devon hissed as he caught up to me. "Don't do this, Emily."

"Don't tell me what to do!" I ground out back at him, still walking.

"I'm the leader of this family, and you will listen to me," he snapped.

"No," I said back simply.

"Emily, you can't go storming in there- fuck," Devon said as someone shouted just ahead as he approached the street that the warehouse was on.

Sterling stepped in front of me and used his own gun to shoot the man who was shouting threats at us. The sound of the shot echoed around us in the alley and likely alerted everyone to our arrival.

Milo met up with us, slightly out of breath from running to catch up. He looked me over to make sure I was alright. I wasn't sure what he saw. "They're on the second floor. I saw them through a window going upstairs. Gregory and Clara are in with Anthony now and as far as I can see, there's been no more arrivals and Randy's people left. I have his people on standby in case we need backup."

I traced my fingers over the knives strapped to my thigh and the small pistol at my hip. I was ready. Without another word, I walked in the shadows out onto the main street. There were a few men here and there, standing guard. It seemed like they hadn't heard the single shot fired in the alley or had disregarded the sound as typical of the city. Sterling was close behind me, not stopping me, and not touching me.

It felt like my consciousness had left my body and I was watching from a few feet above. My hands didn't look like my own as they gripped the gun in what I hoped to be a proper hold. Vaguely, I knew Sterling was trying to relay directions to me for how and when to use the gun, but I couldn't hear him. My ears still rang like I'd been at a concert, and I honestly didn't care. Two men stood in the street, holding guns and chatting. Those guns were there to kill me. To kill my guys. I lifted my gun, aimed at them, and fired. I wasn't expecting more than one shot, so it being an automatic gun shocked me. It took a fraction of a second for me to get back to the target, and I shot both men before they could lift their guns.

Was it merciless? Probably.

Did I care? Not at the moment.

"Jesus Christ, Emily," Sterling said with a chuckle. He took the gun from me and spun me to face him. "What the fuck is going on?"

"Gregory ruined my life. He got me into this mess and I'm going to kill him. Anthony is a horrible human being who deserves to suffer for what he's done to you and Milo and Devon," I said, my voice hoarse and emotionless.

Sterling stared down at me for a long moment. It was like his demons could see mine and they matched. The shadows of the street had his face mostly in darkness, but I could see the fire burning in his eyes. We were twin flames in this need for vengeance.

"Are you sure?" Milo asked. I looked at him and his

expression was like Sterling's. His was tinted with awe. "You want Gregory dead?"

"He's getting into business with a man trying to start human trafficking. He deserves it," I said.

"Emily, you're going to regret this," Devon said from behind me.

"Don't patronize me, Devon," I snapped.

"You don't understand," he said, but I was done listening.

"We have to be quiet now or we'll spook them, and they'll leave," Sterling said, and we started walking again. With Randy's men missing, it was easy to get to the building. Inside was a different story.

The lights were on, and men were everywhere. "What's the plan, then?" I asked.

"You go back to the van," Devon muttered.

"Looks like a spray and pray situation," Milo added dolefully after peeking into the window.

"Dev and Milo take the stairs," Sterling said, gesturing towards the stairs on the right. "Emily and I will take the left."

The building looked and smelled like it had once been a medical facility with multiple offices. Inside the front doors it was an open lobby with a reception desk. Elevators and a door to the stairs were on the right. Devon counted us down from three before Sterling kicked in the door. As men appeared from rooms and hallways, Sterling and I sent bullets hailing in their direction. Sterling was considerably a better shot than me, but I held my own.

With every bullet fired, every spray of blood, every scream, the demon in my soul was fed. And she was hungry. She *craved* this. I had been a sheltered, coddled child who had been denied independence and who grew into a sheltered, coddled woman who maintained relationships where I had no independence and no control. For so long, I was dismissed and diminished to less than a man. Less than Gregory. Now, I was given access to that independence and that control, and it overflowed from me. What came out was a rotten, curdled, and decayed version of that freedom. It turned my blood acidic and came out as frothing violence.

Once we'd cleared the first floor, Sterling helped me reload my gun at the bottom of the stairs. "You good?" he asked as we climbed the stairs at a jog.

"Yeah," I said, not meeting his eyes. I didn't want him to see the fracture within me. The spreading rot.

At the top of the stairs, we stepped over the bodies of the fallen gang members. I should have felt bad that they had gotten wrapped up in something they likely didn't want to contribute to. But I couldn't remove my focus from getting to Gregory and Anthony.

There was another metal door with a window leading to what likely had been a medical lab of sorts based on the items in the room. In the room, Devon was holding a gun to Gregory and Clara, and Milo was tying a barely conscious Anthony to a computer chair. My eyes went straight to Gregory, where he was cowered on the linoleum with his hands up. He wasn't even covering Clara to protect her. She was curled on the ground near Gregory, with tears running down her cheeks.

When we entered, Gregory's eyes widened. "Emily!" he shouted desperately. "Tell them to stop!"

It was a demand. As if we were still in a relationship where he made all the decisions. The rot within me swelled.

"No," I growled. My fingers tightened around the gun at my side.

"Ropes are in my backpack," Milo said, his voice deep and vicious as he finished tying up Anthony. Anthony was quiet but glaring as Milo worked.

Sterling grabbed the ropes and he and Milo tied up Gregory and Clara to two rolling lab stools. Gregory pleaded with Sterling as he wound the ropes quickly and skillfully.

"Careful, Milo. Clara here likes to be tied up," I spat, cutting off a stream of nearly incoherent begging from Gregory.

"There are a lot of women out there like you," Sterling said in agreement.

"*Her*?" Gregory scoffed through the snot and tears on his face. "She's as vanilla as they come. Just you fuckers wait."

Sterling, Milo, and Devon all laughed. Gregory's eyes bounced between all of us.

Sterling stepped back from Gregory as he finished tying him up and said, "You're an absolute idiot. This woman has let me and Milo do *unspeakable* things to her. Together. You never gave her a chance."

Gregory looked at me with anger and regret. I glared right back.

"So what's the plan, Devon?" Anthony spoke up in a taunting, condescending voice.

Our attention jerked to him. I reveled in seeing him bleeding from his nose and lip and tied to a chair. I wanted to see more blood. He needed to hurt more.

"Well, you'll have to understand we weren't expecting to see Gregory and his mistress here," Devon said conversationally. I could hear the bite to the edge of his words, though. "We will have to discuss in the hall. Make yourselves comfortable."

His nonchalance was intimidating, making Clara sob. We walked to the hall and shut the door behind us.

"Can I kill him?" Sterling asked.

"Who Anthony or Gregory?" Milo asked. "I'll take whoever you don't choose."

"Stop it. We need to give them the option to stop their planning and to walk away. We need to give my dad the option to give over control and to stop trying to kill us," Devon said, his eyes flashing with desperation.

"Ugh," Sterling rolled his eyes. "Fine. But-"

I didn't listen to the rest of his sentence. I quickly went back into the lab and shut the door behind me. There was a strong looking deadbolt on the door, and I flipped it. Fists pounded angrily on the window, and I could hear the shouts of the guys. Ignoring them, I grabbed a broom from nearby and put it through the handle. It likely wouldn't hold them for long, but it would have to be enough. The pounding and shouting continued as I turned back to the three people tied up.

"Emily, thank God! Untie us and let's get out of here. Let's get you safe," Gregory said urgently.

I stared at them, looking each of them over. The necklace on Clara's neck looked familiar. "That's mine," I said and pointed at her neck.

"What?" Clara asked, shaking her head.

"That necklace," I clarified and stepped closer.

"It's- I- I was-" Clara stuttered and looked at Gregory.

"She's just borrowing it. You can have it back," Gregory said dismissively.

"Was it my life you wanted or just my husband?" I asked Clara, ignoring Gregory.

Clara squeaked incoherently and shook her head. Clumps of blonde hair stuck to her cheeks. Her tears fueled my rage. She could drown in them and it still wouldn't be enough.

"Emily, untie us," Gregory said and rocked in his ties.

"Are you kidding?" I shrieked at him. "You not only were cheating on me, but you got me kidnapped!"

"I did not get you kidnapped!" Gregory shouted back and tugged at the ropes.

"Anthony, would you like to weigh in on this?" I asked and gestured to him.

"You were a bargaining chip, yes," Anthony said, as if it meant nothing.

"Oh my god," Gregory groaned, grief in his tone.

"I have something of value from each of my deals. It's insurance," Anthony explained.

"But what was that deal for, Gregory? What deal was my life worth?" I asked and got in Gregory's face. The face that once sent butterflies through my belly and was one that I had known almost as well as my own.

Gregory swallowed and looked at Anthony. "Sex trafficking," he whispered.

I stood up. I had known that he knew what he was getting into but hearing him say it was breathtaking.

Clara bowed her head like she was ashamed. She disgusted me. They all disgusted me. I wanted them all strung up and bleeding like I'd seen the guys do in the house's basement. I wanted to tip over that waterfall of violence. They needed to suffer for what they'd done.

The pounding on the glass and the door behind me continued. The rot in my soul drowned them out, and I pulled my knife from the holster.

<h1 style="text-align:center">27</h1>

⚬⚬⚬

<h1 style="text-align:center">Emily</h1>

"Did you even care that I was gone?" I asked Gregory in a hoarse whisper. My vision blurred like there were tears in my eyes. I rubbed across my face with the back of my hand. Wet. I was crying. I hated it. "Or did you feel relieved you could finally have your new girl in our bed without my interference?"

"Emily, that's not-" he started in a tone that made me think he was about to make excuses or gaslight me. It was the same tone he used when he had tried to tell me we could figure out how to move past his infidelity.

"No, I know she's been sleeping there. Do you think I ever once stopped planning this moment?" I asked him. My voice sounded like it was far away. Like my ears had detached from my body.

"Are you going to hurt me?" Gregory asked, eyeing the knife in my hand warily.

"Fucking *duh*, Gregory!" I shouted and rolled my eyes.

Clara let out a squealing cry. She sounded like a pathetic little girl. "Please let me go!"

I laughed. Was she for real? "You were fucking my husband for years. I sent you birthday cards, and gifts, and Christmas cards. I delivered a basket to your apartment after you had surgery last January! Did you ever once feel bad you were screwing my husband?"

Clara only sobbed and looked down.

"How long did you know about the sex trafficking?" I asked, making connections I'd not seen before. She'd been around for two years and was stuck with him through his dealings with Anthony.

"The whole time. She's the one who introduced me to Anthony," Gregory murmured.

Clara let out another squeaking sob. I didn't want to listen to her anymore. I switched my knife to my left hand and knocked her out with a hard punch to her face with my right. She slumped on her stool, the ropes holding her up. Blood coursed from her nose, drenching the front of her blouse.

"Emily, that's enough," Gregory tried to demand. His voice shook, and it disgusted me. He barely looked at Clara, even though she was unconscious and bleeding. We were both nothing to him.

"Anthony," I said and turned to the calm man who was watching me intently. It was eerily like the way Devon watched me. "Do you break fingers in the mafia? Is that still a thing, or is it reserved for the movies?"

A corner of his mouth lifted in a smirk. "We remove them, actually," he amended with a slow nod.

"What?" Gregory shouted and jerked in his seat, almost toppling it to the ground.

"You were supposed to give me safety, a home, a family. You were supposed to give me a peaceful life. Instead, you're going to give me a finger," I said simply, like I was ordering a dessert at dinner. "It's only fair."

"I'm sorry!" Gregory simpered desperately. His voice cracked and warbled.

"For *what*?" I snapped.

"For cheating on you! For getting into business with Anthony! For- for getting you kidnapped!" he listed, his eyes never leaving my knife. "For everything!"

"What about underestimating me? Devaluing me? Not communicating with me? For spreading rumors to our entire town?" I shrieked. I wanted to pull my hair out.

"Yes! I'm sorry, Emily! Please don't hurt me!" He begged, tears and snot ran down his face.

His begging didn't change my mind. Distantly, I knew my mind couldn't be changed because it was rotten. It was decayed. Words evaded me as I stared at my pleading, crying ex-husband with no emotion. I approached him with my knife. The smell of urine met my nose, and I looked down to see he had pissed himself. I scoffed.

He continued to simper and beg as I gripped his left hand in mine. I wanted the finger that still bore the indent and tan line of our wedding band. He screamed before I'd even cut him. Making me even more disgusted with him. His apologies weren't sincere. He was begging for his life and not for me. Not that I'd ever forgive him, but he could have at least tried.

He tugged within his ties, but he'd been tied by Sterling. I knew from personal experience he was going nowhere.

The first drop of blood from Gregory collapsed the last of my tethers to sanity. I remembered in a flash sliding his gold wedding band on this finger in front of the church filled with our family and friends. I remembered holding this hand in a dark theater during our first date. I remembered this hand covered in dirt, helping me replant rose bushes along the back gate. That first slice of his skin had me staggering back. Gregory howled in pain.

"You're not going to slice his finger off at that angle!" Anthony coached over the sound of Gregory's howling and the pounding at the door.

I looked up at him frantically.

"You need it on a table or a hard surface!" Anthony coached. A gleam of demonic glee shone in his eyes.

I held my head with both hands and screamed through my teeth. The handle of my knife was slick with sweat and pressed against my temple. I wanted to gut them all. I wanted their blood to paint the floor. But I also wanted to run away. To never see or hear from any of them again. The opposites of my feelings cracked in my chest. It was now or never to kill them. It was now or never to end this. Whichever way.

Gregory could stand losing a finger. I had lost my entire life. My sanity. He could bear to lose the finger that once bore our fucking wedding band.

With a wild, animal scream, I went back to Gregory. I tried to slice his finger off again, but Anthony was right. I couldn't get through his bone at this angle. Blood flowed heavily from his cut hand. I'd been sloppy and had sliced a few of his other fingers, too. None so deep they couldn't be stitched.

I screamed again in frustration.

"It's alright," Anthony hushed me calmly from his chair. "I'm impressed by you, Emily. Your emotions control your actions, but your dedication to your cause impresses me. I may have acquired you incorrectly, but I stand by my decision to bring you into my family. My son has chosen well to keep you."

"Don't talk to me about him!" I screamed at Anthony, whirling my bloody knife towards him. He didn't even flinch at my shriek or as Gregory's blood flecked his face with my gesturing. He maintained eye contact and looked calm and steady even though he was tied up and at my mercy. "Your son wants to give you a choice."

I calmed my shrieking tone and my breathing. If I was going to give him his options, I needed to be calm. I cleared my throat. "Devon wants to give you the option to give over your control of the gangs and suppliers and leave. You will not pass go and you will not collect two hundred dollars. You will fuck right off and never engage in the family business again. Your other choice is for me to kill you right here, right now. Make good choices, Anthony. You have one minute before I decide for you."

I glared at his face, about an inch from his nose. He smirked and shook his head, but I saw the flash of fear in his eyes. I had scared him. The kindergarten teacher from a suburban nowhere town made a mafia boss scared for his life. Instead of humbling me, this fed the rotting demon in my soul. I smiled back at him.

"Tick tock, friend," I said in my singsong Teacher Voice.

A gunshot sounded from the hall. I looked to see one of them had tried to shoot the window out of the door. It didn't work. The window must have been bullet proof. A second shot sounded off something metallic, like they'd tried to shoot the door handle. It also didn't work.

I saw three wide-eyed faces in the window. In that moment, they looked like scared little boys lined up with their hands and faces smudging the glass. I was so angry. So full of rage now on behalf of these three men and the little boys they once were. Nobody had gotten angry enough for them. Nobody had demanded their well-being. Nobody had taken care of them. I was not their mother or their caretaker. But I was a woman, and I firmly believed a woman could get angry enough and would defend any soul if given enough reason. And I had enough reason.

"What would Matthew say? Michael? Meredith? Owen? Kristen?" I asked, listing Milo and Sterling's deceased parents. With each name, I got closer and closer with the knife. I had it to his throat, a small stream of blood dripping to his collar. "You treated Sterling like trash. You killed every single guardian that loved Milo and Marie. And then you tried to kill us. Your hands are dirty and bloodstained, and you don't deserve my mercy or your son's."

A crash sounded across the room. The window at the back of the lab had shattered. Devon appeared, dangling above the windowsill, before he dropped into the room. Glass crunched under him as he landed on one knee. He didn't even wince before he barreled across the room at a sprint, knocking me away from slicing his father's throat. His jaw was set hard, and his eyes shone with fear as he took me to the hard ground.

28

Milo

We had let her go too far. I realized this as I watched Devon tackle her to the ground. Her scream when she realized she was done was gut wrenching. My breath left me in a *whoosh* and it fogged the window before me. How did I not see she was hurting this badly? How did Sterling and Devon miss it? I felt sick with pain watching Devon wrestle the knife from her. A desperate ache to protect her clawed at my insides.

Sterling, Devon, and I had been together our entire lives. Balancing each other was second nature. How did we forget we needed to balance her, too? Sterling needed touch to bring him back after he sinks into his demons, Devon needed to be obeyed when he felt out of control, and I needed to be forcibly disconnected from my computers and shoved back into my body. I didn't know what Emily needed, but we had failed her by not finding out. I pounded on the cold glass one last time to remind Devon to open the door.

Next to me, Sterling was breathing heavily through his nose and watching the scene unfold with a hand on the door. His fingers curled on the unforgiving metal like he thought his desperation alone could melt the metal and grant us entrance. I knew he realized we had failed her. It was all over his face.

Devon was able to get the knife from Emily and she sat, covering her face with her bloody hands, and crying. He jumped up quickly and opened the door for us. His face was ashen and haunted as Sterling and I rushed in. We both fell to our knees next to Emily, immediately holding her in our arms. She sobbed into my shirt as Sterling kissed her hair and whispered calming praises in her ear.

"Are you alright?" I asked her and looked over her hands. We'd seen her cut Gregory, but I couldn't tell if the blood was all his. I didn't see any cuts on her skin.

She nodded and gasped in her breath.

"Call off the search for Emily," Devon demanded as he untied Gregory. Gregory was watching us hold her with confusion written in with the pain on his face. He had no idea what he'd ruined with her. "She left after you humiliated her. Tell them you falsely reported her missing. She will reach out to her parents if and when she is ready. You are not to contact her. And you are not to speak of this ever again."

"Consider it done," Gregory said and sniffed through his tears.

"Take her and get the fuck out," Devon said and moved over to Clara to untie her.

I ignored Devon as he threatened them both more and focused on Emily in my arms. I shifted on the floor, so she curled up between my legs and rested her head on my shoulder. Sterling came up behind her and continued to stroke her tangled hair. She was still shaking, but the tension had ebbed from her body. Her sobs weren't choking or gasping like before, and I took that

as a good sign. She was coming back to herself.

Gregory carried the still unconscious and bleeding Clara from the lab without a look back at any of us. I didn't bother watching them leave. I knew they'd go without a fight.

Anthony was staring at his son like he was calculating what he was going to do next to get away with murder. When Devon turned to him, Anthony's face changed to one of tired remorse. That fucker.

"You have two options, father," Devon said quietly. "You can hand us control of the family business before leaving and never returning, or you can die today."

"Devon, my boy, this is not how I thought my retirement was going to happen," Anthony laughed, defeated.

"This is not how I saw my family crumbling either," Devon agreed. "You ran this business with an iron fist. You had your people setting up channels for human trafficking. Why? So they could lose their family members to it? They didn't want that. They only did it because you had their loved ones held hostage, or you blackmailed them, or you threatened their livelihoods."

"Our business was crumbling," Anthony explained with a solemn shake of his head. "Matthew and I kept that from you three because we were trying to fix it before you inherited a dying empire."

"Don't bring Matthew into this!" Devon snapped, and I was thankful. "He's more blood on your hands. You've cannibalized this business! It has nothing to do with outside forces and everything to do with your decisions to kill your own people and sacrifice even more to a horrible existence for your own gain."

"You didn't see the profits we'd seen. You didn't see the possibility like we did. The prospects hypnotized us. Even Giovanni and Taz knew Cleveland had the availability of having an organized trafficking business," Anthony reasoned.

"We thought killing Giovanni and Taz would end all of this," Devon laughed sardonically.

"You were partially right," Anthony said. "We built it back up using their proposed infrastructure."

"It's disgusting. I'm disgusted by you," Devon spat. "Even more so by your trying to kill Milo and Emily over and over again."

"For that, I am terribly sorry," Anthony said and hung his head. "I thought she was the person who had you going against my orders and challenging me. I see now she only needed guidance and she would have fit in well with your unit. As for Milo, I knew he was on my trail. I knew he saw what I was doing before I was ready to share with you."

"You could have spoken to me rather than killing them!" Devon shouted in his father's face. "I would have set you straight!"

"I wanted our family back together!" Anthony wailed.

Emily and Sterling turned to stare at Anthony as fat tears

streamed down his face. He stared up at his son, looking all of his sixty plus years of age. I bought none of his alligator tears and false statements.

"Our family has changed. I want you gone. If it's on your feet or dragged out, I don't care," Devon said, his voice dark and menacing.

"I'll give you everything. Son, I'll give you everything you need," Anthony said breathlessly, begging through his tears.

I watched as Devon fell for it. I knew him well enough to see the slight lowering of his shoulders and his brows falling. No. This needed to end tonight. I couldn't go on knowing my parents' and Matthew's murderer was still out there, and I had given up the chance to avenge them. I couldn't go on thinking Anthony was going to turn up at any moment and ruin everything. There was no way I could let this man live now that Marie was having a baby. But this was Devon's call. Devon stepped behind Anthony and began untying him. My heart fell with horrified disappointment.

We hadn't been able to fully strip him of his weapons before we tied him up. It had been a quick decision, and we had only taken his obvious gun. I reached for my gun just in case he made a move. Keeping my eyes on him, I gripped my pistol in my hand and kept it hidden.

Devon untied his father, and they spoke low to each other for a few moments. Sterling looked back and saw the gun in my hand. His eyes met mine, and he understood. His gray eyes tightened with sadness and understanding. I would do anything to keep the three of them alive, even if that meant they'd hate me later. I loved them. They were all I had, and I would burn the world as long as they were safe.

There was barely a second of time that stretched on when Devon looked over at us. His expression was one of relief he didn't need to kill his father. His plan to not be aggressive had worked. But I saw the moment Anthony pulled a knife from his pocket. I saw the evil on Anthony's face as he planned to kill his only child. The person who'd just shown him undeserving mercy.

My gun was up, and I fired. Emily screamed and jumped into my arms. Sterling ducked instinctively, and Devon's eyes went wide. Anthony fell to the ground.

Devon turned to his father with a shout. The knife clattered to the linoleum next to Anthony and Devon kicked it aside with a feral scream as he realized what had happened. My ears rang from the reverberating shot, and I lowered my gun. I had hoped there would be a rush of vindication. A feeling of rightness in killing my parents' and Matthew's killer, but I felt indifferent. Not numb, but uncaring about the death and achingly sad for the pain of the people I loved. Killing Anthony didn't bring them back. It didn't change them, it only changed us. Emily may never forgive us or herself for what happened today, and Devon may never forgive me for killing his father. But we were safe. We were free.

The story concludes with book 3…

Pre-order available on Amazon.

Subscribe at catausten.com/ subscribe to be one of the firsts to hear about reveals and release dates and to get and an **exclusive** sneak peak at the first chapter….

About the Author

Cat Austen is an emerging romance author based in Ohio. She lives with her husband and their two boys. She enjoys gardening and baking and is a voracious reader of romance novels.

You can find Cat on TikTok, Instagram, and Facebook. For updates on new releases, ARC opportunities, and pre-orders, subscribe to her newsletter at catausten.com/subscribe

9 798989 387335